D0522236

NE

Cat Rising

CYNN CHADWICK

Bywater
BOOKS

Ann Arbor
2009

Copyright © 2003 by Cynn Chadwick

Bywater Books, Inc.
PO Box 3671
Ann Arbor MI 48106-3671
www.bywaterbooks.com

All rights reserved. No part of this book may be reproduced
or transmitted in any form or by any means, electronic or
mechanical, including photocopying, without permission
in writing from the publisher.

Printed in the United States of America on acid-free paper.

Bywater Books First Edition: August 2009

Cover designer: Bonnie Liss (Phoenix Graphics)

ISBN 978-1-932859-66-9

This novel is a work of fiction. All persons, places, and
events were created by the imagination of the author.

Mixed Sources
Product group from well-managed
forests and other controlled sources
www.fsc.org Cert no. SW-COC-002283
© 1996 Forest Stewardship Council
FSC

For my best friend,
Lu

NEWCASTLE LIBRARIES	
C457889600	
Bertrams	10/09/2009
	£9.99

Acknowledgments

I don't suppose any book is ever written by the writer, alone; although the task can sometimes be quite lonely. Without first, the unconditional love and support of my parents, Harry and Shirley Chadwick, the opportunity for the writing would never have been realized. For my sons, Zac and Sam, I offer my deepest gratitude for their sacrifice in sharing their mother's attention with an imaginary woman named Cat Hood. This book is, in part, dedicated to those immigrant women who left homelands to cross oceans for the dreams of their fathers and husbands, particularly my grandmothers, Mary Belle Hood-Fredrickson and Mabel Wright-Chadwick. And again, in part, to those women who have pioneered their way into the realms of male-dominated trade-work. Something dynamic happens in the swing of a hammer, the zip of a miter saw, and working *shoulder to shoulder*. I am indebted to my dearest friends Donna McDonald and Lucy Nehls, who gave me the chance to swing that hammer and witness infinite possibility. I have been blessed by the presence of Julie Felton, whose inimitable creative vision, wit, and passion brings joy and inspires awe. I shudder to wonder what would have become of *Cat Rising* without the keen editorial eye of Connie Conway. Thank God I'll never know. In my heart remain those friends who have rocked on my porch, read the rough stuff, and cheered me on anyway: most especially, Karen Essex, my *uber-pal*, who actually *gets* it and without whom my world would be a smaller place; Martha Vanderwolk who has always believed in me; Dave Wills for showing me how to hurl crabapples; Gian DiDonna for driving with me through a blizzard with the sunroof open; Irene Sherlock, who suffered my mania-in-residence and roomed with me anyway; and Ro Hiley who knows me longest and probably best. This would not be a complete acknowledgment were I not to mention my writing mentors: Dr. Peter Caulfield who took a chance on me; Leslie Williams, whose gentle hand guided my first creative endeavors; Bea *(The Velvet Hammer)* Gates, who pointed out the absence and value of stories about women working together; and most humbly to Sarah Schulman—who kicked my ass and dared me to be a writer.

Cat Rising

Chapter One

Cat opened one lazy eye. White walls tinged blue as the room filled with watery twilight, rising from base to crown, swallowing ankles of furniture, lifting the hem of night, skirting her chin, mouth, nose, eyes. She counted: five, four, three, two, one, as morning light divested corners of shadows. Folding forward, she slid wool and flannel from her neck onto her lap, exposing bare shoulders. Elbows resting on knees, she cradled her head in the nest of limbs. She knew by heart the seconds it took for a winter light to fill the room. Spring, summer, or fall, she'd been counting it her whole life.

The quiet of the country is an illusion, she thought; there is never any true silence. Before light, hungry babies disturb sleepy mothers from beds and nests. Calfless cows, heavy with milk, bellow complaints as they cross pastures to barns. Meadowlarks trill, tractors rumble, and voices fill the once still world. The closest it comes to quiet is before a storm, when everything stops, and the air hangs until wind pushes through coves pelting windows and tin roofs with rain and ice and hail. And if you're not paying attention, if you're eating or reading or dreaming awake, you can miss the moment because it creeps and stills the world in a way that tricks you into hearing your own breath so loud that it fills the space of what was almost perfect silence.

Intruding her slow awakening was the rumbling sound of Lily's work van bumping its way over the old bridge. The truck's grumbling engine was as familiar as Cat's own hungry stomach. The sound sent her leaping from the bed, pressing her nose against the frosted window. *What the hell?* She looked to the clock on the bedside table. Two full hours till work. The coffee below wasn't even programmed to start brewing for another forty-five minutes.

She snagged her pinky toe on the corner of the nightstand. Fuckfuckfuck, she swore in time with the throbbing in her foot. The fire in her toe pulsed, pushing her back onto the bed where she held the injured appendage till the pain dulled. Her German shepherd, Mike, lay sprawled on his back in the corner, snoring.

"Hey." She picked up a slipper and threw it at him. "You worthless hound, I'm injured here." The shepherd pulled himself up on his haunches, circled the plaid blanket that was his bed, and curled into a ball, burying his nose between his paws.

Cat pulled on sweatpants, slippers, and a T-shirt, and hobbled down the staircase, making her way through the dark to the wood stove in the living room. First poking coals bright and then punching the brew button on the coffee maker, she turned as the back door swung wide and Lily blew into the house on a gust of cold air. Waving a bundled paper above her head, she stomped past Cat and slapped the copy of the *Galway Mountain News* down onto the kitchen table.

"Did ya see it?" Lily turned on her. "Here, read it. Look. See?" Punctuating the words with a finger stab at the page. "It's you. Can you believe it?" Lily spun around flapping her arms, clapping her hands, knocking her forehead with a bunched fist. "Man oh man oh man, Cat, are you famous!"

She nudged Lily aside and scanned the open paper. The photo from the jacket of her first collection of stories centered the page. She was standing on a granite boulder, left thumb hooking a front belt loop, her long sandy hair whipped wild around her face. She was squinting into the summer dusk.

A review. She'd never been reviewed. There had never before been anything to be reviewed.

"Is it bad?" She looked at Lily.

"*Bad?* Hell no, it's great. You're great." Lily grabbed her arms and danced her around the room. "You are gonna be so famous."

Shaking free, Cat leaned over the paper, running a finger beneath the black type.

Galway's own Cat Hood's first collection of stories, Outside of Everything, *details a series of charming tales about friendships as enduring as the mountains. Although craftily veiled, "Painter's Ridge, North Carolina" bears a striking resemblance to our own little hamlet of Galway. Hood's characters are authentic portraits of ourselves.*

"Gets better," Lily said turning the page. The light from the table lamp shone through Cat's picture to the back of the page, revealing a sketch of a haloed Christ surrounded by small children and baby animals. It was part of an advertisement for Mount Zion Baptist Church. Pinching the corner of the page Lily waved it back and forth. The picture changed, like a hologram, Cat to Christ—Christ to Cat.

"It's a sign." Lily banged her fist on the table. "Even Jesus knows you're gonna be famous." Cat looked over her shoulder and scanned the review.

3

"See, Cat. It's all good." Lily rose, walked into the kitchen, and poured coffee for each of them.

OK, so there she was, flat-out, right in the middle of the *Galway Mountain News,* back to back with Jesus. Cat's knees weakened and she slid into a chair. Someone, a stranger, had read it—her book—all the way through, and they liked it. She skimmed the rest of the review. There was stuff from the jacket bio about how she had been raised by her grandmother and still lived just north of Galway, up in Little Galway. And how she wrote stories in a *remote cabin buried deep in a winding cove.* It made her sound like a bumpkin. Like she'd never left the house and that writing was just something she fell into, like a hobby. Even though she'd gone away (for six long years) to college and grad school over in Greensboro, she suspected that she might still be some kind of bumpkin.

"You thought being a woman carpenter got you looks?" Lily nudged Cat out of her thoughts. "Wait till people start reading your book. I said all along that you'd do it."

Cat rose and flicked a finger at Lily's shoulder. "No, what you've said all along was 'Quit wastin' a perfectly good Saturday on that stupid book.'" She went up the stairs to shower.

"Hey, I've been supportive, always," Lily yelled. "Just remember who it was saved you from Stanley Schmidt."

Cat let the water run hot over her, making her skin pink. Stanley Schmidt. How could she forget? Lily would never let her. A hundred years could pass and still Lily would remind her.

The rescue had occurred on the playground during kindergarten recess when the boy with the yellow eyelashes had jumped Cat and fought her for a brownie. Lily

4

Cameron's kick to his backside sent him scurrying. Her grin had revealed a gap where a tooth had been. She was scabby, knees and elbows. Her long brown braids wiggled as she danced from foot to foot.

She spit into her palm and held it out.

"Now, you do it." Lily had demanded.

Like it meant something.

Cat spit.

They'd been best friends for the next thirty years.

That was her first memory of Lily. Yet it wasn't their first meeting, or so the story went. The pair of toddlers had apparently wandered off during a Baptist tent revival. They were discovered, later, on the edge of a riverbank, battling geese bigger than themselves with long sticks and rocks. But neither remembered it.

Cat's first true memory (ever) was etched from the day she'd arrived in the mountains. It had been winter and had included a blue black dusk, church bells, falling snow, and soft yellow lights filling windows of stone houses with stone chimneys that puffed gray smoke into animal shapes. She was two years old and wedged between her grandmother, Kate, and her brother, Will. The children had been bundled in thick leggings, boots, woolen coats, and hats tied firmly under their chins. The three had ridden in silence.

Orphaned. That was the word everybody had whispered during coffee hour at church. Orphaned explained the presence of the two small children at Kate Hood's knee. They'd belonged to her son, William, killed along with his young beautiful wife, Linnea, in a car wreck on New Year's Eve. A terrible tragedy.

Kate had driven alone the fifteen hours to New York City to retrieve the children. She'd been the sole (closest or otherwise) living relative on either side. Linnea, too, had been something of an orphan; the only child of a widowed roofer whose missed step off the top of a ladder had left him dead the day after Linnea's twenty-third birthday. It had been the same year that she'd fallen in love with William Hood, a fellow law student. They'd married, but only after each had graduated and begun their respective careers.

Sensible, her grandmother Kate had called them. Had they lived, Cat would have grown up in New York City where the words *winding cove* would never have been included in a review of her book. But Cat had no memory of any home before this cabin, any place before these mountains, or any parents before Kate.

Soap slid over arms shaped by years of working carpentry: cutting wood, banging hammers, lifting Sheetrock, pulling plaster. She hadn't planned on being a carpenter. That had been Lily's dream since she had been a *site mite* on her daddy's construction jobs. The work included cleaning up the building materials, throwing away destruction waste: tossed nails, scrap wood, broken shingles, loose screws. Except Lily'd always salvaged the better stuff. When they were eleven, she and Cat had built a wooden castle high in the branches of a fat oak. Running electricity from the garage in Lily's backyard, they'd swayed above the world for that whole summer.

With the exception of Lily and her mother, Sophia, the Cameron house had been filled with the stocky frames of big, black-eyed Cameron boys—*descendants of gypsies,* Lily's dad would tease his darkly hued wife. Lily's six older brothers, all grown men now, with big beards and big laughs, had towered over Cat's childhood memories.

Cat reached for her throat and between her fingers tumbled the small silver thistle on the chain. One Christmas, when she and Lily were ten years old, Jim had, with tears in his eyes, given both little girls the necklaces.

"I love you like one of my own, Mary Catherine," he'd whispered.

And she had felt like *one of his own.*

She did have her own family, of course. But it numbered only three and was quiet and something else ... *temporary.* Even back then, when she was a kid, she'd had a sense of its tenuousness, perhaps even of its inevitable extinction.

Not like Lily's family that had planted and rooted itself in these mountains almost two hundred years before and had grown and spread across three counties. After Will had left and Kate had died, Cat had a hard time thinking of herself alone as any kind of family. She was pretty sure that a family required more than one person.

She knew that her grandmother had loved her *like one of her own* but she never would have said it. It wasn't Kate's way. Cat had somehow understood this; even so it would have been nice hearing it—maybe once.

Kate's love came in the folds of laundry as they snapped from the line; in the light brush of fingertips on a feverish brow; in the scramble of an egg; and in the lift of an eyebrow, raised in suspicion, as Cat spun stories of bounty hunters she'd claimed to have met in the woods. Now, as a grown-up, with that ever-amazing glimpse called hindsight, she understood that the disapproval she once feared in her grandmother's raised brow had been, in fact, amusement. *Ach, go on with you,* Kate would say, shaking her head and turning away.

There had been something in that turn that made Cat think that Kate, in her own way, really didn't want her to *go on.* Somehow, she thought maybe her grandmother liked that she made things up. Most of the time, Cat didn't feel like she was lying. Most of the time she believed her own stories.

She wondered if that made her a liar or a sociopath? Or just a fiction writer whose brain cells were fused at the reality checkpoint in the lower lobe, or wherever it was located.

Reluctantly, she rinsed suds from skin and turned the water off. Twisting hair into one towel and wrapping herself in another, she stepped in front of the fogged mirror. With a finger she swiped an X and watched it fill back up. She waited. Too lazy to swipe with a towel. She was just really that lazy sometimes. It was even probably laziness that had turned her into a carpenter. She liked carpentry mostly, except in extreme heat or cold, or if there might be snakes involved.

When Cat was in college, she and Lily had shared an apartment while Lily finished her carpentry apprenticeship. They were broke most of the time until Lily scored a sideline remodeling job and needed Cat's help. It had been a lazy way for Cat to find a job. After they'd finished that first job, word got around about the two girls with hammers, and suddenly they found themselves booked every weekend. By the time they had left Greensboro, the business, now called Girls with Hammers, was thriving. They brought it back to the mountains with them. But it had always been Lily's business. All the responsibility Cat had wanted was to be the helper.

The tail of her towel smeared the mirror. Vapors skidded into skinny streams and droplets plumped from steam. Wiping again and turning the nozzle of the hair dryer onto the mirror, she appeared almost mystically out of the mist. Unfurling the towel loosened a tangle of wet tendrils that snaked along her forehead. Cheeks pinked against pale skin.

Her eyes, blue slits, creased fan-like into laugh lines—crow's feet. *Denim eyes,* an old lover had once called them. Their shade ranged from the soft sky blue of a worn pair of Levis to the inky indigo of its shelf life. Her moods, the old lover had said, stormed and cleared in the color of her eyes. She slid the flat of her hand over the flat of her stomach, still tight, and so, thank God, were her breasts. Not too shabby for thirty-four. She looked hard in the mirror.

"And *reviewed,*" she said out loud, watching for her own response. It flickered. She glimpsed it behind dark lashes. Deep in the black circle of her pupil was something she couldn't quite name. Shit. It was a pretty damn good review. Why wasn't she jumping up and down about it? Getting drunk? Getting stoned? Getting laid? Again, there was the flicker—*exposed*—that's how she felt. The whole world was about to find out what a faker she was; not some savvy writer from New York City, but a *bumpkin* from the hills. She leaned back as if repulsed, as if something had pulled her away from her mirrored self. Finally she tried a smile, but she could see that she really didn't mean it.

Two banged out beats hitting the bathroom door jarred her out of her thinking.

"What the fuck are you doing in there?" Lily's voice came at her. "We gotta go to work, you know."

"You were two hours early." Cat combed her fingers through her hair, untangling strands that would braid themselves back together by the end of the day.

"Don't expect any special treatment now that you've gone and got yourself famous." Lily tried the locked doorknob, impatiently.

Cat watched it rattle. "Do you do this to Hannah?"

"I don't have to. Hannah knows better than to make me wait all this time."

"Go away; I'll be down in a minute." She listened as Lily mumbled her way back down the stairs. Cat turned the hair dryer onto her wet head. God bless Hannah, she thought. If it hadn't been for Hannah, Lord knows what would have happened to Lily or to Cat for that matter. When Lily was around sixteen years old, she went off on some wild craziness: staying out late, drinking, speeding, fucking around with guys. Cat was right on her tail except for the fucking around with guys part. That part had never happened. Never would for her because she'd always somehow known that she liked girls better. From the moment in the fourth grade that she'd fallen in love with Joanie Miller, asked her to go steady, and kissed her behind the school, she'd known she loved girls best.

It wasn't till later, in the sixth grade, sitting with her arm around Sarah Johnson on the Bible School bus, that she learned from Pastor Bob Handy that God did not approve of her loving Sarah *that way*. Sarah hadn't seemed to mind. And she, Cat, certainly didn't mind. And up until that moment, she didn't think that God minded her loving Sarah *that way*. But Brother Bob had minded, and so she'd removed her arm from Sarah's shoulder and slipped it into a warm spot between Sarah's knees.

Lily, on the other hand, had sworn on the Bible that she liked boys and only boys. She had liked them so much that she'd joined in on their baseball games, taken their shop classes, and practiced shooting whiskey in the tree castle so she could drink them under the table. Once there (under the table) she'd wrestle those poor bastards, sucking their faces purple, proving to everyone, except herself and Cat, that she was not, never would be, no matter how many rumors floated, a lezzie.

For a short period, Lily's fear had pushed Cat from her

life. There had been gossip about them. Ever since Cat Hood had been caught kissing Carrie Smith at an eighth grade dance, everyone just knew she was a dyke and she wouldn't deny it. People started rumors. Was Lily queer, too? Did Cat turn her into one? Did they catch it from each other? But the only thing that had ever gone between them was the night they didn't kiss.

Cat turned the blow dryer off and stepped out into the cold bedroom. Her heated body rebuffed the accosting air. She pulled a pair of gray thermal underwear from the drawer. The task of dressing for a day of winter carpentry work was a chore. Layer upon layer. By the end of the workday both she and Lil would be stripped down to their T-shirts.

The night that Cat and Lily didn't kiss had affected each of them differently. It had come after months of silence, on the eve of their high school graduation. There had been a party in a field with a huge bonfire at its center. Every kid there had known every kid there since kindergarten. It was an ending for most and a beginning for some and everybody was drunk.

It was that night, when Lily had stumbled into Cat and knocked the beer bottle from her grip, that had brought them back together. They hadn't spoken in months and when their eyes met, Lily's began spilling over with tears. She wrapped her arms around Cat and began to sob. Not exactly knowing what was going on, Cat guided Lily to the truck.

She couldn't remember who drove home. One of them must have. There seemed to have been no time between that moment and the next one; they lay on their backs in the tree castle passing a bottle of Jack and a joint. Cat remembered

11

being intensely sober. Her efforts to get drunk as Lily came roaring out of her lesbian closet were fruitless. Lily's fear of being queer had sobered Cat.

"I'm a fucking dyke," Lily had sobbed. "I don't want to be a fucking dyke."

Cat tried to listen, tried to understand, tried to figure out why being a dyke was such a problem. She loved women.

"I'm so sorry I ditched you." Lily pressed her face against Cat and heaved deep sighs into her shoulder. "I just didn't want anyone to think that I was a lezzie like you."

Cat held her, rocked her, and kissed the top of her head. Once quieted, Lily raised her chin. In that moment, the one that hangs before every first kiss, their eyes had searched. Lily's were warm and brown like her skin. The dark waves of her hair softened sharp features. Freckles dusted the bridge of her nose, and when she smiled a deep dimple appeared. And it was in that moment, together without words, that they had chosen not to kiss. Ever.

For Cat, it had been a relief. She had, for a minute, worried that she and Lil might somehow wind up together out of sheer laziness or convenience or for lack of anything better to do.

For Lily, something even better had come from her confession.

Only days later, in a honky-tonk bar with Merle Haggard blaring in the background, Lily had met Hannah Burns and the two had been together ever since.

"That's it, Cat Hood," Lily yelled up the stairwell. "If you're not down here in the next five minutes I'm leaving without you."

According to the clock, she still had fifteen to go.

"You will not," she muttered, clunking down the stairs.

"Don't think I won't," Lily yelled from the back door. "I can't hold up work because of your newfound famousosity."

"Famousosity?" Cat poured food in Mike's bowl and followed Lily out the back door.

Chapter Two

The work van bumped over the bridge and headed down Maskas Creek Road, paralleling the river. Cat lit a cigarette and stared out the window. The mountains were covered in white; a leftover combination of the sleet and snow that had fallen the week before. Black patches of trees and melted snow speckled the humped hills, reminding her of a big black and white cow. Frozen splashes formed ice goblets along the edges of the creek. As if being tugged, wisps of mist rose from pockets and smeared across the landscape.

As Lily guided the truck past the fishing lake where fat carp swam just below the crust of ice, a snapping of reeds sprung loose a great blue heron. Sweeping up from the feathery fronds, he sliced a half moon curve and slowed to a glide directly in front of them, as if he were leading a formation. Lily smacked Cat's arm.

"Are you seeing this?" she asked.

"We're riding the ass of a bird," Cat said.

The van slowed as the heron drifted in front of them. Gently lolling from side to side, but staying in his lane, the bird flapped; a sound like a bedsheet snapping open. Rising occasionally, his wingspan (they'd later swear) was as wide as the truck. He dipped his head twice, veered left, and headed for a frozen swampy tobacco field. Lily looked at her. Cat counted in her mind: five, four, three, two ... *"It's a sign."*

"It's a sign," Lily said and smacked the steering wheel. "Just two days ago, a black snake was coiled up under my porch. So Hannah bought a book about animal signs."

"So, what are you saying?"

"I think it's a sign for you, Cat."

She flicked the cigarette out the window. "Don't be including me in your hoo-doo."

At that, Lily picked up the cell phone and punched in some numbers. Cat hated when she did this. She hated when anybody did this. She hated cell phones and the boorish vulgarians they spawned. She had become a raging anti-cell phone activist. Once in the Winn Dixie she had stolen the half-filled cart of a cell phone-distracted woman and hid it behind a banana display six aisles away. Cell phones were most dangerous to people behind a wheel, especially to those drifters who tended to float between lanes with or without one. The van straddled the double yellow line.

Lily, with the phone clamped between her ear and shoulder, was yelling the whole great blue heron story to Hannah. In her exuberant description of the big flapping bird wings and turtlelike bobbing head, she let go of the steering wheel.

"Hang up the phone, Lil!" Cat yelled over the rumble of shaking tools.

"So, yeah, look up ... great—blue—heron. Bye, Sweetie." Lily said as Cat pulled the phone from her ear.

They left the valley road and turned toward the river. The wide span of the Scots Bourne meandered north through the city, rushing around filtering boulders that littered its bed. Sandy banks and pebbled islands dotted the water, giving sanctuary to golden eagles, white egrets, and the occasional kayaker. Cat had often taken refuge here herself. She'd read once that in Native American cultures there is a spiritual practice called *going to water*. She didn't think it was exclusive to them, though. There was a term for it in every culture: *down by the river, on the lake, beside the sea.* They all went, and whether it was an intentional spiritual thing or not, it became one.

"Hannah's gonna look it up in the book for you," Lily said reassuringly. As if this were all suddenly important. For any other person, seeing a great big bird flying by the car window would just be cool. Something you'd tell about for days. But not for Lil. No, that poor damn bird had inadvertently become some kind of omen, a harbinger, a fortune cookie.

"Jesus, Lil, I don't need you and Hannah predicting my future based on the backside of a bird."

"Not just any bird, Cat. A famous bird. A movie star bird. With a famous movie star bird name, great blue heron. Means something now. You just wait and see."

Cat was already getting tired of the word famous flinging itself out of Lily's mouth.

They parted from the river and headed into town toward Dizzy's Lumberyard. Lily backed the van into the dusty warehouse. Layers of cut board and molding reached from dirt floor to the rafters housing swallow's nests and bats sleeping upside down. Lily got out and headed for the hardware store upstairs. Cat yanked open the double doors at the back of the van and slid aside some tools. Before turning she felt a presence at her elbow and then a hand on her ass. She reached down and clenched the hairy wrist. In a single movement, nails dug into soft flesh where blue veins crisscrossed and pulsed. Cat twisted the hand, grinding it between her knee and the fender of the van.

16

"What the fuck, Cat!"

"What the fuck, yourself, Richie. I told you, keep your fucking hands off me." As she let go she pushed him into a stack of two by fours.

"I was just kiddin'," he whined.

Richie had been working the lumberyard since he was a kid, some forty-odd years ago. He'd lost his two front teeth in a brawl up in Madison County (something to do with a rigged chicken fight), and he'd been to prison for stealing a car. Over the years, both Lily and Cat had shoved, kicked, punched, even once bitten Richie for not keeping his hands in his pockets. It was Lily's whistle from above that sent Cat pushing him, one more time, into the stacked pine so she could pass.

"I'm bleedin'," he said and held out his wrist.

"Good," she said and stomped on his foot as she went by.

She joined Lily inside the hardware store, where the fellas were much more civilized. Every Christmas, Dizzy Junior would even bake them each a fruitcake in the shape of a power tool.

"Here she is, fellas." Lily waved for Cat to come closer while all the guys, Dizzy Jr., Doogie, and Matt clapped. Two other contractors stood off to the side. One looked like a painter by the rainbow spatterings on his clothes. The other—a mason. No mistaking the concrete crusting his boots. Both were staring at Cat. What the fuck was going on?

When she got close enough, she saw that Dizzy Jr. had tacked her book review picture up on the bulletin board behind him. It slid in neatly beside the poster of a big-breasted Makita girl with the tip of an electric screwdriver almost touching an almost revealed stiff nipple. Dizzy came around the counter and hugged Cat. Doogie and Matt knew better, but shuffled toward her and grinned and nodded.

After the only display of affection probably ever exhibited in the store, they all stood around staring at one another and then at the floor. Finally someone cleared a throat and everyone regrouped in their usual spots.

"Take that thing down, Dizzy," was all Cat could think to say.

"No way." The giant bushy-browed man folded his arms, stubbornly. His blond mustache and eyebrows twitched together in protest. "You are our most famous customer." He grinned a great gapped grin.

"What'd I tell ya?" Lily slapped her shoulder. "Famous."

Cat shook her head and separated from them, making her way over to the back wall. From floor to shoulder, rows of skinny drawers held every type and size of fastening device ever invented. There were screws the size of a tiny thumbnail and chunky bolts of turned steel the length and heft of a crowbar. The nut to the big bolt slid loosely over her thumb. Tools and gadgets hung thick on pegboard: shiny steel hammers, vise grips, speed squares, measuring tapes, and leather pouches and gloves layered deep. A tall wooden carousel with a hanging scoop stood, each angled bin filled with weighted nails. On shelves and counters blue Makita drills and saws vied for attention with the bright, yellow and black DeWalts.

Sawdust scattered the floor and the fire in an old pot-bellied stove emitted a band of heat. In the air, new and burning wood mingled with metal and grease, stale coffee, and old paper. It was a place of hope, she thought. That even if the worst thing happened, if your floor rotted through, or your ceiling caved in, or you needed more space or wanted some of your own, this store offered resolution.

18

She glanced back over to the wall where her picture aligned with the ballooning boobs of the Makita girl. It was dumb that she was up there, she thought. Funny that those guys wanted to show her off like that. Again Lily whistled for her and they headed for the yard.

After the door units had been loaded and the frame molding had been tied down, Cat climbed into the van and waited while Lily signed for the lumber.

"What'd you do to Richie?" Lily asked as she headed the van out of town. "He was going on about suing my company on account of my hostile employee."

"Just be glad I didn't kick his balls out his nostrils." Cat cracked the window and lit a cigarette.

Lily laughed and snapped her fingers for one.

"I'm telling Hannah," Cat passed the cigarette to Lily.

Over the years, at one time or another, Hannah had insisted that Lily quit smoking. She'd reasoned, begged, threatened, withheld sex for nearly a month till she, Hannah, could bear it no longer. Finally, they'd come to a kind of understanding, "Like the military's 'don't ask, don't tell' policy," Lily had explained.

"No, you won't tell Hannah. You like me smoking. It alleviates your own guilt," Lily said.

"No. Mainly I won't tell 'cause you get too cranky when you're not having sex."

They turned onto the big highway; the one that bypassed the city, skirting its perimeters, sending travelers around rather than through downtown. The six lanes going east and west made a straight shot through a mountainside that had been blown away by tons of dynamite. The dozens of bore lines were still visible in the layers of rock on either side of the freeway. It reminded Cat of the way she felt when she looked at the scar that had left someone legless or paralyzed or blind.

19

Lily hated driving on the highway. The speed of the cars made her nervous. The energy of people already frantic at eight o'clock in the morning made her edgy. Gas fumes made her nauseous, she claimed. Eventually they exited, but not without horn beeps and flipped birds directed at them. Lily, especially when nervous, sometimes forgot to use her blinker, and worse, never used her rearview.

They turned into a subdivision and pulled up to a modest brick house with a carport and a swing set in the yard. Two small white poodles greeted them at the door. They were followed by a tall blonde woman with long braids wound in loops that hung just below each ear. She was dressed in a pink sweat suit fronted by an apron with an almost life-size Barbie doll decorating it. Barbie's Barbique, it read in hand-painted lettering.

"Now Topsy, now Turvy," the woman said to the yapping poodles. "These are the nice carpenter ladies who've come to replace our doors."

Heidi (that was the woman's name) invited them in. As her eyes adjusted to the dimness, Cat saw that along the walls were stacked rows of dolls. All sorts of dolls: Barbies still in their boxes, babies that talked and wet and cried, Madame Alexanders behind glass cupboards, old dolls with peeling plaster faces, and waxen dolls whose heads seemed just a bit misshapen. Upright in the corner was a perfect Chatty Cathy, like the one Cat remembered coveting in the Sears and Roebuck catalog one Christmas.

Making their way to the back of the house required some maneuvering. They dodged miniature cribs and cradles. A playpen full of posed plastic toddlers centered the room. There was a bald baby doll propped in one of many tiny high chairs. A bib that read "Got Milk" was tied around its neck and a bowl of toy oatmeal sat on its tray. Cat nearly knocked over a two-foot tall stuffed child as it leaned against a wall, its face buried in its arms, as it either counted off a game of hide and seek or wept; this wasn't entirely clear.

"This is the little boys' room." Heidi gestured to the left. "And this is the little girls' room."

Their heads swiveled in sync to the right and left again. Inside the red, white, and blue striped walls was a set of bunk beds and a toy box spewing blocks, bears, and trucks. Squatting over a game of marbles were three stuffed dolls dressed in overalls; one had a forked twig slingshot poking from his back pocket. Heidi marched to him and removed the weapon. She held it up.

"Now, Roddy, what have I told you about this?" She turned back to the carpenters and sighed. "Boys will be boys," she said.

Cat glanced at Lily who avoided her eyes.

Across the hall, all in pink and white, there was a fluffy canopy bed centering the room. Two tufted girl dolls in frilly frocks were seated at a small table serving tea to a brown bear with a loose red tie around his neck. Heidi raised a finger to her lips, hushing the women.

"Girls are so much easier," she whispered.

They went back through the maze of inanimate children and out to the work van.

"Lily, what the fuck is going—"

"We ain't talking about it."

The doors they had picked up at Dizzy's were Dutch. Split neatly in half, each door required twice the work of hanging a regular one and ten times the trouble. As they made their way through the house with the heavy door between them, Lily accidentally kicked a stuffed child down the hall, sending it into the wall. Heidi's shriek nearly sent the pair tumbling after it.

21

"Mikey, Mikey!" Heidi's voice was panicky as she rushed to the tumbled toy boy. "Stay out of the carpenter ladies' way, now." She lifted Mikey and tucked him under her arm

"Kids," Heidi said, shaking her head in exasperation.

They finally got down to work. As was the routine, Cat measured the opening of the doorway and Lily measured again after her.

"Measure twice, cut once," Lily said, as she always said, the click of her retracting tape punctuating the didacticism. Ever since Cat's eye on the tape had missed one calculation and had caused them to "eat a window" as Lily had put it, she never truly trusted her again.

The first door took twice as long as Lily had expected and half as long as Cat had feared. The second door was easier once they'd gotten their system down. Throughout the day, Heidi's looped braids bounced around her shoulders as she scurried back and forth: changing empty diapers, feeding bottles that never really drained, comforting babies whose cries came from speakers in their backs.

Heidi looked whipped when she handed Lily a plate of hot chocolate chip cookies covered in foil. She waved them good-bye with an ancient tiny Thumbelina doll cradled against her breast.

It wasn't till they'd reached the highway that Cat cleared her throat. Before she'd voiced a word, Lily held up her hand.

"Don't even say it."

"Did you not know about this?" Cat turned on her.

"Look," Lily defended. "If I turn down every nutcase out there, we'll both be on welfare."

"Lil, there's got to be other people out there. Not everybody's a loony tune."

"That woman ain't any different than you, Cat Hood."

"You're kidding me, right?"

"Well, what's the difference between that doll lady playing with those make-believe babies all day and you sitting at your computer writing stories about people who don't exist anywhere, 'cept in your own mind?" She pulled the van into the parking lot of Garden Festival and turned off the motor.

She and Hannah had become health food converts years before; only Cat knew that Lily cheated with packed chili-dogs from the Mr. Weiner drive-thru.

"I gotta pick up some tofu and seaweed," Lily said now. "Need anything?" The question was out of politeness. She left without waiting for Cat's decline.

Was that how she seemed to Lily? Cat wondered. Like Heidi-the-doll-lady, living in a world of make-believe?

All those years of being holed up in her bedroom, declining invitations to movies, kickball games, hikes in the woods, all so she could write stories. She had to admit that there were times when the life and the fantasy were inextricable. Maybe it was the same for Heidi-the-doll-lady.

Cat looked across the street and watched a small yellow-haired boy pulling a red wagon that was hauling a large papier-mâché sculpture. An art project. Cat smiled. A passerby, an older man, paused to point admiringly to the piece. The boy nodded, shy at first, and then he was gesturing, clearly explaining his work. It was only a moment. The two soon parted, heading in opposite directions, but Cat recognized the bounce in each of their steps.

She cracked the window and sniffed the air, detecting a hint of snow. The airy chill carried with it a feeling of expectation, something revelatory—something prophetic. She gulped in a breath and held it, filling her lungs with the possibilities.

Lily yanked open the door and jumped in. She threw a silverwrapped candy bar across the seat into Cat's lap.

"What's this?" Cat held up the gift, inspecting it from a distance.

"Carob," Lily said. "It's just like chocolate." She ripped the wrapper off her own bar with her teeth and bit a chunk. "Try it."

Cat unpeeled a corner and sniffed. "Whatdya mean it's just 'like' chocolate? Is it chocolate or isn't it?"

"Jesus, Cat, just try it."

As her teeth broke into the waxen bar it caught in her molars the way a Crayola crayon had, once, when as a kid she'd chewed one on a dare. Closing her mouth and poking the debris from her teeth with her tongue, she waited. When the bitter chunks refused to melt she spit the whole mess out the window.

Lily was affronted. "Why'd you go do that?"

Cat spit twice more and wiped her mouth, handing the carob bar over to Lil.

"That's your idea of 'like' chocolate?"

"Well, it ain't exactly like chocolate. It's better for you." Lily pulled the van up into the driveway and Cat climbed out.

"You know what, Lil? I liked you better when you ate real chocolate." She closed the door and walked to the house.

"Oh yeah?" Lily stuck her head out the window. "Well, I liked you better when you weren't such a grumpy old sour-puss super famous stuck-up writer."

Chapter Three

Outside a wind was blowing through the night air, causing the pine branches to flail against her kitchen window. She leaned against the counter, thinking about Lily's parting shot that evening. *Stuck up*—it's what Lily always said when she didn't know what else to say.

Inside the cabinet, on a shelf of its own, lay the shiny gold bag of fresh coffee beans. Cat pressed it to her face and inhaled. She slit the bag neatly across the top, burping its enticing aroma. The beans ground fine and black, almost sticky. The whole thing was foreplay.

The light on her answering machine was still blinking. The message that had awaited her when she arrived home was from Marianna, the owner of Mari's Café and Bookstore. They wanted her to do a *reading*. To be the *featured* writer for an upcoming open mike. *To take comments and answer questions from the audience,* Marianna had whispered as if it were a secret. The whole idea of it made her just as ill as if she'd been asked to belly dance on *Leno*.

She poured the black coffee into a thick mug and followed it with a swirl of cream and two sugars. This was better than sex. OK, maybe not better but close, she thought as she sipped.

Stepping out onto the porch and into the icy night, her breath hung and mingled with the heat of the coffee. Stars punctured the blackness of the sky. Rising fast and blue into the night, the waxing moon erased them in its ascent and cast shadows across the hard frozen earth. In the distance echoed a barn owl, its cry the stuff of scary movies. From far away came a rustling and crunching of leaves—maybe a dog or a deer wandering the crest of an icy ridge above, Cat thought.

Cracking tree limbs and a lone howl cut through the crisp air, ricocheting off hills, rolling through valleys, grazing craggy bluffs toward heaven. Every creature, she imagined, was burrowed or nested or curled in some cozy crevice, wings and paws and arms hunched around bodies warmed to stillness. None would leave for unknown warmer places. For most, there was ease in the known, even if it chilled them. They knew how to keep from freezing to death in it.

She longed for spring when the air wouldn't sting; when sweetness would fill it with moist loose dirt and worms and green shoots twisting up through the earth. She awaited each season with the same desire, like a kid waiting for Christmas, and always at least a month before its turn. She didn't have a favorite. She was an egalitarian in her longing, welcoming the heat of summer and the cold of winter with the same enthusiasm. Maybe it was the relief in knowing that nothing ever stayed the same. Or maybe it was the comfort in trusting that, in fact, it really did.

Soon, she knew, there would begin a buzz whirring through the valley. Humming over the rushing creeks, out-lasting bleating sheep, hanging above the barks of distant hound dogs. It would come from a chorus of tiny cheeping peep frogs hanging in trees. It was a sound that was old in her. That reminded her. As kids, she and her brother Will would crouch beside the stream that bordered Kate's farm and catch the little peepers. For days they would keep them in shoeboxes scattered with grass, a jar lid serving as their pond. By the third day the frogs would be *bakin' and stinkin',* as Kate would say and then order their release. Memories. They were like pieces of short stories strung together and pinned to the sounds of the seasons.

Her cabin was settled into the bowl of a spoon-shaped valley whose blue ridges rose and stretched into a silhouette of a woman lying on her back. The sun that pinked over her shoulder each morning met the cabin's face. The stones and timbers used to build it had been plucked and cut from the land on which it sat.

Back in the late thirties, her grandparents, Kate and Angus Hood, had been the last of an exodus of Scots who'd migrated to western North Carolina. They'd bought the farm cheap from an old black tobacco farmer broken by the Depression. They'd landed in these mountains, Kate had once told her, because it reminded them of home. Cat later learned from her school books that these Blue Ridges had once, millions of years before the glaciers had sliced them apart, joined the Hebrides of Scotland. The nexus was uncanny.

Angus had been a farmer and a cabinetmaker. A great strapping man, Kate had said, with green eyes and a giant red handlebar mustache that matched the curls upon his head. Cat had never met him. He'd died before she was born. She thought she would have liked him, mainly because of his silver harmonica, tucked in a corner of his old rolltop, in a worn blue velvet case, as if only moments before he had placed it there himself. She'd discovered it one rainy afternoon.

Sneaking into the forbidden realm of her grandmother's bedroom, she'd stood on tiptoes to see the blue case inside the oak desk. In her remembrance she recalled the feeling she'd had upon cracking its hinge, revealing the shiny harp for the first time. For Cat, it might as well have been set with diamonds. Her heart had quickened with urgency as she held the smooth cool metal in her small hands. She brought the harp to her child's lips and blew a soft shy note. A slight whiff of sweet tobacco blew from the sound. It was her grandfather, she'd been sure.

"Like an angel."

The voice of her grandmother came whispering behind her. Cat fumbled the harmonica, bouncing and spinning it across the wood floor. It bumped to a halt at Kate's feet. Bending slowly she retrieved it, cupping it to her own nose. Cat watched her grandmother sway to a tune playing only in her mind.

"He blew tunes like an angel," she said. "Do you think you could play it?"

The question had been heavy on her small shoulders. She'd wanted to play it. Like an angel, if she were to be specific. The weight of this new responsibility had nudged a place in her.

A year of hiking, at first deep into the woods away from the world, to settle on a sunny rock or lean against a mossy tree, where she'd practice. Scaling the harp, tongue and lips rubbed raw in the repetition. Later, she'd settled high in the rafters of the barn. Once, she'd peeked out and caught a glimpse of her grandmother, poised with arms outstretched, a sheet waiting to be clipped to the line, her head cocked, listening.

Now Cat shivered in her rocker and sipped the steaming

coffee. She remembered cold nights like this one that had beckoned Kate with her yarn and Cat with her harp to the porch, where they'd sat in a comfortable quiet together. She recalled the night Kate died. It was while she'd been playing *Amazing Grace* that her grandmother's soul had left her body.

There was a crunching of footsteps coming closer from up the cove—a deliberate march of an upright creature. The rising moon had spotlighted the shadowy figure making its way down the long cove road. Cat recognized Delores, not from the glimpse by the moonlight, but from the sound of her stride. Long and easy. There would be just enough coffee for Cat to top off and Delores to warm up. She lit a cigarette and watched the approaching figure.

Delores's name had appeared in a letter addressed to Kate that had arrived a week after her death. It was Cat who had opened it and first read the words written in Delores' hand.

Dear Mrs. Hood, ... My name is Delores Marley-Stevens ... I'd like to purchase a piece of your property. Not just any piece, but a small plot of ten acres at the base of Marley's Mountain ...

Cat had known exactly where this piece of property was located. It was only a quarter mile up the cove where an overgrown rutted drive lead to the dilapidated homestead of Gabe Marley, the old black tobacco farmer who'd long ago sold Kate and Angus his farm. *Our family wants to return to the land that my grandfather, for a lifetime, wept over losing. It's important ...*

Will had fought Cat on it. Said that they didn't have to make up for a deal that went down decades ago. Said that they didn't owe anybody anything. But Cat hadn't been so

29

sure. It was *important*, the letter had read. That morning, she had decided to hike up to the old shack falling in on itself.

Cat had approached and circled the old homestead, envisioning it upright and permanent. Imagining, as she did, the old couple out in their yard, scattering chickens, splitting firewood, mixing lye soap in a big black kettle, scolding children weaving chases between the swinging axe and the scalding water. Under her feet the ground felt different, Cat had suddenly noticed. There was another belonging here. Different from the traces of ore that led to her own roots. Generations of a family had left the imprint of a life here, she'd decided.

As Delores made her way closer to the cabin, Cat went inside and poured the second cup of coffee and then waited for Delores to join her. She was tall and dark and beautiful in the moonlight, her head wrapped with a colorful African print scarf, the pattern repeating in her mittens. It had been an unexpected visit like this one that had decided their friendship. They'd rocked in silence for nearly ten minutes before Delores finally turned to her and said, "Let's talk about *anything* except kids." And this had become the terms of their friendship.

"Been hearing you coming for the last twenty minutes," Cat said as they settled back into the rockers. Soft clouds blew across the moon, flickering the landscape before them, like an old silent movie. The air was colder now. Cat lit an oil lamp hanging on the wall behind them.

"I came to rest with you a minute," Delores said and lit a long white cigarette, a holdover from her New York City life.

"It's pandemonium over there." Behind curled lashes her black eyes cast back a sliver of moonlight.

It was always pandemonium over there, Cat thought. Three growing boys and Mamma and Matthew were often enough to bring Delores along the road between their homes, to rest on this porch with Cat. Especially in the winter when everyone was stuck in the house together.

Every woman needs a single girlfriend to crash with, Cat had decided. And she was often glad for the company. Even the quiet kind. Conversation came slow between the silences. Giving each time to drift and gather thoughts. Like writing, Cat thought, without the dreams in between there would be nothing to put on the page.

Behind the sifting clouds, Cat glimpsed Orion's belt in the sky. It hung just to the left of Snowball Mountain. "Snow," she said, sniffing the air.

"They're not predicting it."

"That's 'cause they're inside and can't smell it."

The women smoked and rocked and watched the sky grow opaque with clouds.

"Saw your picture in the paper." Delores broke the silence. "How does it feel to be famous?"

Cat rocked forward and tossed her cigarette over the rail. "Man, I'm getting sick of hearing that word. One blurb in the *Tattler* doesn't make me famous."

"More than you were yesterday, it does."

There was no arguing with that. At least it was so down at the lumberyard where she was now pinned, breast to breast, with the blonde Makita girl. But she didn't guess that those fellas' eyes would do more than glance over the skinny-ass little writer as they settled on the pair of ballooning tits beside her. So much for fame.

"So, what are you going to do?" Delores interrupted her thoughts.

"Whatdya mean, *do?*"

"Cat, your life is about to change. Book tours, travel, money—all those things that change people's lives when they get famous. You're probably going to have to give up carpentry." She laughed softly and then grew serious. "Maybe even move away."

"I think you should be talking to Stephen King, not Cat Hood. This is one little book in one little town. Lucky if I see enough money to buy myself a steak dinner."

"That's what you say now, but things are going to change for you, just wait."

Something nudged her. Maybe change was coming just as surely as the signal of snow in the air, she thought.

The phone jangled inside the house and Cat listened as the machine picked up. It was Matthew's urgent voice telling Delores to come home quick; a blizzard was on the way—they'd just heard it on the news.

Cat wondered what kind of sign Lily would make of that coincidence.

The women looked at each other and then to the heavy sky. The moon was entirely gone now. The temperature had dropped and the wind had picked up and flakes were beginning to spiral heavily downward, caught in the shafts of the cabin's lights. Cat thought how funny it was that city people relied more on the Weather Channel than they did their own senses.

"It's pretty dark, want to spend the night?" Cat asked. "Or shall I drive you?"

Delores stood and stretched her long thin frame, fingers nearly touching the ceiling. "No, I got to go back to all that noise. I think I'll prolong it with a walk. You just pray for me."

"You know I don't pray, Dee."

"Yes, you do. You're a good person. Mamma says you must be Christian."

Mamma, a big round woman, would grab your face between her thick palms and press it between her pillowed breasts, squeezing till you gulped for air. When Mamma proclaimed something, mostly everybody agreed. It was just the easiest thing to do.

"Not all good people are Christians and not all Christians are good people," Cat said.

"Now, what would Jesus say about that?"

"Jesus ..." Cat stomped her foot. "Jesus was this poor bastard carpenter who hung out with drunks, prostitutes, and queers. He goes and beats up some punk loan shark, who sounds off to some dirty politician, next thing Jesus knows he's pinned to a cross and on his way to becoming a cult hero. I'll tell you what Jesus'd say, he'd say, Fuck me, man."

"Blasphemy." Delores stood with her hands on her hips, a familiar stance.

"Now, if I were black," Cat teased. "I'd be a Christian."

"What now?" Delores eyebrows shot up.

"I'd go down to the AME, listen to the Martin Luther King Choir, clap and sing, Amen and Hallelujah, all over the place. Hell, I'd even dress up and wear hats." Cat lit another cigarette with the one burning in her hand. "But, I won't 'cause it's not the same for white people."

Delores shook her head. "*God* is not the same for white people? What kind of thing is that to say? You got some kind of God I don't know about?"

"Look, if I was black and Christian people'd respect it. Like they did with Martin Luther King Jr., Rosa Parks, and the brigades of domestics who walked their feet to bloody blisters in the Montgomery bus boycott."

33

"Girl, where do you get your ideas?"

"It was noble, righteous, spiritual. But if I call myself a Christian now, being white and all, people'd think I listen to Rush Limbaugh, vote for Jesse Helms, and tithe to the fucking Christian Coalition. It's shameful and political. You think I want to be associated with that mess?"

"You might have a point, but not one that I want to discuss with you." Delores leaned over and gave her a quick hug around the neck. She stood for a moment and gazed out to the hills. White flakes of snow had begun to fall, collecting on her head like tufts of down. Wrapping her scarf tighter, she headed for the steps.

"Well, at least send some good vibes out into the universe to see me home. Isn't that what you pagans do?"

"I'm not a pagan, either." Cat yelled after her. "Don't you want a ride? I can give you a ride."

Delores waved. Seconds later, the snow-filled darkness swallowed her.

The wind had picked up and had begun a low moaning howl as it cut corners around the cabin and blew through cracks in the old barn siding. One thwack of the maul axe loosened firewood from its ice entombed stack. Fists of wind punched at her as she split kindling. Before entering the house she heard a sharp report, like the crack of a rifle sound in the woods. Then a muffled thud. The trees were breaking. They were in for it, she thought.

The power had cut off in the crack of a snapping hemlock. It had closed the creek road, but no one knew it just then. They wouldn't know it for hours. Outside, wind whirled snow into banshee-like figures clawing and screeching outside her window. When she pulled away the curtain—it was her own reflection she saw in the lamplight. The world beyond these walls was white and impenetrable. She went upstairs to gather her pillow and blankets. Her room was an icy chamber, warmed only by the stove heat rising up the stairwell. Frost crackled on the insides of windowpanes.

The plump brown couch took up the whole wall in the living room; opposite the fireplace, it often served as her winter bed. Sometimes she wished for a storm, just so she could sleep downstairs. Mike had joined her, literally, up on the sofa, curled in a ball on top of her legs. It was their ritual. She rubbed his golden tummy with her socked feet.

"You're a good old cowboy, ain'tcha." He wiggled on top of her toes. "Saving your mamma from the cold. A regular John damn Wayne, you are." And she stretched to scratch around his ears.

Eight years ago, in the parking lot of OzGirlz, a dyke club where she'd sometimes bartend for extra money, she'd found the puppy stuffed into one of the saddlebags of her motorcycle. It was his little nose poking from under the flap, bumping her leg that nearly toppled them to the ground. The brass heart on his collar read simply, *Mike*. Not counting Lily, he'd pretty much been her one and only long-term relationship.

Girlfriends had never been long-term for her. When Lily had met Hannah, Cat thought it would be a similar passing thing. When it kept going, she got jealous.

"How come you spend every second with that girl?" Cat had huffed. "You never did this with guys."

"Guys were a phase," Lily said. "I'm in love with Hannah. We're gonna be together, forever."

"Forever? How long is that?"

⌘⌘

In response to Cat's inability to stick with one girl at a time, often Lily would accuse her—*You are nothin' but a slut.*

"You think you're gonna fall in love by sleeping with every girl in town?" Lily had asked, disgustedly. "It just happens when you're least expecting it," she said.

But Cat wasn't sure she really wanted it, anyway. Relationships, as far as she could see, weren't all they were cracked up to be. *Do this. Don't do that.* That kind of stuff just wasn't going to work in her life.

Cat had been convinced that Lily just wanted her to *suffer*.

But it was a rainy night in the emergency room, after Lily had run her bike off the road and it was determined that, in spite of some bruises and a chipped ankle bone, Lily would live to be a mean old woman, that Cat had made her peace with Hannah. In their shared relief, Cat could see that they were bonded by their love for the same woman.

The kettle whistled and Cat made herself a cup of black tea. From the time that she was a small child, she had suffered its bitterness. It had made Kate smile the first time Cat had ever turned down sugar and lemon to temper the dark liquid's bite. She had laughed at Cat's pinched lips. *It's the Scot in you,* her grandmother pronounced, making her willing to suffer the bitterness.

Outside, the wind intensified, if that were even possible. It slammed against the house, racing up and over its peak, prying its tin sheathing with swift malleable fingers. Snowdrifts had crested windowsills. Every now and then the cabin would quake. *Shiver me timbers,* her brother would say on nights when he and Cat and their grandmother gathered near the fire as gusts shook the eaves.

Haloed oil lamps cast shadows on books, glancing and sparking their gold-lettered spines. These were leather-bound books. *The Classics,* Kate would declare, pulling one from its slot, smoothing her palm over its cover as she opened it, careful not to crack its binding. After the supper dishes were washed by Will and dried by Cat, the three would bring blankets and pillows to this winter nest and settle in, each eager to hear the next chapter. Well into a winter's evening, the soft trill of Kate's brogue would narrate the tales of pirates and damsels and knights. Later, when they were older and Will had moved his pillow and blankets to the thick rug in front of the fire, and Kate's eyesight had begun its fade, he and Cat would take turns reading to their grandmother. Later still, when Kate's eyesight was gone and Will had left for good, it was Cat's voice alone reciting more grownup tales of crimes and punishments, ladies and their lovers, and lost generations.

But as kids, Will and Cat would lie toe to toe on the long couch, scrunched beneath quilts, listening to the story until Kate fell asleep, stretched out upon the recliner with a book flapped open on her lap. Soon after, Will would drift off, too, and in those quiet moments, long into a dark and snowy night, Cat would lie awake, listening. Will and Kate's sleeping sounds followed and teased each other, reminding her of the seesawing snores of Snow White's dwarves. The fire crackled, battling the cold, flickers of orange against the glass door of the woodstove.

Cat stood for a moment in the middle of the room whose dark pine walls merged into the planking of the floor. The rough stones of the fireplace absorbed the heat and blocked the cold. In this room, the hands of three generations had poked coals bright, pulled classics from shelves, and cupped thick mugs of black tea. The collected memories of this one family had blended and cozied themselves here. Now, it was mostly Cat's memory that recollected them. Will had left so long ago that the burden of keeping the remembrances seemed left to her alone. A wave of fear passed through her. What if she forgot? Not just her own memories, but the ones given her by Kate. Memories of Angus, the handsome boy who'd stolen Kate's heart and carried her with his dreams to America; and those of William, Cat's father, who'd escaped his mountain home, northward to the city, discarding his overalls and accent with the same urgency. And hadn't she'd even been the keeper of her brother Will's memories? The ones of an earlier time when they were children and Will was happy, before his anger had gripped and pulled him out the door, away, forever.

Mindful of her tea, now, Cat curled back under the blankets and Mike's toasty body. The memory of that day brought with it a sickening feeling, even long after the deed was done and the news was spread.

"If you go through that door, William, you'll not return in my lifetime." Kate had stood squaring off, facing the young man, arms folded across her chest. Her long gray plaits hung down her back, tips nearly touching the belt of her robe. It was late, and the old woman had already been asleep when the drunken stumbling of her grandson banged her awake. As was becoming the ritual, Kate had flown from her room in a rage.

"You dirty stayout, you!" Her voice rising to a shriek as Cat climbed from the loft.

"C'mon, Gran, leave him be. He's home. He's safe. That's all that matters."

Kate had yanked free of her granddaughter's grip and reached for the hanging leather strap that served as a tether for straying animals. Kate's intent had not been to tether Will, but to whip him. He ducked the slap to his shoulders, taking it instead, across his cheek; the gash poured blood. He'd landed on the floor with a look of surprise on his face. He lifted his fingers to the sticky wetness puddling in his sprouting beard.

"Jesus, Gran." Cat pushed past her grandmother. The cut was deep and long, from cheekbone to dimple.

"No, lemme go." He shoved her from him. Struggling to his feet. Will swayed and then stood. Straightened to his full height he towered over his grandmother's small frame. Holding his shirtsleeve to his face, he had raised his chin and then took a step toward Kate. His sister moved between them.

"Stop. Now, Will." Cat placed her palms on his chest. He stared at the woman behind her. Cat had begged. "You two have to quit this." Shaking, Kate pulled a pointed finger and wagged it at him.

"You'll get out of my house. Now," she'd growled. "And you'll stay out, forever." Her face had grown ancient and tired, filled with a kind of stony defeat.

Cat felt the swallow in Will's throat as he mustered the courage to stand defiant, to claim his victory. But in that moment it was more a surrender than a win.

"Naw, Gran, you don't mean that." In the moment that she'd turned on her grandmother, Will slipped past her and out the door.

He had been eighteen years old. There was nothing, not even the law, to keep him there any longer. It was a long time coming. Drinking and drugs had increased both his anger and his apathy. This strap was the proverbial straw, she knew. She had watched him roll the bike down the drive, hand pressed to his bloody face. She did not see him again for nearly eight years.

He was like his father and his grandfather before him, Kate had once said, although he'd never admit it. The Hood men had each fled their homelands to follow dreams that could only be realized in other places. Ironically, it was the very life of a mountain farmboy, the one that Will had so disdained, that prepared him for what awaited him as an adult. Not the corporate, city life pursued by his father, but the "career" he forged as a wilderness guide and, eventually, a bush pilot, long after he had escaped his grandmother's care.

Just as Kate's looks had skipped a generation and reappeared in her granddaughter, so too had the dreams of Angus Hood passed over his own son, only to arise with renewed spirit in the heart of his grandson. Like his grandfather, Will had traveled far, eventually landing in Alaska where he'd led hunting expeditions through the big thick cold landscape of the north. He had followed Kate's orders. He did not return to the mountains until after her death.

Cat had hated him for that. She'd hated the lines that had deepened with regret across Kate's brow. Hated that Will didn't know, couldn't know that every now and then she would catch the tilt of her grandmother's head as she listened for the sound of his old Electra coming up the cove road.

It had been Kate's death that finally brought him home. Cat cringed to see the long white scar that crossed Will's cheek. It was his grandmother's mark, the last she would ever leave on him.

Chapter Four

With morning had come a slight reprieve in the weather. The wind had let up but the snow continued to fall. Cat was going to be stuck out here for days. The cold was bitter. When they'd awakened and Mike had whimpered his call to nature at the back door, it had taken her nearly thirty minutes to shovel through the hip-high snowdrift to the hedgerow beyond which there was a valley in the deep layering. Mike waited, howling his impatience. If a dog could stand crosslegged, this would have been Mike's position.

"The things I do for you," she said as he brushed by her, ignoring her efforts. He had to *go,* for God's sake.

After she'd scrambled eggs on the stovetop and toasted wheat bread on skewers against the flames, she poured the coffee that had been brewing on the old kerosene camp stove her grandmother had bought for such times. Cat guessed that for some this storm was fast becoming a disaster. She'd set the milk and butter and two steaks outside the door in a cooler. She was set to hunker down. Even her laptop was battery powered. She could write uninterrupted for as long as the juice lasted.

Outside, the snow was deep, burying the road. The plows wouldn't make it here for another two or three days.

Nothing, not even a rabbit, could be seen moving about. She was trapped in a weird kind of freedom. When the weather blew like this, it limited everyone's ability to do just about anything normal or expected. It was a time when games and jigsaw puzzles were hauled from closets and attics, silver got polished, stitches sewn, letters written, and books read. And, for her, it was free time to write. Something that was usually accompanied by guilt. Kate used to sniff her out of whatever dusty corner she had become invisible in, pencil and tablet in hand, and command her to abandon her writing.

"Get out! Go get the stink blown off ya," Kate would order as Cat sat hunched, just beginning to fill a fresh white page. With fists planted on bony hips, the old woman had squinted at the child who sighed and waited, hoping for a reprieve. The words clicking off Kate's tongue had matched the sharp angles of her chin and nose, and the bent elbows that formed matching triangles. "It's a beautiful day. Get."

This had made Cat long for rainy days and snowstorms, the safest time to lock herself away in her loft. As long as she stayed quiet, Kate would usually let her be. But on warm, sunny days, Kate's constant nagging locked in her guilt with its repetition. Reluctantly, she would fold the tablet closed and head outdoors. Often, if she were caught dawdling or wandering aimlessly around the farm, the stink she was supposed to be ridding herself of would be replaced by that of manure after she'd been ordered to shovel out a stall or two. Her grandmother would mutter about idleness and the devil's work, and that would be the end of it.

Later, to avoid this inevitability, she would sneak her pad and pen and hide up in the barn or down in the spring-house, ignoring the summoning calls of Kate's search. With each muster the sweat of guilt would bead on Cat's brow and the lies would come forth. No, she would assure her grandmother, she had not been *scribbling stories*. In fact, she'd been out getting the stink blown off her.

The biggest lie, however, had occurred when she went off to college. Kate had wanted her to study law, like her father.

"You'll not waste the money on writing stories. They'll lead you nowhere," Kate had warned, straightening Cat's shirt collar. The warning went beyond the skeptical future of a fiction writer. There was some kind of dismay in it, and it had urged Cat to lie and ease the foreboding behind her grandmother's cautionary words. Cat remembered looking away, not wanting Kate's fear to *get in* her, as Lily would say.

"*Law,*" Cat had assured, perjuring herself to her grandmother's accusing finger. "I'll be studying law."

There had been no tears at this departure. Kate hadn't been given to tears. If the Scots were anything, they were stoic. Her grandmother had practiced it to an art form. And, as Cat herself had learned long ago, tears were not tolerated in anyone else, either. Especially anyone related to Kate Hood. And so, heading east with Lily, out of the mountains, away from home and family, Cat had cried. Another deception. Another disappointment. She was not the Scot Kate believed her to be.

Leaning down from the sofa, careful not to disturb Mike as he snored loudly at the other end, she searched the floor until her hand caught the corner of the book that had been kicked, but not retrieved, from beneath the couch, and pulled it to her chest. It was hardbound. Like a real book, she thought. Its cover offered a drawing of the view from her own porch. It was the silhouette of the woman-mountain, sketched by an ex-lover that Cat still kept up with. Riding the curved ridges of the mountainous breast and belly was the title and then her name—*Outside of Everything* by Cat Hood. She opened the cover, careful not to crack the binding (in case it were to become a classic). With her palm, she smoothed the dedication page flat. *For Lil, my best friend.*

Her thumb ruffled the pages, watching them peel from each other, separating and slipping back together. She caught glimpses of words she'd written, images she'd conjured, and stories she'd told. And yet here in this form, upon these pages, between these covers, none felt as if they had belonged to her. She could never fiddle with them again. No matter how not right they were. It was a done deal.

On the back were the nice things she'd had to beg (OK, maybe not beg, but ask) some people to say about the book. The first and her most prized was from a teacher, her mentor, Peter Cummings. He had guided her through the first and final drafts of the collection. And then there was one from a literary critic: a friend of a friend, who'd agreed to read it and review it and, thank God, said nice things about it. Finally, her most desperate plea of all: a published poet she'd slept with one time, mostly (she admitted only to herself) so the woman's name would adorn her book jacket.

"What would you say now, Gran?" Cat asked aloud, addressing only a ghost. There was silence, as there had always been silence from Kate when it came to the writing. *If you can't say anything nice, don't say anything at all.* Kate Hood lived by her adages.

Long before Cat's letters curled cursive, she had given up reading her stories to her grandmother. They had been met with silence and a set jaw. It was wrong, she'd always thought, how Kate, who had been so fond of the stories on the bookshelves, seemed to detest Cat's. It didn't make sense. Maybe it wasn't the stories themselves that Kate had despised, maybe it was the very act of Cat's writing them that had irritated her grandmother so. *Writing's a way to waste a day.* But Cat had come to think that this was the least of her grandmother's objections. Writing was intimate. Cat suspected that it was this intimacy that Kate so loathed, rather than its frivolity. The Scots were no more given to inward emotions than they were to outward demonstrations of them.

She opened her notepad. It was a small wire bound top-spiral that slid neatly into her back pocket. She preferred it to the side-spiraled ones that pressed into the cheek of her left palm and made messier the ink that had permanently (she was sure) stained her pinky blue. Within the pages of the notebook were her familiar scribbles. Words and symbols, doodles and scratches. Stolen conversations and usurped actions of unsuspecting people were snatched while she eavesdropped in coffee shops, airports, and street corners. It was all up for grabs. Even the gems of wisdom and silliness that dropped from Lily's tongue were hers for the taking.

Lily had once accused, "It's like you steal souls."

Cat thought of herself as a collector. After all, it wasn't whole people she'd based her characters on, it was parts and pieces of many, and mostly (she hated to admit) the truth about herself. And, so she collected: a curl of hair, a hint of a lisp, hairy moles and sprinkles of freckles, even a finger sneaking up a nose were free for the gathering. These bits would be pocketed along with stories of a neighbor's moonshinin' grandpa or a friend's crazy Aunt Lyda or a scene from someone else's kitchen or bedroom or barn. She'd scribble in haste between sips of tea, shovels of shit, and too-long sermons.

45

Cat skimmed through the notebook, searching the entries, which upon collection had seemed perfect fodder for her fiction. As usual, at second glance, most were just *You had to be there* kind of moments. Sometimes these turned into material; more often than not they were just exercises, bench presses for the mind.

She paused at a page in the center of the notebook. In her long scrawl was written, *Mother was in trouble. She got kicked out of Montreal.* Where had that come from? she wondered.

Tapping the end of her pen against her front teeth she searched her mind and recalled the late afternoon sun steaming through the café's window where she'd sat *sippin' and spyin'* as Lily would accuse. Now she remembered. They were seated at a nearby table, sitting across from each other: an older man and a young woman. The white-haired gentleman had tipped his cappuccino, nearly dunking his neat goatee into the tiny cup.

Leaning across the table he had whispered to his companion. Cat's practiced ear perked at the softness of the words, *Mother was in trouble,* he'd said slowly. Cat honed in. *She got kicked out of Montreal.* She looked over her page. At the top she'd written, *dapper.*

Cat stood to clear the breakfast dishes from the table and Mike, who'd been patiently waiting at her feet, rose with her and nudged her knee. He looked up wearing his *I haven't eaten and aren't I pathetic* face.

"OK, OK." She rubbed his head and filled his bowl with dry crunchy nuggets. He sniffed and turned up his nose.

"What? You don't want that?"

He glared at her. Was that really possible for a dog?

"Look, you're getting a little chubby here. No more meat for you." The shepherd grunted and then clunked, with a sigh, to the floor in front of his bowl. His chin dropped to his paws and he whimpered.

"Pitiful, you are," Cat said. "Think of it this way, if you were human, this would be a rice cake. Be grateful."

The dog snorted and slowly lifted himself. He slunked past her, head lowered, tail drooping. The clicking of his toenails meant that he was making his way up into the cold loft. She called after him.

"It's freezing up there." She listened for his return but he wasn't coming back. He was sulking.

Kate's voice entered her head.

"So, it's off with the nose to spite the face, is it?" Her grandmother would toss the phrase into the midst of one of Cat's own adolescent sulks. But what the hell did it mean? Thank God, she herself would never have any kids to torture with that kind of shit. The abuse stops here, Cat thought. Almost, she corrected herself. Poor old Mike was now her victim, probably up there right now, freezing his ass off, pissed about his new crunchy food. Everybody had the right to sulk now and then.

She went to the table and picked up the notepad, taking it and a cup of tea to her chair by the fire. She read the words again. *Mother was in trouble.* Cat guessed that *Mother* must have been kicked out of Montreal about the same time Kate and Angus had arrived in America.

The snow was falling heavier now. Rather than clearing with the stretch of morning, the storm seemed to be regrouping, readying for round two. Cat tried to imagine Kate and Angus' first winter here. The story of its bitter cold and chest-high snowdrifts, and of the small square hut that was their first home, had become family legend. They had arrived at an unlikely time, it occurred to Cat, for starting a new life. Late October.

She added wood to the stove and eased herself back into the scoop of her reading chair. The legendary winter, the story went, had begun only a matter of weeks after Kate and Angus' arrival in the mountains. They had hunkered down in a hut no bigger than this room for a long dark winter. In that little makeshift shelter, Cat's father, William, had been born. The first of January. The first of January? The question sent her from the chair to the bookcase, scanning the spines with her finger. It was a heavy leather satchel she pulled free, instead.

Inside the folds were the "family documents," as her grandmother had explained soon after her sight had faded. Cat rummaged past the deed to the farm, two ancient and tattered passports, titles to old trucks long since rusted to skeletons behind the barn, and a bill of sale for a young bull named Teddy. The blue-covered wills of Angus and Kate and William and his wife, Linnea, were all neatly packed together. So many dead relatives, Cat thought. As she lifted the stack to her lap, a small black and white photo slipped from the pile and landed at her feet. She bent to retrieve it. She'd seen it many times before and as always, she fixed on it. It was her mother.

Linnea was young, younger even than Cat, right now. Her dark hair was gently swept back, caught in sea breeze. She was leaning on a railing, Cat noticed, paused and pensive, staring over the expanse of a calm ocean. The sharp angles of her profiled nose and chin were lifted up, and Cat wondered what her mother had been thinking just then. Or had she been thinking anything? Maybe someone, an old friend, or maybe even William, had posed her like that. After the click, she might have lifted the Budweiser Cat imagined hidden from the lens and slammed it back, wiping foamy guzzle from her mouth with the swipe of sleeve.

48

But no. This did not look like a Budweiser slammin' kind of broad. Linnea was delicate, refined; Cat imagined that her mother would have understood elegant table settings and misted herself in fine perfumes.

She brought the photo to her nose and sniffed, waiting for some distinct smell that would suddenly, after thirty-two years, evoke a flood of infant memories, connecting her to womb and breast. But there was none. There had never been one. This mother of hers was foreign in more ways than by the simple fact of death.

Cat suspected that this mother would never have allowed her to trek barefooted through fields and streams or to climb a tree. This woman seemed the kind to let out a shrill squeal at the sight of a mouse, like ladies leaping on chairs in old black and white movies. Or worse. Cat grinned, recalling the time Kate pulled a handful of dead pollywogs from the pocket of a crumbled pair of shorts. What would this sophisticated New York attorney have done if her hand had sunk into a mass of jellied froglings? She pictured the faint, the slow swoon to the ground—graceful.

No, she was pretty sure that she was meant to have been Kate's daughter by default. When the glob of stinking tadpoles did slap to the floor, Kate had first chased her through the house with a wooden spoon, landing two or three stinging swipes across her thighs. Finally, after the collaring, she'd been sent to the springhouse to wash the reeking shorts. Kate had been tough. But they had always understood one another. Cat slipped the photo back into the pouch and returned to the stack of papers and certificates on her lap.

Births and deaths and marriages were authenticated on these pages. She found the rigid yellow paper testifying to her grandparents' nuptials. She skimmed the fading ink with a cautious finger, pausing under the date. September 20th, 1938.

The document had been signed by Captain Ian MacDonald. This was something she hadn't known. Hadn't ever questioned or wondered about. This was something she never would have expected. Kate and Angus had been married aboard the ship that had carried them to America.

October, November, she counted on her fingers. January, she stopped. It had only been nearly four months later when her father had been born on that next New Year's day, 1939. Holy shit. She laid the paper flat. Her grandmother had been pregnant. Unwed. A girl in trouble. *Mother was in trouble ...*

Where was a telephone line to heaven when you needed one? But this explained the look that sometimes appeared on Kate's face on those rare occasions when she spoke of her home and her family in Scotland. It explained the longing fed by exile, by loneliness, by isolation, that had eventually enveloped the three of them, Will included.

Cat rifled through the rest of the pouch but there were only more records and a yellowed newspaper article featuring her grandfather and one of his prize-winning heifers. She frowned, trying now to recall the family that Kate had so painfully remembered.

Stewarts, Kate had once confided with a small note of pride. That meant royalty, way back. There was Kate's father, Malcolm, and her mother, Agnes. An older brother killed in the First War and a younger sister, Mary Catherine, for whom Cat had been christened. More wee ones followed, some still in nappies when Kate had left. Cat couldn't remember how many had been boys or how many girls. Only that there had been many. But there had never been word from any of them. Only Kate's memories. Why? This question had plagued her as a child and she in turn had once, but only once, plagued Kate with it.

"Do you write to them, Gran?" she'd asked, pondering the stern faces that stared from graying photos in the album. Her grandmother had sighed. Cat raised her head to the old woman's chin. Kate's bottom lip was trembling as the only tear Cat had ever seen escape her grandmother's eye ran its course along the crevices in the old face, dropping hot onto the back of Cat's hand. "Do they not write to you?" she had pressed. When again her query had been met with silence, Cat flipped the page. Even at seven years old, she knew better than to ask any more questions.

But, now, now, this old news. Kate had been something of an orphan, exiled, *kicked out of Paisley.* She'd been *in trouble.* Cat breathed deeply, clearing out other clutter.

"Mother was in trouble," the old man had said. Cat imagined his trembling hand reaching across the table, touching the fingers of his listening daughter. *"She was kicked out of Montreal."*

Accompanying this thought came that flutter inside her. The one that always came when a story was hatching. A *strange longing,* Cat thought, recalling C. S. Lewis's words, aptly describing her own rising muse. Humming from within.

Cat fiddled with a candle. It was only three o'clock; the blustery air outside had gone dark and heavy, and inside the shadows were taking over. Blowing out the match, she closed her eyes and imagined the young troublemaker—Kate. But it wasn't Kate. Familiar and unfamiliar, shifting and changing, the way the features of Cat's own characters always shifted and changed at the beginning, until her mind could settle things. Like those police composites where you pick and choose a nose or chin. Although the remembered face was vague, its expression, Cat could feel, was sad. Then the image slowly faded.

51

A sudden slam against the back door made Cat jump and spill hot tea down the front of her leg. She yelled and danced around the room. Another quick thud landed against the frame and she limped toward it, smoothing her thigh as she went. Pulling aside a curtain, she looked out. Big fat flakes fell and splattered against the pane. Again, a loud punch to the wood below her knees jarred her. She glanced down for the source and saw the tip of a single black boot in the snow. Yanking against the ice that had sealed the door closed, she loosened it with a crack. With the help of a wild gust of wind, it popped open. She stuck her head into the snowy evening, squinting against the blinding white. Suddenly, from below, a gloved hand grabbed her around one knee, buckling her out, rolling her off the threshold and into the snow. Cat tumbled and landed on her side. Slowly righting to her seat, she traced the path her somersault had cleared. Her ass was wet and her shoulder throbbed and she was scared.

"You fucking bastard!" Cat stared at the figure on the ground, half-propped against the cabin's wall. With already numbing fingers she balled a wad of wet snow and threw it, missing the bearded face. A great laugh rumbled from him and his grin revealed a gold eyetooth.

"Gotcha, didn't I?" He pulled his knees under him and lifted his big frame. Kicking packed snow from the soles of his boots, he walked over and extended his hand to her.

"Leave me," she said, swatting her brother's glove away. Standing to her full height only raised her chin to his chest. "You big jerk." She brushed wet snow from her legs and rear end. A cold chunk had slid under her sweater and inched up her back, melting to an icy trickle that was now beginning to stream down her spine and into her jeans.

"Aw, I'm sorry, kiddo," the giant consoled. "I forgot what a wimp you are."

She pushed him aside and made her way back into the warmth of the living room. He followed her. "Take all that wet stuff off. Right there." Cat pointed at the entrance. "I'll get you a towel."

"Brothers," she muttered as she stripped off her wet clothes and slid into a soft sweatshirt and pants. She didn't hurry as she toweled her damp head dry. And she didn't hurry while rummaging for an old sweatshirt and an over-sized pair of flannel loungers that a skinny girlfriend had once given her, without checking for size. When she returned, Will was standing in his long johns in front of the fire.

"Here, try these," she said, pushing the clothes at him. After he pulled them on, fitting everywhere except at ankle and wrist where inches of skin lay exposed, he turned to her. Opening his arms wide, he gathered Cat up in a bone-crushing hug. He smelled like baby powder. She breathed him in. Will always smelled like baby powder. She pulled away.

"What the fuck are you doing here?" She looked out the side window—and then out the front. Only white snow and black trees were visible. "How'd you get here?" There was no sign of a car.

A mass of wild reddish brown curls hung below his shoulders and his beard, stiff and frozen, was beginning its thaw, dripping onto his big chest. He eased himself into her chair by the fire, his long arms dangling, looking silly in the too-short sweatshirt sleeves.

"Walked," he said finally. "All the way from Macon's Bend." He grabbed the quilt from behind his head and spread it across his lap, wrapping his feet in a corner fold. Macon's Bend was a good three-mile hike, up and around a curve that daunted even the most agile four-wheel drive

53

vehicles. "I'm froze." He grinned when the impact of this trek finally landed on Cat's face. "Hey, wilderness guide extraordinaire, that's me." He shrugged and lifted his palms.

Cat held up her own palm to ward off the story of his adventure, but he ignored the gesture, regaling her with his journey, as she made his tea. His flight from Anchorage had ended east, over in Charlotte, a good three hours away. Will had driven the rental car into the storm of the night before, inching his way into its thickness, more often than not alone on the highway. Finally, sometime past midnight, he had skidded into a drift of snow. His efforts to dig out had been futile.

"Like trying to bail a fuckin' canoe with a big damn hole in the bottom," he said. He'd slept some in the car, with heat on, until the headlights of a lumbering snowplow woke him. "I gave the guy twenty bucks to get me to Galway; took hours."

"No wonder—in this storm." She handed him his tea, thinking how these antics of his were predictable. She could imagine her brother standing in the middle of a frozen highway, flagging down the truck, pulling himself up and jumping in before the driver even had a chance to realize what was happening.

Once he'd made it to Galway, he said, it was only a matter of finding a cop who, like the plowman, allowed himself to be cajoled into bringing him as far north as his cruiser was allowed.

"He even gave me some hot cocoa. Had a big ole thermos full of it."

At the Little Galway exit, Will had thumbed down a black Jeep with chained wheels.

"You'll never guess who it was ..." but he gave her no chance. "Billy Rutherford!" As if this were a surprise. Of all the

54

people in the valley who'd be stupid enough to be out driving around in a blizzard, Billy Rutherford would have been her first guess. He was an old buddy of Will's from high school, one of those fellas who still sported the long sideburns of his youth. Will shook his head. "Of course he was half-tanked."

Cat rolled her eyes.

"Gotta admit the Jack warmed me up better than the cocoa." He grinned. "Got as far as Macon's Bend. A big hemlock's down across the road, so I had no choice but to walk."

Will and Billy had parted, shaking hands and making tipsy promises to do it again, sometime. By then, dawn had broken and Will, warmed by the whiskey, had trekked the last few miles on foot. Hypothermia was never a consideration, of course. Not for her crazy brother.

"I was doin' OK once I got around the hemlock. The road was iced so I slid a lot. But after the gap, the drifts were deeper and that slowed me way down. Saw a bloody deer carcass. Maybe wild dogs, I'm guessin'."

Cat cringed at the image and settled into her bed on the couch and pulled the comforter up around her chin, balancing her teacup on her knees.

"So now I know *how* you got here, but *why* are you here is the bigger question." She watched him swipe at his big red mustache, feathering it away from his mouth so he could blow on the hot liquid. As he got older, she thought, he looked more and more like his grandfather, Angus.

Will looked hurt. "I can't surprise my own sister?"

"How'd you know I'd even be here?"

He snorted. "Where else would you be?"

"Well, for all you knew, since I haven't heard from you in six months, I could have moved out. Left for places unknown."

"Right. Like you ever go anywhere."

This had been part of their opening conversation ever since the first time Will had returned from Alaska. Her brother's wanderlust had not been hers and somehow he had held her in contempt for staying in this *podunk town stuck in the ass-crack of a mountain.*

"Yeah, well, I'm thinking about it."

"Well, good. Hell, you're nearly thirty-five years old. It's time you did something with your life."

Cat sighed. "Speaking of doing things—why are you here, anyway, Will?"

She hadn't seen that grin for years. It began slowly and met resistance at the dimple, barely cracking creases around his eyes. His mustache twitched, and he looked everywhere but at his sister.

"A girl?" Cat sat up. Will stared into his teacup.

It was true. Written all over the beard scruffy face. His mouth trembled beneath his thick mustache, like it did when he was a boy and his upper lip sported only yellow fuzz. He fumbled with his teacup.

But this couldn't be. Both she and Will had long ago agreed that getting too involved brought nothing but trouble.

"I like girls better," she had confided to him, one night, while they lay on their backs, staring up into a black, star-filled sky.

He was silent for a minute and then said, "I like girls better, too." And then added, "Be careful. They can be trouble."

But now something was different. Will was acting like some weak-kneed school boy all ga-ga over the head cheerleader.

"I don't get it," Cat said, confused. "You met a girl, but you're here?"

"The girl is here," he said. "I mean, she lives here. Over in Sellarsville. I couldn't get that far."

Cat sank into her cushions. This story, she could tell, was not going to be quite as linear as the travel adventure Will had just spun. This one would take a little time to actually iron out.

Sure enough it had been a girl that had brought William Angus Hood back to these mountains he despised. A *woman,* he said. "Her name is Marce and she's *everything,*" he swore. "She's a little older than me, but just two years."

Marce, it turned out, was an anthropologist at Galway's own university. It was while she was on a tour of Alaska, picking bones out of the ice, that she and Will had met. He'd flown the team of researchers out to some frozen tundra that was still practically unmapped. Marce was the only woman among them. That was over six months ago.

"We got married," he said.

Cat choked. Not a little. Not a sputter that goes up your nose and makes your eyes water. The tea drained down her windpipe, filling it, near drowning her. Her brother jumped up and took her cup. He grabbed her arms and held them over her head.

"Don't talk," he kept saying as she tried to take back possession of her arms and wave him off. But his training as a wilderness guide had prepared him to react to all emergency situations and he wouldn't let her go until he could hear her passages were clear.

"You OK?" he asked, hovering.

"Married?"

"We eloped. Last month. Met in Vegas. I wanted to surprise you."

"Well, you succeeded."

"Cat, you'll like her."

She hated the goof on his face. Next, he'd be saying this Marce-person was different. Beautiful. Smart. Wonderful. All the stuff she never wanted to hear out of her bachelor brother's mouth.

She said, "What about our agreement?"

He frowned and looked as if he'd never heard of it.

"You know."

"To *Independence*," they had cheered, tapping glasses together, years ago, in a seedy bar, after they'd been dumped by women who wanted more.

"What agreement?" Will asked.

"About never getting tied down. Why would you want to go ruining a perfectly good life by getting yourself married?"

He was quiet, staring down into his tea, running his thumb along the rim of the cup. Finally, he looked up at her and smiled. She shifted uncomfortably.

"I'm in love with her, Cat."

Envy reared. It was the same envy that sometimes got out of hand when she watched love pass between Lily and Hannah or Delores and Matthew. The same she'd had when the scent of Angus' pipe tobacco had made Kate sway with his silver harmonica pressed in her palms. It was an envy for something she'd never known.

"I want you to meet her."

Cat nodded.

There was nothing else to do. She would meet this woman who'd somehow managed to touch a place in her brother that had been buried. Some kind of tender spot. She wondered if anyone would ever touch her that way.

How many girlfriends had there been? A *million,* she

heard Lily's voice in her head. *You gotta settle down, Cat.* But she didn't want to settle down, and she didn't want her brother to either. And Lily's voice again, *Quit bein' stupid, Cat. Everyone wants someone to love.*

Chapter Five

Will had fallen asleep where he'd plunked himself hours before and Cat gently removed the tea cup from his big hands before it slipped to the floor. She probably could have wrenched it from him and given him a good smack on his lovesick smug puss without him even stirring. She hummed to herself, trying to drown out his snores. His presence was familiar. Comfortable. She hated to admit it, but she liked having him around. The lights flickered, teasing, and then went dead.

The wind had ceased and the snow had waned. Only a flutter or two, every now and then, were the last trailing slackers on the heels of a great snowy race through the frozen valley. The end would be out of sight in the falling dusk. By morning, she figured, the sun would break through the last of the storm clouds and everything would glitter.

She'd gotten over the shock of Will's news that soon she'd meet her new sister-in-law. A woman she would definitely *adore.* And then she thought about her own sorry *herstory* when it came to women. *Sorry-ass* was more like it when describing her past relationships.

Girlfriends had come and gone quickly in her life. Lily maintained that once one of Cat's *girlfriends* could locate the sugar bowl without first looking through six cupboards, she was out. Cat had denied it, of course. She just didn't like anybody messing with her space. They start moving things around on you, as if your idea for where to put a dish is stupid. It usually begins right after they've slept in your bed for the third time, according to her experience. But, if she were to psychobabble herself, she'd guessed it had something to do with her *fear of commitment,* as Lily would say. She'd been alone so long that she couldn't imagine having to check in with somebody. Like Lily and Hannah did all the time. Lately though, she'd found herself feeling that it might be nice to have some one person who actually cares that you're just still out having fun and not dead on the side of the road.

She'd always felt that she had that with Lily. Lily would care. But Lily wasn't calling her up every night making sure she was safely tucked in. Lily would start to care when everybody else did—when they noticed her absence. Which, in their case, would be on a Monday morning when Lily pulled up for work and came inside to discover her cold dead body on the floor and the place ransacked.

If Lily had had her way, Cat would have been settled years ago. It wasn't for Lily's lack of trying. When she met or spotted or heard about a single dyke, she was hot on the trail. There was no stopping her once she'd got the notion in her head—*get Cat hitched.* But it was only after one particularly bad blind date that Cat had put her foot down. No more matchmaking, she'd told both Lily and Hannah. No more fixing her up with every dyke, chick, and clown in town.

As darkness swept in and covered the valley, the electricity hummed back on and tiny yellow lights appeared across the clearing in the hills. A milk barn glowed on a knoll beyond the river and the stained glass windows of the stone church down the valley road were, she could imagine, lighted to color. She cracked the window and listened to milking cows bellowing and church bells ringing out the dinner hour. The dark beefy stew she'd prepared soon after Will fell asleep bubbled to thickness on the woodstove.

She went out to the porch and lit a cigarette. Funny what kind of people your friends think you should be dating. Lily knew her better than anybody in the world and yet she had actually fixed her up with a *clown*.

"A *professional* clown," Lily had said with a straight face. "Good lookin', too."

The idea was so preposterous that, at first, Cat had thought she was kidding. But Lily was serious.

"Her name's Rosie."

If Cat remembered right, she'd gotten suckered into the dinner mostly because she'd been stoned.

She and Lil were sitting on her porch swing when the subject was broached. A touchy one for sure. Cat had become picky in her choice of women and so Lily had been sneaky in her proposal. She let Cat smoke most of the fatty before she brought it up.

"Seriously hot," Lily said, passing over the joint.

"Are you hearing yourself? You're not truly suggesting I date a *clown?*"

"I'm telling ya, she's cute." Lily insisted.

"She'd have to be, wouldn't she?" Cat toked again before handing back the joint, her own common sense was heading for the door. "How do you even *know* a clown?"

Lily waited. There was cunning in the pause. "Hannah met her," she finally said.

Hannah-the-psychologist met her, is what she really

meant. And not just your ordinary *lie on the couch let me get you some Prozac* kind of psychologist. Hannah had embraced the new age movement back before it had even been called a movement. She'd complemented her practice with crystals and chakras, herbs and flower essences, meditation and drums, all to better serve her growing granola-crunching clientele. As much as Cat respected her, she knew that a lot of the women Hannah treated were (in Lily's words) *corn-flakes*. She had imagined that clown. *Bozo*: honking red nose, spiked orange hair, floppy shoes, smelling of patchouli. A *dream* date. But Lily had worn her down.

These had been her thoughts that night, as she pulled her Harley up into Lily's driveway. Parked next to the work van had been a bright yellow VW Bug with a big daisy attached to the antenna. *Oh boy.* Cat climbed off the Glide, shaking hair out of her helmet. *Rosie the Clown—Professional Entertainment Services*—big letters painted in rainbow colors. She remembered measuring the distance between herself and the bike, contemplating escape, then Lily's voice had come from the window above.

"Don't even think about it," she laughed. "Get up here."

Cat had tried to forget the rest of the evening, tried to erase the image of the small woman with short spiked orange hair clutching a wineglass in both hands, knees pressed tightly together. She had tried to put out, altogether, the rest of the memory of that evening which had ended in the disaster that would forever become known as The Clown Incident.

It had been later, at the dinner table, when the proverbial excrement hit the propeller. Or, as she liked to remind Lily, when the clown went crazy. To give herself credit, Cat tried to make conversation. She had thought: for a clown you sure don't say much. It had made her wonder if the woman was one of those mime clowns.

"So, you're a clown?" she asked.

The silence that followed had caused Lily to tap her foot against the table so that their drink glasses nearly tipped before Hannah's hand had steadied her knee.

"Yes," Rosie said. "I'm a clown."

"How, exactly, does somebody become a clown?" Cat asked.

"How long does it take to be a clown?" Hannah inquired, interested.

"Are there degrees of being a clown? Like in karate?" Lily pressed.

"Have you ever worked in a circus?"

"Do you get to ride an elephant?" Lily leaned forward. "And, how do they get all those clowns into that one dinky little circus car?"

The woman had pushed her chair away from the table and stood.

"Look," she said, addressing them all. "This is why I don't date. All anybody cares about is me being a clown." She threw her napkin down. "I'm sick of it." She pushed back the twists of her spiked hair, and as big tears welled and spilled, she turned and ran, muttering, *I fucking hate clowns!* out the door, never to be seen again.

Cat couldn't help but laugh, even now, many months later. It wasn't funny at the moment but got more so with the remembering. She finished her cigarette and threw it to the snow below, watching it fizzle and sink into the wet. Was that her last date? Oh God, please say it wasn't. Please remember something since then—a roll around the cabin? A wink or a flirt would do. Nothing. It had been months since she'd had a date.

Across from her in his chair, Will stirred and stretched and finally opened his eyes.

"Is that Gran's beef stew I smell?" He smiled.

"Hey, sleepyhead." Cat dipped the wooden spoon into the broth, cupped her hand beneath it, and guided it to her brother's mouth. He blew twice, then slurped. "It is," he declared and swiped his mustache. Squinting around the room, he rubbed his eyes. "Electric's back." He stretched again. "Must've cleared that downed hemlock away."

Will sopped the broth of his third bowl of stew with the last thick slice of bread and pushed back from the table. He rubbed his belly with both hands. "And that's why I'm sure you'll like her," he said, concluding the second boring round of Marce stories. The whole sappy fairy tale made Cat lose her appetite; leaving half of her first helping of stew still in the bowl. She was not convinced she could even be in the same room with this woman, never mind like her.

After dinner, the same way he would as a kid, Will claimed a shower before he could get stuck doing the dinner dishes. Some things never change, she thought as she dried the last dish and brought her coffee mug to the chair by the fire. She'd never seen her brother so ... *giddy* was the word she wanted to use, but she knew that it was just the meanness in her. In fact, Will was happy. Happier than she'd ever seen him. Ever. Such a little word—such a long time. But this Marce-person had done it; brought back that sweet-tempered boy, not the bitter teenager Cat had last known. Was she really jealous or was she afraid? In all her thirty-four years had she never been in love?

⌘⌘

65

An image of Jamie came floating across her mind, long strands of dark hair teasing over Cat's body as they made love, hovering and then fading, but the accompanying feeling of grief lingered.

She rarely thought about Jamie anymore. She really didn't know why she thought about her at all. It had been a few months after Kate had passed away when they'd met. Cat had just started tending bar at OzGirlz.

Ruthie, the owner, a big old dyke with spiky gray hair, had hired Cat to bartend for one reason only, she'd said.

"I want good-looking women working my place."

"I don't have much experience," Cat had said.

Leaning over, pressing her big breasts into Cat's chin, Ruthie whispered, "Don't worry about the experience, kiddo ... I provide that for free."

She took the job because the work was OK and the money was better. She even managed to ignore Ruthie's overly familiar touches until one night after hours when Ruthie had tried a big sloppy kiss.

"Ruthie, I like you." Cat slid by. "I just don't like you like *that.*" When the hurt showed in Ruthie's face, Cat put an arm across her shoulders. "I mean," she whispered, "I like you like a mother. You know I'm an orphan. You're like the mother I never had." Right then Ruthie shifted from predator to protector. And it was Ruthie who claimed credit for fixing up her bartender with her hot new piano player.

The night of Jamie's first gig, the two had watched each other surreptitiously across the bar. Jamie cast glances from beneath heavy black lashes shading light eyes, while Cat poured drinks.

She sat at the piano, small and sexy, and sang through curls of smoke and strands of hair. The big voice that came from the little body was deep and husky, made so by the packs of cigarettes she smoked between and during songs. It had been Cat's job to make the gin martinis for the musician—stirred not shaken, three olives not two. It was the final rendition of Jamie's second set that had clinched the romance. From across the room, over the heads of a few straggling revelers, came the familiar tune of Cat's favorite song. She turned and looked toward the singer. Jamie's eyes were closed and a secret smile played on her lips. The lyrics to Tom Waits's melody, "ol' 55," cut smooth through the smoky air of the bar.

Oh, my time has come quickly,
I go lickety splitly . . .

That had been a long time ago. For barely one summer the two had been together, Jamie moving into the cabin where they had fantasized about becoming famous artists together. They'd create some magical life that, years down the road, each would recall in *Rolling Stone* interviews. Except the wild thing that had kept them together wasn't their creativity but the sex that eventually only distracted them from their work. In the end, neither produced a lick of new material and this, becoming more frustrating and burdensome each unproductive day, had been the thing that had caused the split, although this truth was only just becoming evident to Cat. Most obviously, the breakup had come directly on the heels of her walking in on Jamie, drunk, with some woman named Suzette, naked and rolling around in their bed—*her* bed.

What a miserable night to be remembering, Cat thought now. A drama. No, a comedy: two naked women caught in their skins. It had reminded her, even in that horrible moment, of the time she and Lily had caught Brother Bob Handy and his secretary, Marlene, scrambling out of a closet in the church vestry. Weird how your mind works in a crisis.

"Get the fuck out. Tonight," she had yelled, not to the quivering Suzette, but to Jamie, whose small body had trembled, as if she'd turned suddenly cold. But there were no tears. That's what Cat mostly remembered: that overwhelmingly sickening disappointment that arose when Jamie couldn't even produce one single teardrop. She did recall her own tears, streaming and splashing against her cheeks as she raced the Glide to the top of Fordham's Creek. She drove to Lily and Hannah's house where the windows were dark and the two had stumbled to the door in matching Winnie-the-Pooh pajamas. She didn't think that the crying had come from love, though; she thought it had come from anger. She'd never been so pissed.

Will's big voice, above her, was belting out the words to "Camelot." Her brother was a closet Broadway show tune aficionado. He had actually played Rip in the sixth-grade production of *West Side Story*. Finally, he thumped down the stairs. The air filled with the smell of the J & J powder he'd sprinkled all over himself. Cat pointed to the kitchen where the coffeepot was still hot and motioned for him to get himself a cup. Dinner was all she was going to do. She wasn't going to suddenly start waiting on him.

Before he sat, he leaned over and picked up her book from the table where she'd left it earlier. She watched as he examined its cover, turned it in his palm and read the backside. Slowly, without taking his eyes from it, he sat and placed his cup on the floor at his feet, opening it, skimming its pages, frowning as he stopped to read a passage here and there. Cat felt a nervous jump in her stomach. This was the first time he'd seen it. She waited, suffering. When he finally did look up, he was nodding and smiling. It looked like a toy book in his big hand.

"So, this is it?" He kept shaking his head, looking from the book to Cat and back again. "What's it about?"

"Here," she said. "This place."

He thumbed the page back. "Hey, how come you didn't dedicate it to me?"

"'Cause you're a jerk," she said.

Finally, his new kinder, gentler, unselfish-self emerged and he nodded, flipping through it again.

"Good for you, Cat. You did it. Now you'll *have* to leave this podunk town," he said. "Get yourself a life."

"What are you talking about?" She pulled a wooden box out from beneath her chair and flipped it open. "I have a life." She rummaged for a packet of papers and the bag of pot. "This is my home. I wrote the book. What more do I need? I belong here. My life is here, my job, my family, my writing, Lily, and ..."

"And nothing." He leaned forward. "You could have saved yourself some breath and just said the truth—Lily. You don't belong to any of this." He lifted his palms to the ceiling. "It's Lily that keeps you here, little sister. Can't you see it?"

Her cheeks burned.

"First it was Lily you latched onto, then her family, then her job, Jesus ... It's a fuckin' miracle you can have one fuckin' thought that doesn't begin in Lily Cameron's head."

"Fuck you." She threw the joint at him and headed for the stairs.

"You're an orphaned daughter of an orphaned mother

69

raised by an old bitch who would have died unnoticed had it not been for you sticking around to mark the date. Show me where you *belong* in that picture, Cat."

She turned on him. "I fucking hate you. Now I remember why—you're a prick." In frustration, she landed a punch to her own thigh. "There's something fucked up about you, Will, and it's only a matter of time before this Marce-woman sees it. If she's all that you say," she held back tears, "she'll figure it out before she winds up making the biggest mistake of her life."

She stormed up the stairs and threw herself on the bed. What just happened? What the fuck just happened? How was it only five hours into the visit they could have wound up like this? God, Will could find that soft spot and with one quick jab, poke it open and watch it ooze.

It wasn't that she didn't know, on some level, that she was attached to Lil. She had counted on her, sure. She had, she supposed, as her brother contended, squirmed her way into the Cameron clan. She sometimes, in a scary moment, wondered what her life would have been like without Lily. And then she'd shake that thought free because in fact she had never been without Lily. She couldn't imagine it.

But that didn't mean she needed to have her nose rubbed in it. That didn't mean that Will had the right to walk in here and start pointing at every little thing he didn't like or had never liked and pass some kind of judgment on it. Anyway, the way he made it sound, it was like she was nothing without Lil. And that just wasn't so. She wrote a fucking book, for God's sake.

She heard him start up the stairs. Wiping her eyes and sucking in a deep breath, she decided to let him apologize and have it be over. Maybe she was overreacting, maybe he was overstepping. Was she really going to let it begin all over again like this? *If it's not working, try something different,* Lily's words came to her. She sat up waiting for the top of Will's head to emerge above the landing. But before it happened, the telephone rattled for the first time in two days.

She looked over to the bedside table: nearly ten o'clock. Who'd be calling at ten o'clock? She heard Will turn on his heels and race to answer it.

"It's probably for me," he called behind him.

She leaped down the stairs and saw his face as he lifted the receiver.

"Hello?"

Cat watched the grin spread, deepening his dimples. His eyes (she checked) sparkled. She didn't have to hear him name the voice to know it was *that* woman. He turned his back on Cat and walked down the hallway to the room that had once been Kate and Angus' and latched the door behind him.

Latched?

She folded her arms across her chest, feeling her own rising temper again as Will's big laugh broke through the closed door. She fell into the couch and curled under the covers.

An hour later, when he finally emerged, he'd awakened her from her moody doze with a kick to her foot. She looked up to see him poised, like a boxer, taking punches at the air above her head, bouncing from one springy foot to another.

"C'mon, let's go sledding." He punctuated his words with a swipe at his invisible opponent.

"It's eleven o'clock at night, Will. And I'm mad at you." She pulled the blanket off her legs. "I'm going to bed." She rose and pushed passed him, but he grabbed her around the neck and held her in a headlock.

"Aw, don't be mad. I'm sorry. I didn't mean it. You know I love Lily. Come on, Cat, let's go sledding. It'll be great, like when we were kids. I'll even let you take the Flyer."

She stopped. The Flyer? He'd never before in all their lives, ever, *let* her take the oldest fastest sled in the valley, the sled that was, in fact, his prized possession before he left to go wander. So maybe this Marce wasn't such a bad thing after all. Maybe there were some advantages to her brother becoming a big, soft, stupid marshmallow.

The moon was high and bright in the sky, waxing almost full. Everything was eerily visible, exposed in the light reflecting off the white snow. They made their way to the top of the knoll behind the cabin to rest on the narrow bench outside the family cemetery plot. With gloved hands they pushed snow from the bench's concrete surface. The air was thin. White puffs of breath hung and haloed their heads as they sat.

The cold made Cat's eyes water and her nose run. There was a silence surrounding them, the kind that only comes with deep snow. Heavy and insulating, so that in spite of its cold, Cat could imagine burrowing into a drift and keeping warm in her own little cave. How many nights had they made this trek in this same kind of weather? To do this very same thing? With Kate yelling at their hurrying heels—*"Don't be goin' and harmin' your-selves, now."*

And they hadn't. Cat shuddered, thinking, except for once on a snowy winter night when she was twelve. They had misjudged the depth of the snow, not expecting its dip toward the ground just as they began their flight on their bellies toward the top string of a barbed-wire fence

72

that had in winters before been buried. She'd caught sight of it first, just as she crested the slope. She was sure she had yelled—warning her brother to duck, as she had done, but her words had been muffled in her coat sleeve. It was his scream that went through her, flinging her from the runaway sled, tumbling her into a rocky crag whose top was poking through the snow.

Cat had pulled herself straight up into the moonlight, searching the bare hill for her brother. Then she saw him, crumpled in a ball, his arms curling around the top of his head where blood was pouring and staining the snow a terrifying red. On that night Cat learned the meaning of adrenaline rush. In a burst of super-human strength, she'd rolled Will's body onto the nearby toboggan and hauled him home. Pulling his weight as much with her imagination as anything else. She was a reindeer, a team of huskies, an ox. Never would she feel that kind of strength and power again.

Will had been scalped, more or less, by a jagged hook of wire. His white skull lay open beneath the flap of torn skin and hair. The sight of it had caused bile to rise in her throat and her feet to move faster. All the way back to the cabin, Cat screamed her gran's name at the top of her voice. By the time they'd made it, Kate was dressed and bundled and warming the truck. She had known there'd been harm done.

Cat shivered with the memory. Will put his arm around her shoulders.

"Cold?" he asked.

"No, just thinking about your scalping."

His hand raised to his head where, she knew, the scarred ridge hid just beneath his curls. "Ouch, let's not talk about it," he said, and winced.

"I saved your life." She leaned against him.

"You're always saving my life, Cat. That's why I'm glad I found Marce." He squeezed her. "Now you're off the hook."

She smacked his chest and got up.

"Come on, you take the 'boggan, first. I'll be right on your tail."

Three runs down and back up the long stretch of slope had exhausted them. Not like when they were kids who wouldn't quit until their toes had numbed and their gran had called.

"Must be getting old," Will huffed on their way back home.

"Speak for yourself." Cat smothered her belabored breathing into the folds of her scarf. "Fun, though, huh?"

He smiled. "Yeah, I want to take Marce for a ride when she comes over, tomorrow."

So it was imminent, she thought. The phone call must have decided the plans. And there'd be no getting out of it. She couldn't claim having to work. Lily'd never make them work in this kind of weather.

Don't believe in it, Lily had declared. Cat remembered those days when Lily'd come home from her apprenticeship with fingers bloodied from pulling steel bolts off frost-stuck tips. *I ain't ever gonna work in the cold when I have my own business,* she had sworn back then, and she never did.

Brother and sister propped the sleds against the house and kicked the snow from their boots.

Cat had set up the wooden rack in front of the stove and they stripped down to their long johns and hung their wet clothing on it. She was suddenly overcome with exhaustion and crawled under the covers on the couch.

"How's *your wife* gonna get here?" She asked, feeling those words crawl over her tongue.

Will grinned, "I'm gonna take the truck and go get her."

She sat up. *Truck? Her truck? What made him think that she'd let him take her truck?* But it wasn't totally hers. It had been Gran's, and like the rest of the family property it had been left to them both.

"Wanna come along for the ride?" Will's tone was hopeful.

"No," she said. "I'll stay here and clean up a little. I'm sure you'll want some time alone."

He went upstairs and brought down a comforter and another pillow from the big closet under the eaves. He didn't ask where they were. Instead of spreading out on the floor in front of the fire, Will kicked the old recliner back, stuffed the pillow under his head, and pulled the comforter to his chin.

"'Night, Cat," he whispered into the darkened room.

"'Night, John-Boy," she answered. Soon his snores filled the air, familiar as they'd been when he was a boy stretched out on the floor below her.

There were no snores from Gran to follow his, though. It was like listening to a familiar song playing in mono instead of stereo; you only got half. Maybe that's what happens when someone dies or the relationship breaks up—you're left with half. Is that how she'd thought of herself? As only half of something? Like that Shel Silverstein book, *The Missing Piece*. But what happens if you never find it? Are you never whole? Wasn't Kate whole, even after Angus died? Cat didn't think so. She didn't think that Kate had been whole when Angus was alive either, although this was not something she could prove. She thought maybe Kate hadn't been whole since she'd left Scotland.

75

But the rest of them—Lily, Hannah, Delores, Matthew, and now Will. She did have to admit, there was a certain kind of rounding out about them all. Nothing drastic, only something you'd really notice if you were listening—kind of that subtle difference between mono and stereo. It only mattered if you were listening for the harmony.

Chapter Six

Just as she'd expected, sunlight had broken into the morning. The valley glowed and glistened busily as rays of light struck and bounced off snow-and-ice encased trees and barns and mountains. It stung her eyes to look out the window. When Cat turned and faced away from the sunlight everything in the room went dark and she had to steady herself until her pupils readjusted. By noon, the snowplows had made it to the creek road. Power lines dripped snow and chunks fell, landing in soft thuds. Ice crystals swirled in tiny tornadoes and then on gentle gusts. Everything glittered.

Will had risen early, bringing the scissors to her for a beard trim. By the evidence in the bathroom, she suspected, he'd plucked his nose hairs with the tweezers he neglected to return to the drawer. Shortly after the first plow had swung by, he left and said not to expect them back till later. A drive by the old elementary school and general store to show Marce the old hometown were in his plans for the day. *Old hometown,* were the fond words he'd had the audacity to use, as if he'd ever given the place a tender thought in his life.

After his departure Cat scoured the fridge to see if there was enough of anything to make dinner for this woman. God, she couldn't believe she was cooking. Eggs and breadcrumbs were the only things lacking in the preparation of chicken parmesan, one of the four dishes she could actually make.

Out the window, she saw the smoke curling from Delores' chimney. She could just walk over there for the missing ingredients, she thought, and then imagined the scene that she'd be walking into: Delores, at her wits end, standing outside in the freezing cold, chain-smoking cigarettes, trying to get away from the three little wild boys home from school because of the snow. Mamma baking; she'd insist that Cat sit and eat some big fat piece of cake or pie. She'd stuff herself sick, for sure. Shaking her head, she decided against it. Instead, she called Lil for the missing ingredients.

Dressed in coveralls and jacket, Cat strapped her feet onto her cross-country skis and set her sunglasses on her nose. It would take about an hour. The trail that led from Cat's farm, across the valley, through a stand of pines, over a tobacco field, and into Lily's apple orchard, was an old one. Made long ago, legend had it, by the Cherokee who had once, hundreds of years before, traveled their trade through the Fordham Creek Valley.

She headed out, down the drive and up the lane. So packed was the snow on the paved creek road that she glided across it without having to remove her skis. The old timber bridge that linked the banks of the wide creek was untouched by footprints, neither human nor other. As she reached the stand of tall dark pines, a flap of a great wingspan snapped and shook the treetops. Just in time, she paused to see the underbelly of a big golden eagle fly over her. So easy, she thought. Just spread your wings and go. It swooped down and over the hillock ahead.

Her aching thighs were relieved by the declining slope and she hunched low, feeling the skis carrying her swiftly. Entering the clearing, she startled a bunny across her path. His long hind feet kicked tufts of new snow into the air. The last stretch of land before reaching Lily's back orchard was the most rigorous. Deep ruts of tobacco rows dipped and sometimes sprouted tips of old dried stalks, slowing her pace enough to force her to walk the last hill, skis slung across her shoulders.

From the distance, Cat could see the rise of smoke from the rock house's chimney. Cat crossed the small wooden footbridge that Lily had built over the rushing creek cutting the orchard in two. Above her was the back porch of the house, screened against the mosquitoes that each summer hovered in black clouds above the water.

As kids, she and Lily would ride their bikes past this house, sometimes stopping to rest against the low field-stone wall that corralled the yard and outbuildings. She remembered leaning their ten-speeds and chugging water from canteens. Lily's two braids, which she'd worn until the eighth grade, had been woven into one long one that hung down her spine.

"I'm gonna live there some day," Lily had said between sips from her canteen. Cat hadn't paid much attention, passing off the wish of a teenager, similar to the one she dreamt about living in a castle some day. As her gran would say, *Get your head out of the clouds before you fall over your own feet.* It just so happened that the old deaf woman who'd lived in the house had passed away just as Lily and Hannah had begun their house hunting.

Cat propped the skis against the wall and kicked the snow from her boots. Without knocking, she twisted the knob and pushed the door open into the warm air of the house. Neither Hannah nor Lily moved from their spots.

Hannah, dressed in overalls, a turtleneck, and orange fluffy slippers, was perched at an easel. Her long brown curls cascaded down her back, curving to a point in the middle of her spine. She was sketching a pastel of Lily who was seated beyond, in a pair of burgundy silk pajamas, unbuttoned, revealing a little of the crevice between her breasts. The tips of her hair were wet from an earlier dip in the hot tub, Cat figured.

Planted in an armchair in front of the silent television set, Lily's eyes never left the flashing screen. There was a plate bearing the juicy remains of a persimmon, which, Cat figured, might have been some kind of sex prop that Hannah had insisted Lily indulge in while she was being sketched. Knowing Lily, she probably popped the whole fruit into her mouth and swallowed the seeds without one lip-lick. With the exception of her socked feet, which wiggled with minor restraint, Lily was still.

"Hey." Cat closed the door behind her and hung her wet clothes on the hooks on its back. She wandered over to Hannah's shoulder and looked from the picture to Lily and back again.

"Well, she got your mustache exactly," she said. Lily's eyes widened.

Hannah laughed. "I did not, sweetie," she said.

Cat bent and hugged Hannah around the neck and kissed her soft flushed cheek. Hannah patted her arm, smudging a pink chalky imprint on her sleeve. "Nice to see you, McCat," she said. It was Hannah's own version of Mary Catherine and she was the only one in the world who used it, thank God.

Cat made her way around to the back of Lily's chair and looked at the TV. A man in a turban was walking toward a gold-domed mosque. He was miming and gesturing left then right, highlighting his surroundings. The camera followed him, swinging back and forth, lingering on palm trees and a green monument with foreign lettering at its base.

"Travel channel," Lily mouthed the words through clenched teeth, like a ventriloquist trying to throw her voice. "Saudi Arabia. Hannah, can we quit now? Cat's here."

Hannah leaned back, cocked her head, gave one last swipe with the crayon and nodded. "All right, go ahead. I swear."

Lily jumped up and shook her limbs loose. With her palms she adjusted her jaw, popping it. Her bloused shirt opened.

Cat pointed at the suddenly exposed left breast. "Wanna cover up your little friend there?"

Lily looked down and jerked her shirt closed. "Hey," she huffed, "it's not like you got anything to show off either."

Hannah stood and stretched and wiped her hands on her jeans. "All right, you two; breasts are not for comparing." She made her way to the kitchen. The coils of the brown curls sprung and bounced with each step.

The house was warm. Firelight flickered against the pine that paneled the walls. Only two pictures were hung in the whole place. Lily didn't like clutter. It made her feel dyslexic, she claimed. The first picture hung above the mantle, a photo of the house taken by Lily's brother, Kevin, who'd managed to catch the yellow stone in a pink glow of a sunset the first summer the couple had moved in.

The second wall hanging wasn't a picture exactly. It was a bath towel-sized chart of every yoga position into which a body could bend. Hannah was a devout practitioner of the meditative form. Lily, however, followed the movements in spurts, usually after some hedonistic consumption of food, alcohol, or sex. *Cleansings,* she would call them. Cat thought that it was just some leftover Baptist.

Hannah carried the tea into the living room and Cat seated herself, as she always seated herself, in the big gray leather chair that they'd inherited from Lily's Great Aunt Lyda. It still smelled of that skinny old lady's pipe smoke. She had been a spinster who'd sit on her porch, rockin' and whittlin', with a silver flask in her front dress pocket. When they were teenagers, Cat and Lily had liked visiting Lyda. She'd let them smoke cigarettes and would sometimes pass them a sip or two from her little flask.

It was Hannah who'd delivered the news that made Cat nearly topple her teacup to the floor.

"Heard you're doing a reading from the book down at Mari's Café next week," she said, as if this weren't news.

What? No, Cat explained. She'd been asked but hadn't agreed. "Where'd you hear that?"

"On WNW, the radio station," Hannah said over her cup. "They announced the readings for this month. Like they always do."

Cat closed her eyes. She had avoided returning Mari's blinking message on her machine. In fact, she'd decided to pretend she'd never even received it. Suddenly her book was on the radio and she didn't even know about it.

"Can I use your phone?" She was definitely not going on a book tour. Definitely not. She was too busy, too tired, too shy, and too attached to her home to leave it to go selling books. Especially when it involved standing in front of a bunch of people, exposing herself to public scrutiny. As she skimmed the phone book and dialed the café's number she realized that her thinking on this was already flawed.

Public scrutiny had begun the minute the book had made that first journey to her agent. By now, she was being judged by anybody who'd take the time to pull it off a shelf and read it. It had even been reviewed.

Mari herself picked up and Cat led with outrage: "How dare you ..." and "Nobody told me about it ..." and "I'll call my agent ..." Then there was silence while she paced around the kitchen. The conversation wound down on her end with quieter responses: "Hmmm," and "Oh," and "She did?" Finally, "I see."

When it was over, she replaced the phone in its cradle and wandered into the living room where Lily and Hannah sat waiting. She flopped back into the big leather chair and stuck her bottom lip out.

"Well?" Lily asked.

"It was Candace. She got some hot idea I would actually *want* to read. Just because she's my agent, she thinks she can run my life."

Mari had waited for Cat's call but by chance, it turned out, Candace had wandered into the bookstore that very same day and they got to talking.

"Candace told Mari that I would be delighted to do the reading. *Delighted*. Can you believe it?" Cat shook her head. "More like sick to my stomach."

"C'mon, Cat," Hannah said. "Aren't you just a little excited about it? I mean, isn't this what you've been working toward?"

"No. Not this. I knew I'd have to do readings, sure. But talking about it? Questions flying? No, that's not what I signed up for." She looked at Hannah and shook her head. "They're gonna expect me to know something."

Hannah laughed. "Aw, sweetie, you do know something. Lots of somethings. You wrote and published a whole book. Not everybody's done that. It's something."

Cat chewed on her thumbnail. She guessed Hannah was

83

right. She guessed it wasn't going to be an inquisition like she had been building in her mind.

"So, are you gonna do it?" Lily slid forward, planting her elbows on her knees, waiting as if a Solomon-like decision was about to be made.

"Looks like I'm going to have to. Either that or wind up looking like a big fat jerk."

"You're gonna hafta get used to being famous. It's fate."

Her whole life, Lily had believed in fate. It was her answer for all the whys of the world. It had been fate that she and Cat had become best friends. Probably, Lily had imagined, their great-great-great-great-grannies had been best friends back in Scotland. It had been fate that sent that old lady to heaven just in time for Lily to buy her house. And fate had been at work when she steered into that straight honky-tonk bar where she had first met Hannah.

"What else could have given me the courage to talk to her?" Lily had asked. *"Don't I know you from somewhere?* That's what I said. Can you believe that I actually came up with that line?" Lily believed that it was fate's handiwork.

Apparently, that night, Hannah had looked Lily over, grinned, and asked, *"How old are you?"*

"Twenty," she had lied. She was only just seventeen.

Months later, when Hannah had discovered the truth, she had been furious and had broken off the romance. Lily had been heartbroken. She moped around for weeks, cried day and night, got and stayed drunk. And then, all of a sudden, she stopped; stopped the moping, stopped the crying, and she quit getting drunk.

Instead, she made a box. A wooden box: dark mahogany, carved and tooled, polished to a soft sheen; shiny brass hinges and a delicate lock and key to finish it off. She'd worked on it for nearly three months. When she was done, she went to the creek and walked its middle. It had taken her hours to find the stone, so long, in fact, that her toes had numbed.

The stone was the size of a silver dollar—shaped like a heart—translucent, honey-colored. Upon its smooth flat surface, in black ink, she'd written *My Love.* And then she'd placed it inside the box lined with black velvet. The note attached read, *Don't open this box unless you're willing to accept what's in it,* which of course, deep down Hannah was. And from that moment on they'd been together. That had been over fifteen years ago.

Lily put a platter of cheese and fruit and small round crackers on the coffee table and Hannah followed with more tea.

Cat sat back listening while the pair discussed her life, as they often did, as if she were not in the room. They predicted her rise in the literary world with the same misinformed wishfulness that Will had reckoned her forthcoming fortune. Booksignings all over the country. Probably even a movie deal, Lily insisted. Cat listened, as she always listened, half amused, half annoyed.

She interrupted them, "Guess what ... Will's in town."

The two women stopped and looked at her.

"He got married!"

"Will Hood is married?" Lily asked, not once, but twice. These were words that had never before gone together in the same sentence; had never joined the man with the act. After Cat had spilled the details, it was Lily who declared it a victory. A softer, kinder Will Hood could only be an improvement, she said. "Now all that's left is to get you hitched."

Cat shook her head in disgust.

"Maybe you ought to take notice of your brother," Lily said, pointing the cheese knife at her.

"What's that supposed to mean?"

"He's growin' up."

"Oh, and I'm not? Just because I don't have a girl-friend?"

"Exactly." Lily stuffed a cracker in her mouth. "It wouldn't hurt you to start thinking of settling down with some nice girl here. Especially now that the book's done."

Cat jerked forward. "Now that the book's done is exactly why I'm *not* supposed to be settling down. I'm supposed to be going on a tour, thinking about my next project, traveling! *Remember?*" She sat back exhausted by her own admonishments.

Lily frowned at her. "What do you mean, *traveling?* Since when have you wanted to travel?"

This was not a fantasy that Cat had shared with Lily.

"I don't know," she said quietly. "Doesn't everyone want to travel? I've just been thinking lately that I might want to go somewhere. You know, like on a vacation to anywhere other than Myrtle Beach."

"What's wrong with Myrtle Beach?"

"Nothing, Lil. But there are other places."

Lily leaned into the cushion behind her. "You just need a girlfriend. That'll help you settle down."

"Maybe I don't want to." Cat looked to Hannah for help.

"Leave her alone, Lily. Not everyone wants to settle. Some people want to travel."

"Only crazy people don't want a girlfriend," Lily mumbled.

"I didn't say I didn't want a girlfriend." Cat sighed and

blew across her teacup. "Let's face it, *they's slim pickins* in this town. Maybe I'll travel and meet someone," she said, more hopeful than she felt.

"Now why would you want to go getting hooked up with some foreigner when there's a perfectly good new single lesbian right here in this very town?"

"Not again."

"You'll like her, Cat," Lily said. "She's a doctor. Really. And, if you like her and get into a relationship, and settle down together, you won't want to go off around the world." She got up and walked over to Hannah, putting her arms around her. "Like me and Hannah, we never want to go anywhere!"

Cat frowned.

Hannah patted Lily's arm. "I don't think you're doing anything for your cause, sweetie."

"Just what I need, to be shackled here for yet one more reason."

"Whatdya mean shackled?"

"I mean," she felt herself edging into some sensitive territory. "I mean that I wound up here because my parents died. I stayed after college to take care of Kate."

"And because of the job," Lily reminded her.

"Yes, and because of the job. And what I'm saying is that maybe I should be thinking of doing something else, somewhere else."

There was a silence that fell over the three of them. Cat and Lily avoided looking at each other.

Finally, Hannah said softly, "It might be good for you to get away for awhile, Cat."

"Maybe so, Hannah."

"You just need a girl," Lily muttered.

⌘⌘

"She is an interesting person, Cat," Hannah (of all people) said. "She's a doctor from Boston."

Cat held up one hand. "Stop, stop, stop."

Hannah did not stop. "Just moved here. She's really sweet and very funny."

"And hot." Lily chimed in.

"Her name's Melissa. She's an artist, too."

Cat grinned a little. "Which is it? Artist or doctor?"

"Both," Lily told her triumphantly. "That's the beauty of it."

"I think you'd really hit it off," Hannah added.

"Oh yeah, just like I hit it off with that damn clown," Cat said. "You two just keep your hands off my love life. I'll get my own dates, thank you very much."

"Oh, like you've been so successful in that department," Lily said.

Cat got up and went down the hall to the bathroom, knowing that they would go on about her whether she was there or not. She imagined another excruciatingly painful dinner; this time, her new soul mate would be dressed in scrubs, stethoscope draping her neck, palate and brush in her rubber-gloved hands. The image made her laugh.

But what *was* she looking for? This question winnowed its way into her.

When she returned, Lily and Hannah were bent over their fat beagle, which was spread-eagle on his back, eyes embarrassed by his exposure. Apparently their discussion of Cat had been interrupted.

"The only digestive problem this dog's got is trash consumption," Lily was saying, rising and wiping her hands.

"What's the matter with your dog?" Cat asked.

"It ain't my dog. I keep telling' ya." Lily loaded the fireplace with more wood. "It came with the house. It's fat, is what's wrong with it."

Hannah argued, "It is *too* our dog. He's just a little over-weight."

But on this one point, Lily was right. Tubby old MacDougal, as a puppy, had been left behind with some of the old deaf woman's furniture. Hannah had found him in the barn in a quilt-lined drawer of an old dresser. The woman's family had said that Hannah and Lily could keep the dresser *and* the puppy.

While Lily carefully wrapped and bagged the eggs and breadcrumbs, Cat unhooked her coveralls from where they hung, and as she did, a navy blue New York Yankees cap fell to the floor. She bent to pick it up and turned it upside down to look inside its brim. Tiny initials were faded along the edge, but they were hers all right.

"Hey, this is my Yankees cap." She frowned and looked at Lily, who made a grab for it.

"No, it ain't."

But it was. Cat slapped it onto her head. It was her cap, all right. Its familiar weight and shape, now years older, still fit perfectly on her head. What a little thief. Although Cat had told no one, the cap had belonged to her father. She'd found it in an old trunk in the attic. It had been a personal thing for her, not telling anybody where she'd got it. It was sort of like a secret shared between heaven and earth. She'd been devastated when it disappeared.

"I can't believe you stole my hat," she said.

Lily folded her arms across her chest. She knew Hannah was watching from the kitchen.

"Hey, at least I didn't steal your car."

She was referring to the time, after Kate's funeral service at the church, when Cat had fled from the building and into its parking lot. Unable to bear it any longer, she had jumped behind the wheel of the MG, the key in the ignition as always. She had raced away in a storm of dust that matched her mood.

"At least I gave it back," Cat defended.

"A car is a way bigger theft than a hat."

"Only if it doesn't get returned." Cat stepped out onto the porch. "Five years is a long time to wait to get your property back." She pulled on her gloves. "You should be grateful I don't have you arrested."

"Yeah, yeah." Lily waved her away. "Hey, we working tomorrow?" Her tone held the hope that the roads might still be too snowy and the air too cold to be doing any carpentry for a couple of days. Surprise vacations, Lily had called them. Best part of being a carpenter, she'd always say.

"Not sure," Cat said, but thought they weren't going anywhere for awhile.

"Anyway, I'll call when I get home," Cat said, "once I see what the conditions are." Meantime she'd let Lily stew in the possibility of having to work in the morning.

By the time Cat had made her way back across the valley to her farm, the light was dimming and soon night would fall. The cabin was dark. No sign of the truck. Good, she thought, she'd have some time alone, get stoned, and cook dinner before she'd have to start being polite.

When Will and his wife (so strange an image, she thought) finally did pull into the driveway, darkness had indeed fallen, as were some tiny flakes of snow. The wind had whipped up and the temperature had dropped. The roads, Will said, were turning to black ice. They (meaning he and Marce) would be spending the night, here, together.

Marce didn't look the way Cat had imagined. Then again, she wasn't entirely sure what it was she had really been expecting.

Marce was tall, taller than Cat but not quite as tall as Will. And thin, in an elegant kind of way. Her features were almost sharp but softened just before they got there. When she smiled her eyes sparkled hazel. The long braid that hung down her back, Cat noticed, was a weave of silver and gold. She was dressed in jeans and a heavy wool sweater. On her feet were a pair of kick-ass leather boots laced to the knee, which Cat immediately coveted. She found herself returning the warm smile that greeted her.

Awkwardly, the three moved around the kitchen until she made them go sit in the living room while she finished cooking dinner.

It had begun over dinner, the shift in Cat's heart. But she'd resisted it. Tried to find things to pick at: watching Marce eat; waiting for flawed table manners, but there were none. She listened for professorial pontificating she didn't hear. Instead she caught the soft easy laugh of a woman who knew and liked herself. Occasionally, Marce would send Will a playful wink across the table. Cat found it more difficult to hate her.

Later, after the two women had quietly washed up the dinner dishes while Will snored away in the living room, Cat suggested they take a walk up the cove. The air was cold but the falling snow was light, dusting a sugar coating across the already frozen landscape. Their walk began in silence. Cat searched for words, something, anything, to engage. But it was Marce who finally broke their shared quiet.

"I read your book," she said, almost shyly.

This startled Cat. As if Marce had gotten one up on her. Mindstalked her via her book. She felt vulnerable in the woman's knowing. She didn't know what to say.

"I love the stories," Marce said. "Made me laugh and cry, sometimes at the same time."

Cat smiled.

"Is there a real Lucy in your life or did you just make her up?"

As if anyone could "make up" Lily.

"She's kind of based on my best friend, Lily—my only long-term relationship, well, if you don't count Mike the dog."

"And this is by choice?" Marce asked, carefully.

Cat laughed. "I'm not so sure I'd call it that. Of course, Lily'd call it my *fear of intimacy choice.*" Cat stuffed her mittened fists into her pocket. "She'd tell you that as soon as somebody starts getting too comfortable, I sabotage the whole affair."

"And would Lily be right?" Marce's step did not slow with the question, as Cat's had, taking her out of the rhythm—Marce's long-legged rhythm. Cat double-timed and caught up, but she was no longer in time with her companion's footfalls.

"I'm sorry." Marce shot her a sidewise glance. "Was that too personal?"

"No, no," Cat shook her head. "I kind of asked for it, didn't I?"

Marce smiled.

Cat bent and scooped snow with her bare hand, and tightened her fist, melting the fluff to an icy chunk, then popped it into her mouth and let it melt.

She said, "Lily doesn't understand. For her it was simple. She met the love of her life and they lived happily ever after—the end. I've never seen two people more perfect for each other. They're symbiotic."

"And you think this is a good thing?"

"It's a perfect thing. Rare. That's why it's taking me so long to find one. That's what Lily doesn't realize: that they're one in a million."

"Sounds like they're more than that; sounds like one of a kind. Do you really think you can replicate it?"

This surprised her. She wasn't sure if she could—just always thought she should. And then this struck her.

Did she want to live like Lily and Hannah? She'd always thought she did. But did she want one hand knowing what the other was doing all the time (or however that went)? And this was the irony. She'd spent all this time thinking she'd been searching for the perfect Lily/Hannah look-alike relationship but the minute she even sniffed one like it, she'd run or kick it out.

"OK, I admit it." She threw her hands up. "Maybe I do sabotage things when the going gets close because I—I'm not sure that I want to *get* that close."

Marce nodded.

"Don't tell Lily, though. She'll just call it semantics but it's more than that."

"I guess people find their own perfect relationships. But you won't find one if you're not open to more than one possibility."

"There's nobody worth dating around here, anyway. I haven't had a date in months. And I won't even go into the last one I remember."

Marce raised her eyebrows in question. "Let's just say it involved a clown."

Marce giggled.

"Not funny. Truth." Cat raised her palm in a solemn oath. "*A professional* clown. Can you believe it? Is there anything about me that gives you the impression that I would even consider dating a *clown?* I'd be more likely to date a snake handler than a clown, don'tcha think?"

In a few seconds Marce had doubled over and was laughing uncontrollably. She went down in a snow bank and lay on her back, holding her stomach. Cat plunked down beside her, grinned, and pulled a joint out. She passed it over, but Marce waved her decline.

"I'm not kidding now," Cat kept going, enjoying the peals of laughter coming from the body next to her. "She came to dinner. I guess we weren't too nice to her. She ran out of the house screaming *I fucking hate clowns!*"

Marce looked skeptical.

"I swear," Cat defended her sincerity. "Big shoes floppin'— slap, slap, slap, across the driveway."

"Quit!" Marce smacked at her.

"Okay, her shoes were regular but that big red nose ..."

"Enough, no more about the clown."

Cat shrugged and toked on the joint.

"Ever considered personal ads?"

Cat threw her a scornful look.

"What?" Marce became serious. "People do place personal ads."

"Yeah? Well, not me. What kind of loser puts herself in an ad? Here's mine: *GWF*: (you know what that means, right?) *writer—smoker, pothead, insomniac, bi-polar, obsessive-compulsive, liar. No PDA* (public display of affection), *junk-food junkie, no religion, must be willing to go downtown.*"

Marce looked confused. *"Downtown?"*

"Straight girls—don't you know anything? It's a euphemism."

Marce's brow had not smoothed with the clarifying.

"Think about *sex.*" Cat waited.

Marce shook her head as she finally got it. "You really are bad," she laughed.

"I'm not kidding. I went out with a girl one time for three whole months who never hailed the cab."

"Another euphemism?"

"What kind of selfishness is that? Talk about sacrifice."

"Oh God. Who knew?"

"Who knew what?"

"Who knew you'd be so funny." Marce pulled herself up and held out a mittened hand for Cat, who gratefully yanked upright.

They turned and began their trek anew. They were each quiet in their thinking. Cat deciding—she was liking this sister-in-law. They both kicked at the fluffy snow.

"This kind of snow reminds me of Alaska," Marce said, tossing some of it in the air. "Deep and silent. Like Will."

Cat frowned. "We talking about the same Will? Big furry guy?"

"Yes. He is." Marce smiled. "And sure of himself."

This could be pretty true. "From the time he was a little boy," Cat said, "he could make you believe he could do anything."

"And could he?" Marce asked.

"Almost. One time, though," she laughed, "he dragged home this old tired plow horse. Paid our neighbor, Charles Wyndom, ten dollars for it,"

"For what?"

"He was going to train him." Cat laughed.

"To do what?"

"This we'll never know, because when he actually mounted him, the old bugger took off at full gallop with Will on his back, through the woods, down the cove, right into his old stall in Charles Wyndom's barn. Practically beheaded my brother on the crossbeam."

Marce stopped in her tracks. "Then what happened?"

Cat shrugged. "It died. The horse dropped dead right there with Will on top."

Marce pushed her. "No—more—stories!"

95

Cat put up her hands. "OK, OK. But it seems to me you might wanna know some of the history."

In the distance, they could see the soft lights glowing in the cabin's windows. They were walking toward it now. The cabin was cozy, Cat thought. She didn't often get to see it from this vantage. She imagined herself not of this place, seeing it for the first time, maybe like Marce was seeing it. She would feel a tug of envy for whoever lived there. That would be me, she thought.

They walked in easy silence for awhile.

"Your brother really loves you," Marce said finally.

Cat nodded, knowing. "I just wish he liked me better."

"Why do you say that?"

She scuffed at the clumps of ice sticking to her boots. The air was still. Thick snow hovered above in the tree branches. This and the rise of drifts around them made Cat feel like she was in a lofty winter cathedral.

"I don't know." She shrugged. "Sometimes I think he wishes I were more like him and less like Kate."

"And *are* you more like Kate and less like him?"

She had to think about it. She wouldn't have thought of herself as closely resembling either one of them. She never really felt as if she and Will were alike, but she always felt they were close in some fucked up love/hate sibling kind of way. She didn't really know who she was like. The Kate that Will remembered: the controlling one, the bitter one, the one who had somehow stopped feeling ... well, she had hoped she wasn't like that. And the Kate that she knew: the strong one, the stoic one, the one who always did the *right* thing, Cat didn't think she could ever live up to that.

Maybe Lily's edict about her intimacy issues was true. It had probably been created by the coldness in Kate that had chilled Will. Her grandmother loved her, of this she was sure. But it was a kind of subtle love whose proof was in the everyday business of caring for their lives: sheltering, feeding, educating, and then dragging them to church.

Of course, there had been good moments. Like Christmas. She'd almost forgotten about Kate and Christmas. She paused in the road and Marce stopped beside her. They stood haloed in a pool of moonlight whose glow was grayed by the falling snow.

"Kate loved Christmas." Cat swallowed and then smiled. "If she'd had her way, she would have started getting ready for it the day after Thanksgiving."

They both turned and began walking again, only this time more slowly.

"She'd cut holly and evergreen sprigs and weave the most amazing wreathes. She'd hang them on the door and above the fireplace and give them away to neighbors. Our tree would be cut on the first as well, but she'd wait until the fifth to put it up. I have no idea why. Then all month we'd listen to carols, bake mounds of cookies and shortbread, string popcorn and cranberries and lights everywhere. Once, she got Will to crawl up the barn roof and wrap the cupola in red and green lights, which, by the way, never came down. The wires are still there, but most of the bulbs are busted. You're surprised by this." Cat more stated than asked.

"Well, it doesn't sound like the grandmother Will described."

"Yeah, well ... Will doesn't seem to remember the good stuff." She glanced to see that Marce was listening. "Or, if he does, he can't admit it because then he'd have to admit that some of that whole mess was partly his fault."

Marce nodded but didn't speak.

"Kate wasn't a monster," Cat said, after a minute, adding softly, "and neither is Will."

Marce touched Cat's arm lightly. "So you're a little like both, but nothing like either."

Cat smiled. "Maybe so. I'm the good, the bad, and the ugly, and a little of my own yuk fluxing the mess together."

They walked along a fence line, where on the other side, two horses puffed clouds of smoke and snorted as they passed. By the time they reached the house, Cat felt her defenses peeled away. She liked this woman. Maybe, Cat thought, as they stood side by side, she would even come to love her. Right now she loved that this was the woman who would be taking care of her brother.

"I think I'm going to like having you for a sister-in-law," Marce said, giving her a quick hug, surprising Cat out of her thoughts.

The next morning, Cat woke to the smell of coffee and eggs and bacon as it drifted into the living room. They would be leaving today, her brother and his new wonderful wife. They'd be going over to Sellarsville to stay in the old Victorian on Main Street.

"It was my grandmother's house," Marce said. "I love it but sometimes I feel like I'm living with a ghost."

Cat nodded. "Once in the middle of the night, a couple weeks after Kate died, I could have sworn I'd heard her having a coughing fit."

"How long did it take you?" Marce asked, knowingly.

"Two seconds. Then I'm standing in that empty room, looking at that empty bed, and feeling like a fool."

"I know what you mean. I lived with the sound of a respirator for nine months. The first time I heard its silence, I freaked, like I was hearing a train coming through the living room."

Will was quiet, Cat noticed, while they talked of dying old women.

His head was down, she saw, as she spoke about Kate. When he did finally look her way, it was actual sorrow shadowing his eyes. She wondered if he had never felt that before just now, at least about Kate.

After breakfast, Marce said she'd clean up while sister and brother headed to the barn to take a look at the motorcycle, which, Cat told Will, was making a funny noise. The Duo Glide was wrapped under an old blue tarp that Cat pulled back, cracking the coating of ice that had frozen it there. Its chrome forks and spoked wheels shone in the morning light. Cat wiped the black saddle with soft lamb's wool.

She had been fourteen when she and Will had dragged the bike from the dump and pushed it, flattened tires and all, the four miles home. When they'd first retrieved it, it had been nearly indistinguishable as a Harley, never mind a classic '59 Duo Glide. For nearly a whole year they had worked on it together. Mechanics books and old Harley photos littered their shop floor as they took it apart and put it all back together, replacing some parts, cleaning or repairing others.

Now, as she gave the taillight one last swipe, Cat nudged Will. "Remember how excited Kate was to make these things?"

The shiny black leather bags had replaced the rotted ones. Kate had cut and soaked and sewn the new ones, duplicating the originals right down to the fringed flaps. She'd once made a similar pair for Angus' horse.

"Its name was Mackie, wasn't it?" Cat wondered aloud. "The horse, I mean."

"No, it was Jacko," Will said.

"Are you sure?"

"She told me," Will said. "She named all the farm animals after her brothers and sisters back in Scotland. Jacko was the baby."

Cat was stunned. How could she not have known about this, and why did Will? She looked at her brother. He was remembering something about his grandmother. Something good, something that even she, Cat, hadn't known. Something *tender*.

The summer of her fifteenth year, she and Will had finished the bike, painting it in its original colors of calypso red and birch white. It was a beauty and a *babe magnet,* Will had declared, after he'd tooled it around town that first week. Two years later, after he'd won a '67 Electra Glide in a card game just over the border in Tennessee, he'd thrown Cat the keys to the old Harley saying, "Whatever you do, don't wreck it."

Will laid down on his back to check the panhead of the bike. Cold, Cat filled a rusty steel drum with wood and paper and threw in a match, sparking only enough heat to warm her hovering palms. She watched her brother tinker.

Using their hand signals from the old days Will held up two fingers, and she handed him the small wrench. She squatted and watched. Knocking a frozen knuckle against cold metal, he cursed. With blackened fingers he carefully pulled on a capped wire and sat up, inspecting it. Digging out the crusty threads with the tip of a screwdriver, he blew the red dust from its hollow.

"This might be the problem," he said, tilting the tube toward her. "Corroded."

"Where the hell'd you find that sucker?" She crouched, trying to see its housing.

"Oh, this little sonofabitch likes to hide up in there." He blew again and scraped the end of the wire shiny. "Same thing happened to mine last summer. You wouldn't think to look. Took my whole damn bike apart before I found it."

He slid his big body back under the bike and clanked around, grunting a few more times. "That ought a do it," he said, and climbed on board, cranking the engine to a smooth, low rumble. "Like a top." He grinned at his sister and then joined her by the fire. They stood quietly together for a while.

"Am I like Kate?" Cat asked him.

He looked hard at her, searching her face as if he would find the answer there. "Maybe," he said.

"Maybe? What kind of answer is that?"

"You're easier than Kate." Will said. "But—in some ways you're harder."

"Geez, Will."

He shrugged. "I don't know, Cat. Sometimes you scare me."

"Scare you? How?"

"Well, if I die before you, I know you'll be OK. I know you can live without me. But if you die first ..." He looked away and up into the belly of the barn above. "Shit, Cat... it's just ... you're always *here*. You know? Pretty much the one thing I can count on."

She didn't know what to say. How could this be? He'd left her. Years ago. Struck out, surviving just fine on his own, without even a backward glance. She said as much.

He shook his head. "That's my point. You did just fine without me. You didn't even know where I was half the time."

"Seven-eighths of the time. Might as well call a spade a spade."

He laughed. "But I always knew where *you* were. What you were doing, who you were doing it with." He shook his head. "I never lost you in the same ways you lost me, Cat."

"And this is why I scare you?"

"Yeah. That's a hard heart, Cat. The heart of a survivor. Like Kate's heart. It's good and it's bad—and in that way you're like Kate."

Cat found herself smiling. "My brother the psychologist," she said.

But Will's face was serious. "I just hope you can soften enough to allow some love into your life, Cat," he said.

"Like you?"

"Yeah, like me. I fell in love and I'm different. I hope you can be so lucky."

Marce had wandered up the path and joined them. Placing both arms around Will's middle, she laid her cheek against his back and he smiled.

He pointed to the place on the rafters where the tattered remains of a rope had been knotted and hung. With giant sweeps of his arms to dramatize, he launched into regaling Marce with tales of the trapeze stunts he and Cat had performed as kids. How the two of them had swung across the width of the barn, nearly killing themselves at least a dozen times. Cat pointed to a thin scar across her left brow, just above her eye.

"This is where his giant boot landed, nailed me on a downswing, opened my face like a faucet. Blood everywhere." She punched him.

"Shoulda got outta my way," he said, as he had said from the moment his boot and her face had made contact. Before they could turn the story into an argument, as they had so often done, Marce tugged on Will's arm, reminding him that they needed to leave.

"I'll come by," he said to Cat, not looking at her as he pulled on his gloves. The close moment between them was gone. Marce was taking his arm, taking her brother away.

"Out of sight, out of mind," Kate had shrugged once, when Cat had asked if she missed her grandson. But he'd rarely been out of Cat's mind, and she didn't believe that he'd *ever* been out of Kate's.

Chapter Seven

The *Storm of the Century,* as Lily liked to call this last snowy blast of winter, had quickly melted off, leaving the ground spongy and muddy. Small streams forged new rows through cornfields; treetops cracked with the weight of the wet snow; rivers crested banks, and everything woke up. Spring had arrived in one fell swoop.

Cat smoked out on the porch waiting for Lily to pick her up for work. She was dressed now in only jeans and a flannel shirt, the winter layers having been stripped with the rising temperatures. It was a relief to be back to work, she thought. Lily had decided to extend their storm-surprised vacation. *So you can get ready for your reading down at Mari's,* she had magnanimously offered.

Knowing it was now impossible to escape the performance, Cat practiced: in front of the mirror, in front of Mike, in front of Delores and Matthew and Hannah, after dinner at Lily and Hannah's house. She'd felt dumb about it. They had cautioned her to read slower, louder, and to make eye contact and breathe. It wasn't like she had never read in public before. But somehow this felt different. For the first time she'd be reading from her own published book.

Tonight would be a kind of debut. Even if it was only for

herself. When she'd first heard the promo on the radio, calling her *the author,* she was startled. There was some kind of difference (in her own mind) between *writer* and *author*. She was the former, but suspected that she would be expected to sound like the latter.

As if she should know something more now having crossed the threshold into print. If anything, it had made the unknown all the more frightening. This was what had been digging at her as she mulled over the idea for a new story. All the old fears were chipping away at its fragile truths. She had an image of a young Scottish woman exiled to America. It was a novel, her first (of this she was sure) that had begun rising in Cat.

She'd been visited in her dreams, as she shoveled snow, and soaped herself in the shower. How was she supposed to explain that kind of *thing* to people? It would make her sound nuts.

"Yes, yes, I hear voices," she imagined herself explaining.

Cat picked up her cooler as the white work van made its way to her driveway. Clicking off the lights, she headed for the front door. Mike stood and stared at her as if he were unsure about what he should be doing. It had been so long since she'd been to work that he'd forgotten his job.

"Watch the house," she said as she pulled the door open. He jumped to his spot on the couch and grunted into a ball. He was miffed. She only hoped that his German-shepherdness would be enough to scare away a prowler.

Cat settled into her seat in the cab and Lily patted her shoulder. "Ready for your reading tonight?"

Each morning for the past week, Lily had posed this question. Counting off the days for Cat, just in case she didn't remember. Five more, two more, one.

"Ready as I'll ever be," she said. But the only thing she was really ready for was to have it be over.

Yesterday, Candace had called to say that the publisher was pleased with the opening sales. That she, Candace, had gotten a call from a bookstore in Raleigh and another one in Atlanta; and there was an email from a college that wanted Cat to speak at a summer writing seminar.

"Email," Cat had murmured, marveling.

"Just wanted to let you know." She could actually *hear* her agent's grin through the phone.

Lily had declared that Cat was on her way to the top.

"We'll all be there tonight, buddy. Me, Hannah, Delores, Matthew, even Mamma."

Cat could feel the fear rising as she pictured them all in a row—probably smiling. She shook the image from her mind.

"Is Will coming?" Lily asked, stopping the van at the light and letting it roll back as diesel smoke from a dump truck ahead threatened to fill the cab.

"I doubt it." Cat lit a cigarette and tossed the match out the window. She hadn't mentioned the reading to Will. He'd once told her he couldn't read her work because it made him feel like he was reading her diary or something.

"Did you even tell him about it?" Lily looked over as she turned onto the main road, nearly swiping a speed limit sign in the swerve.

When Cat had been silent long enough, Lily pulled the cell phone from its cradle and punched in her own home number.

"What are you doing?"

"Hey, baby," Lily said to Hannah over the receiver. "You need to call Will. He doesn't know about the reading tonight." She turned to Cat. "What's his number over there at Marce's?"

Cat shrugged.

"C'mon, Cat. He'll be hurt if he misses it ... Hannah says so." Cat gave in and reeled off Marce's number, by now imprinted in her mind. He wouldn't come, anyway. But if she didn't give him the chance, he'd probably hold it against her. Let 'em all come. Fine. She'd humiliate herself in front of everybody all at once.

The van pulled up behind a row of stopped cars. Ahead, a farmer in overalls was waving his cap, slapping the hindquarters of a cow that had broken a fence. Farmer and cow were not budging from the middle of the road.

"Moooooooo!" Lily called out the window as they skinnied by the shaky bovine.

They pulled onto the highway and began heading north into the mountains. Lily reached into her pocket and pulled out a crumpled piece of paper. She passed it over to Cat, who unfolded it. "Directions."

"I'm supposed to read this?" Cat squinted at the paper. "Your handwriting is worse than a doctor's."

"I was in a hurry. I can read it."

"Furry Fox Road?"

Lily leaned over, slid her finger under the blue ink and frowned. "That ain't Furry Fox ... that's Slippery Rock." She tapped the paper as evidence. As if, just because she wanted it to say it, it would.

"How the hell do you get Slippery Rock out of that?"

"No cussin'," Lily said.

Cat looked up at her.

"Seriously. No cussin' on the job," Lily explained. "New company policy."

"You gotta be kidding."

"Nope. Can't change company policy."

"Lil, *you* are the company, for Christ's sake."

"Ahht ... no cussin'."

"*Christ* isn't a cuss."

"It is when you use it like that."

"For cryin' out loud." Cat slouched back in her seat. "What's this all about?"

They were off the main road and headed into a low-lying valley. "Cussin' only brings out negativity. Me and Hannah are gonna quit."

"Well, good for you and Hannah. Leave me out."

It was the weekend, Lily went on to explain. The retreat they'd gone on. It had changed them.

"There we were, way out in the country, in a cabin. With a bunch of other women, all of us on the same quest for peace and tranquility—a life void of negativity."

Cat yawned. "Another retreat? Haven't you guys been changed enough?"

"This is serious, now. It really showed us how to be more positive."

"You and Hannah don't need any fixing, Lil. For God's sake."

Lily looked at her. "Right." She was smiling. "But you shoulda seen this Sister Boogie Woman, Cat. She knew all about what she was saying. And it showed, 'cause she did her whole workshop with a smile on her face and that's the first step toward positivity—smiling."

"Please tell me you are kidding."

"God's truth," Lily said. "Sister Boogie Woman says—"

"Sister Boogie Woman?"

"—says our souls are like a box of Tide."

Cat stared at her.

"See, the soul," Lily hesitated, "is the detergent for all the dirt and stains that go into the mind and the heart."

"You sure you've got this right?"

"Something like that, anyway." Lily cocked her head, thinking. Then her voice pealed out for a second. *"Use your souls to cleanse your hearts!"* She waved her hands, in the same manner (Cat suspected) that Sister Boogie had. *"Wash your mouths with the cleansing awareness of positive energy; refuse to allow negativity to guide your days. Allow NO MORE SWEARING into your world."*

It was this that had convinced Lily and Hannah to quit cussin'.

This was one more juncture on the couple's spiritual path, Cat figured. They had gathered in fields with other naked women, beating on drums, sweating in lodges, and calling to the four corners. In circles, they had sat cross-legged, passing talking sticks, peace pipes, and communal ablutions.

"I'm not quittin' cussin'," Cat finally mumbled.

Lily ignored her. She slowed the van as a flock of ducks waddled across the road. They had come to a fork and could not make out the way from the directions scribbled on the ragged paper.

"We'll go this way," Lily decided. "I feel the Universe's pull, strong today." She looked over at Cat. "See how not having negativity around you can make things exceptionally clear?"

Cat shrugged. She'd give this no-cussin' policy exactly two weeks.

Lily said, "Might help with your reading, too."

Cat snorted slightly, in spite of herself. "You mean the Universe will guide me through?"

She leaned across the seat and pulled at a wooden box on the floor of the cab. It was filled with white rectangular pieces of plastic stamped with black letters. After snapping them back and forth, clicking them like dominos, Cat held one up.

"What are these for?"

"I am the new official sign manager for the Fordham's Cove Community Sign," Lily said, happily, and blew across the mouth of her coffee cup. "You know, messages, birthdays, anniversaries ... they all go on the sign."

"Why you?"

"I volunteered. Sister Boogie Woman says we should do good in the world, no matter how small the contribution. Just doing my part," she said, and then smiled and kept smiling.

The old truck was bumping along now, kicking up clouds of red dust as they made their way deeper into a darkening hollow, whose end would be soon or, she was sure, they would be swallowed. Lily handed her a worn leather folder pulled from beneath her seat. Opening to the middle, Cat noticed each square date box was filled with Lily's scratchy handwriting. *The Ponder Family Reunion. Sarah Emily's third birthday.* These were written in black. Red ink messages filled her squares. *Lost: black and white tabby named Heifer. Found: One lady's red high heel, in good shape.* Filling the remaining spaces, in purple ink, were quotes: *A smile a day keeps the doctor away* and *Every good turn deserves another.*

"You're a regular Paul Harvey." Cat shook her head. "Aren't you?"

"No," Lily looked at the sky. "But I love going out early in the mornin'. Mist pockets driftin' up out of the hills. Everything shinin'. Big dewy spider webs sparklin' in the early light. David Collar's peafowl runnin' ever'where." She headed the van onto the graveled road. "It smells so sweet and clean out here, like cut grass, new milk, wet dirt. You know—all those memory smells."

"Did Sister Boogie Woman say you should write poetry?"

"And," Lily said, ignoring her. "I like the letters. I like the way they feel. And I like making them into the signs."

Cat held one between her fingers. It was thick and heavy and, Lily went on, when you clicked them all together they said something. *Meant* something. Not all stuck in the box that way, she clarified. Together they made words, sentences. She seemed awed by her own revelation.

She nudged Cat's elbow. "You know what I mean about the letters?"

Cat thought she did. Like writing, you pick the words because of the way they feel, how they make you feel, and how you think they'll make somebody else feel. Yes, she did understand that.

The van was now at a dead stop. "We're lost," Lily said.

Cat looked around. The mountains rose steep above them. Damp green forest air clung to her, even through the truck, making her shiver. An ancient rotting barn had crumbled to its knees next to a chimney stand in a sloping field beyond. Lily sat back against her seat and lit a cigarette. Cat stared at the abandoned structures, testaments of neglect. She thought suddenly of Kate. How the memories in her were gone now into death. A lifetime's worth of experiences and feelings—gone. Except for a few remnants, flashes of scene or sense she had conveyed to her grandchildren—pieces of her experience that, any moment now, might slide out of Cat or Will forever to be left to decay in the dark. Cat looked out at the stone foundations of the buildings. Someone's hands had placed each rock. And those hands belonged to a life. She wondered if there was anyone still around to remember it.

"I've had to be tough about that sign, though," Lily was

111

saying. "Right off the bat, people tried to take advantage of my good nature."

Cat looked away from the barn, back at Lily.

"Neighbors calling me up for every single event going on in the community." Lily told about Nora Loftin wanting to advertise her February Tupperware party, to which Lily had put her foot down. And how during her first day on the job, she'd followed the directions in the leather calendar book and put Coy and Bertie Martin's anniversary congratulations on the sign. "Then I find out the Martins split up two years ago. So now I've got to double-check all the damn information."

Cat raised an eyebrow. "Damn?"

Lily gave her a dark look. "I ain't on the damn job yet." She stared at the steering wheel, obviously thinking about her sign problems. "I mean it, Cat; there are just some things a person has got to be sensible about." She started up the truck and turned into a rutted drive whose humped middle grew thick with long grasses that skimmed the underside of the truck.

Cat could see that being sign manager had its downside.

"Take this fight I had with Lonny Buckner last week."

"You fought with little-old-wouldn't-hurt-a-fly Lonny Buckner?"

"Well, she wasn't being reasonable."

"She must be going on ninety, Lil."

"Don't matter. She's ornery, kept yellin' at me."

"I think she's deaf."

Lily ignored her. "Calls me up and says I should put, *Deepest Sympathy to Eurna Collar on the death of her daughter, Lorry Jean*. Sounds like a congratulations when you say it like that—*on the death of her daughter*. I got a problem puttin' Lorry Jean's passing on the sign, anyway. I mean Lorry

Jean Collar hasn't even lived in this valley for nearly twenty years."

"Aren't you being just a little *negative* out in the *Universe* today?"

Lily justified by whispering that Lorry Jean had moved up north. Cat was appalled.

"Lily, Lorry Jean went to school with your daddy. And Eurna, well, she'd make us those candy apples on Halloween." She gave Lily a stern look. "Remember how she'd sometimes give us two?"

Lily's jaw was set.

"For cryin' out loud, Lil, the woman is going to be grieving for her daughter no matter where she died. There isn't some rule that unless you die up Fordham's Cove you don't get your condolences up on the sign, is there? I mean, if Will went and got killed in some car wreck wouldn't he make it up on the sign?"

Lily was silent.

The tools in the back knocked together as they bounced across the farmland. Cat looked over at her friend, thinking funny how sometimes you can see someone's face nearly every day for most of your life and then suddenly it's like you've never seen it before.

Lily cleared her throat. "She did have Lorry Jean brought back home to the Collar Branch Cemetery Plot. So, she's *sort* of back in Fordham's Cove."

"There you go." Cat leaned over and patted Lily's shoulder. "If you want, you could put *Deepest Sympathies, Eurna Collar* or *Welcome Home, Lorry Jean.*"

They never did find the job site. Lost as they possibly could be, they wound through mountain coves for nearly three hours pulling into dead ends that looked like someone had just given up, returning the neighborhood to the belly of the beast. Cat saw the hills with an awe she had somehow never felt before in all her years of living here. She imagined those first settlers, machetes in hand, hacking and beating their way into the thick brush and dense bramble that proceeded forests, all of their primeval world now darker and thicker than *the fur on the back of a bear,* as Lily would say.

"I'm giving up," Lily said, suddenly, plaintively, after one last wrong turn. The journey out, a little less contorted, took them another hour. All she wanted to do, she said, was get home and take a nap before she had to go back out to hear Cat's reading.

At the cabin, she stopped Cat before she climbed out of the cab. "You want me and Hannah to pick you up tonight?"

Cat grinned, "Afraid I'm not going to show up?"

"You've been known to be a little flighty."

"Don't worry, I'll be there. Four hours of riding with you in the truck has given me new positive energy, Lil."

Inside, Cat flopped down on the couch, exhausted. What was she thinking? She was sick as a dog. It had come in waves all day. Every time she thought about standing up in front of all those people.

She reached across the couch to the phone and hit the play button on the answering machine. Both Delores and Candace had left offers of rides to the reading tonight. Did nobody trust her? She knew they were all afraid that she would chicken out. But she wouldn't.

By the time she'd finally showered and dressed, she'd had to blow-dry twice. After the first round of wrestling herself in and out of shirts and sweaters, jeans and other jeans, she'd settled on a black turtleneck and a pair of worn Levis. And then she wondered if she looked like a beat poet.

She'd left her reading upstairs, twice. Its pages were

highlighted to signal pauses and possible places of laughter—Delores's idea. Cat held the book and stared down at the cover as if she were seeing it for the first time.

Her keys were left behind on the counter and she went back for them. Dropped her lighter into the bushes. Finally she got on the Glide and managed to flood it. If she weren't careful she would miss the whole reading altogether. Everyone would just think she'd chickened out. She'd have to take the truck.

Although it wasn't the same truck as the one Kate had driven to New York City to retrieve Will and Cat when their parents died, it was similar. Same tan color, same plaid bench seat, same lingering smell of lilac talc that Kate would dab at her neck and between her breasts. For some crazy reason Cat found herself remembering that first ride, snuggled into a deep warm nest of blankets between her grandmother and her brother. The quiet of that journey had been complete. Each in their own thoughts, Cat imagined now, although she had no recollection of her own. Will would have had his own, she was sure. The faint image of his arms wrapped around her little form, pulling her to him even as he slept, hanging on to her, was more sensory than remembered. It had been to the old woman that Cat had wanted to be pulled.

Old woman, Cat thought, now. But Kate had just turned fifty when she came to claim her grandchildren. Still, to Cat she'd always been ancient: a stringy woman with lines etched around old eyes and a lean firm set to her jaw. It was during that first journey that she had imprinted on Kate's lilac smell the way a duckling imprints on the sight of its mamma.

She tried to imagine her grandmother's thoughts as she'd driven those many miles to New York City. Had she been afraid? Had there been any time for her to have mourned the loss of her only child? Mourned the loss of her own independence, now that she'd taken in these two little burdens? Cat slowed as the truck approached the café, thinking, it's no time for worrying about whether you wrecked an old woman's dreams. We didn't choose to be orphans, either.

She pulled into the space in front of the café for the *visiting writer,* as the sign read *(Gawd,* thought Cat). Delores and Lily were standing outside smoking cigarettes and waiting for her. She suspected that they were deciding who would leave to hunt her up in case she didn't show. She looked over their heads and in through the café's windows. The place was jammed. She recognized a bunch of faces: flirty women from OzGirlz; a couple of old high school friends she no longer saw except at the grocery store.

Cat cringed—over in the corner, heads together, were two women she had dated, once each. Delores's husband Matthew and Hannah were getting Mamma settled with a cup of something hot; and beside her, low and behold, was Jim, Lily's dad.

When she was a little girl, Jim had promised to never miss anything that was important to her. And he hadn't. He'd been to most of her high school softball games, all of her graduations, Kate's funeral, and once he said (hopefully) that he'd walk her down the aisle as soon she got out of that lesbian phase.

Candace was in deep conversation with Mari and a gray-haired gentleman in a suit. That sight was even creepier than the two ex-dates in the corner who were (she imagined) barbecuing her. Who was this stuffy old guy? Cat wondered.

When she walked through the door both Mari and Candace rushed her, pulling her through the crowd. A smile and one or two familiar hugs later she was sequestered in a back room where the gray-haired gentleman was now seated, evidently waiting for her.

"David Webber, host, *Stories and Writers,*" he said.

Cat allowed him to shake her hand. "The—uh—WNW thing?" she asked stupidly.

He had a fake smile and shifty eyes. "I'd like to invite you to come on for an interview and a reading."

Words were not managing to push past her lips. Candace nodded and assured Mr. Webber that indeed, indeed, Cat would be *delighted.* There was that word again. Webber pulled open a small notebook and ticked off a bunch of dates, times, a pre-interview interview, stuff.

All the while, Mari was standing beside Cat, fluffing her hair, pinching her cheeks, whispering that she was *on* in *ten.*

Lily said, "Here, I'll hold this," taking the book out of Cat's hands while Mari primped.

The whole thing was surreal; Cat excused herself to the ladies room and locked the door behind her. She leaned and breathed deeply. Sweat collected and slid down her back and legs, gathering in her socks. What had she gotten herself into? No way could she go out there. She had no voice. She pressed her forehead harder against the door and opened her silent mouth, as if to prove it.

A click from a stall door pulled her around. A woman emerged. Long copper-colored curls framed her face, teasing at the corners of a pair of green eyes.

The woman smiled almost apologetically, then made her way to the sink and washed her hands. She didn't look up. Even on the verge of hyperventilating, Cat noticed how long and slender her body was, and the way she washed her hands, each caressing the other under the running tap, lathering soap in one pass and rinsing it clean in the next. Cat realized she was still leaning hard on the door.

After drying her hands, she pulled another towel from the holder and ran it under the tap, then twisted it damp.

"Here," she said, handing Cat the cool paper. "You look like you could use this."

She hesitated, then took it and patted her neck.

"Breathing will help," the woman advised.

"Yeah, sometimes it's hard to remember." She patted her face, as neither of them spoke.

The sweet smell of Plumaria drifted into the space between them. And there was a heat. An unmistakable heat. Cat felt almost sheepish—*this girl knows what I'm thinking*. Then she felt as if she were being pulled into the twin seas of those eyes. She patted the cool towel to her face more firmly.

"May I leave?" The woman pointed at the door.

Cat shuffled, nearly bumping the wall and tugging on the handle, which stuck. The woman reached around her, brushing her shoulder.

"Here," she flipped the latch. "I think you locked it."

"Sorry."

The woman released the door. Before crossing the threshold she placed her hand lightly on Cat's shoulder. "You'll be fine." And she was gone.

Cat made her way to the sink. Her eyes looked suddenly big in a face that seemed to have grown small. Her heart was still chugging hard in her chest and so she waited for it to slow. She brought the towel to her nose, catching the hint of Plumaria. Breathed again, and then tossed it into the trash.

The bathroom door swung wide and Lily marched in. Then Candace and Mari.

118

"You OK?" Lily asked. She was holding the book, cradling it carefully against her chest.

In unison Candace and Mad attacked. What was Cat doing? People were waiting. Where had she been? David Webber was worried. They were practically introducing her that very second. Finally, Lily turned on them. Raising her arms, she pushed them back.

"Give her a break. Go on. I'll bring her out in two minutes."

The women eased out the door and disappeared. Lily put a hand on her friend's shoulder. "'Bout ready?" Her voice was soft. She was smiling. "You can't fight this, Cat. It's part of it, what you've been workin' for your whole life."

Cat nodded.

"It's just fear. Cat, you've been up two stories high, hangin' off a scaffold with a bucking Quickie saw in your hands, for cryin' out loud. What's scarier than that?"

Cat shrugged, then pulled away, breathing deeply, and gave one last fluff, as Lily would say, in the mirror.

Lily handed her the book. "You'll kick ass," she said, and was out the door.

Cat smoothed the pages of the story with her damp hands. She stared down at the print and then closed the book on a finger to mark her place.

They had not, as Mari had threatened, already introduced her. The crowd had mostly settled into café chairs, couches, and on stools along the bar. Others, who'd come late, lined the back window, packing the place like the proverbial can of sardines.

She dared look out over the crowd. There were her people in the second row. At the end of the line, right next to Hannah, were the smiling faces of Will and Marce. Her brother waved the flyer, dancing her picture like a paper doll over the baldheaded guy in front of him. Cat smiled, seeing Marce slap his hand down. But Will kept on grinning.

There were clusters of people she knew from her whole life. Ruthie must have shut down OzGirlz to come with her entourage of wait staff and patrons. Standing in a separate little group were a bunch of women from The Pocket, where Cat and Lily spent most Tuesday nights shooting pool. She glanced across the crowd, fixing on some faces more happily than others. She was startled to see Dizzy and the guys from the lumberyard looking uncomfortably awkward but all neatly dressed and spit-shined. Dizzy held a bouquet of daisies, which trembled daintily against his big muscular chest.

Just before David Webber finished his winded speech about the work of *this author,* Cat caught a glimpse of the woman from the bathroom standing toward the back. She was holding a copy of the book now. Maybe, Cat hoped, she would want it signed after the reading.

Clapping started up.

As if she were no longer in her own body, Cat watched herself make her way to the stage. It was odd, not feeling the floor pass by under her feet, not sensing the shift of her body as it stopped just behind the podium. And even though her voice, once it started out of her mouth, *sounded* like her own, it was as if she was hearing it OK—just not speaking it. There were things she had meant to say: how the mountains had given her the stories, how her family and friends had endured her endless efforts to get them to sound right. Something about history never quite losing itself in the Carolina consciousness.

But she had clean forgotten the little speech. Instead she was quiet, then sipped from the glass of water placed inside the podium, and took a deep breath, imagining herself high atop a shaky scaffold. She began to read.

"In the blue bowl of a valley whose ridges rise to etch the silhouette of a woman lying on her back, in early dawn the sun pinks over her shoulder and greets the cabin's face. Andrew Hooker was watching that pink slide of light right now, from the field where he had just begun to plow. It was a dwelling place, he thought. It was his dwelling place. He shaded his eyes and watched a different womanly figure closing in on him, making her way through the wheat field toward him. Her long body moved in rhythm with the windblown grasses ..."

The room had quieted. It was now only Cat's voice filling the void. Delores had urged her to pause, breathe, and drink water in a way that would not interrupt her reading. She gave moments of laughter and quiet a chance to resonate. And throughout she remembered to slow down, breathe, and to make eye contact.

She'd caught Will wiping a tear, Lily wrinkling her nose, and Mamma's big jolly laugh bouncing her massive breasts like molded Jello. Toward the end Cat looked to the back corner, catching a glimpse of the green eyes, watching intently. *Still there.* She read the last sentence and allowed herself the hope that the woman would stay to have her book signed.

The applause came and the audience got to its feet. It was embarrassing. The crowd was descending upon her. She felt besieged, cringing against her own ego, but happy, too—astonished. People were shaking her hands, hugging her.

Lily thumped her back saying, "What'd I tell ya?"

Then Will was lifting her into the air like a rag doll until she pounded on his shoulders and made him put her down.

Mamma had grabbed her, crushing her to her bosom.

And finally Jim held her and told her how proud Kate would have been.

She was suddenly whisked, between Candace and Mari, to another part of the café where a table was surrounded by stacks of *Outside of Everything*. Three chairs had been set up.

Mari and Candace were in charge of selling the books. Cat was in charge of signing them. Not an easy task, she was left-handed, her writing—hazardous.

At first, she did her best in her most careful hand. But after the eighth one, she looked up to notice that at the very end of the long line was the beauty from the bathroom checking her watch. Cat gave up any attempt at neatness and began scrawling.

After Lily had her book signed (she owned three copies, already), she opened the jacket.

"How can a writer have such bad handwritin'?"

Cat waved her away as she reached for the next one.

It was old Cora Jones, from up the cove, who brought the line to a standstill. Cora had been an old friend of Kate's. From time to time, they hadn't much liked each other but they'd always been good neighbors. Cora began to chat.

"Did you know that Lester's bull got in my garden last week?" she asked, handing Cat the book. "Et all my corn, it did."

Cat shook her head in sympathy.

"Been at your field, too." Cora leaned over. "Your granny would a shot it, you know."

Cat smiled politely.

"Is that character, *Wesley,* after my boy, *Warren?*" Cora asked narrowing her voice to a whisper. "'Cause it shore do sound like him."

She tried to keep a watchful eye on the redhead, now just a few signatures away. Finally, Cat pointed to the line behind Cora and she left. But it was too late, so too had the woman from the bathroom. Cat vengefully pictured spinning wheelies through Cora's tobacco field sometime after midnight. Damn it.

Her hand was numb. She pried the pen from her atrophied fingers and cracked her knuckles to free up the joints. Mari had told her, twice, that they'd sold every last copy of the book. And Candace had exacted her agreement to appear on the David Webber show.

The crowd had dribbled away. Finally, she was left alone with Lily and Hannah, relieved to step into a conversation that was not about her performance.

"Didn't you see her?" Hannah was asking Lily, who shook her head and looked around the empty café. "She's gone, now."

"Who?" Cat looked around with Lily.

"Melissa," Hannah said.

"That doctor we told you about," Lily added. "Right here and I missed her, dang it. We could have introduced you."

"You don't need to, I saw somebody else I might like."

They walked out into the cool night, Lily scanning the vacant sidewalks. Only an empty plastic bag kicked along the street. "Who?" Lily asked.

Cat shrugged, thinking about the green eyes. "I don't know."

Lily and Hannah looked at each other.

"Whatdya mean, you don't know?" Lily asked, following Cat to her truck.

"I mean I don't know. I saw her in the bathroom. I didn't ask her *name*, Lily. But she seemed nice. Pretty." Cat rolled down the window and yanked the door shut. She waved to Hannah, patiently waiting for Lil on the sidewalk.

"You met a woman in the bathroom?"

Cat turned the key, bringing the motor to a coughing start, tapping the gas, waiting for the cranky old engine to catch. Hannah gestured for Lily to come along.

"Hey!" Lily shouted over the truck's roar, "We'll be talkin' about this first thing tomorrow!"

She rolled up the window, feigning deafness, and steered the truck toward home.

Chapter Eight

Cat dreamed of her grandmother. Only different. In the dream, Kate was younger and had wild red curls and green eyes. She was in love with a young man who might have been Angus, except he kept changing, sometimes looking like the real Angus, sometimes looking like Will. He appeared as the man in the photo album, said to be Cat's father. The dream had carried the different Kate and the morphing Angus first across a great rollicking ocean, which turned to rolling hills, which climbed to rocking mountains. The lovers wore kilts, red and black plaid. They hacked their way through a deep forest, swinging machetes in front of them. Once, the Will-looking Angus swung a baseball bat.

The young woman was Kate; a Kate she'd never known, younger, sitting beneath the great oak tree that still shaded the family plot behind the barn. Only there were no headstones or iron-gated fence. In her lap, raised and angled by bent knees, was a writing tablet. The yellow pencil in her hand moved quickly along the page. She was deep in thought. There were no sounds in this dream.

Then—in the dream—Kate's chin jerked and she jumped up. Folding the tablet, she quickly stuffed it into the branches of the tree. A man with long brown hair approached. It was the real Angus, but then not. Everything about him changed. He shape-shifted into someone else, someone familiar, but in the way that someone reminds you of another, in mannerisms but not looks.

Pushing the woman aside, he reached and pulled out the entangled notebook, waving it above his head, as if in evidence.

Cat woke with the kind of start that punches your heartbeat into reveille. She pulled herself upright and wrapped her arms around her bent legs.

Kate. This name didn't come out of her mouth although she would have sworn she'd heard it. The dream was diminishing, Kate disappearing. Cat tried to hold onto the man's face, the one that reminded her, but it was too distant already. In the blankness she searched for something in the dream that would comfort her, make her see the light, prophesize her future, but there was nothing. She tried to receive the message by staring out her window at the sole star glowing above the mountains.

It was only midnight, she saw by the numbers of her clock. After tossing for another hour she decided to get some tea and go to her office. The small room at the back of the house had once been Kate and Angus' bedroom. It had taken Cat a long time to claim it as her own. It had been Lily and Sophia's arrival on her doorstep, one wintery morning, a good long year after Kate had died, that had helped her recover the room.

They'd come equipped with boxes and bags and stacks of newspaper. "Your granny wouldn't have wanted you to clean out this room all by yourself," Sophia had said.

The memory of that day seemed illuminated with the click of the light switch. The room warmed in the yellow glow. Cat eased herself into her grandfather's oak swivel chair. The soft gold of its rubbed finish matched the rolltop desk; he'd built it himself. Lifting the knobs, the smooth slats easily rolled back into the belly of the desk, revealing Cat's laptop humming in its sleep. She flipped the screen open and tapped a key, listening to its slow awakening. Swiveling around, she caught her tripled reflection in the corner vanity that had once belonged to Kate. Angus had made this too, from a walnut tree that had, one stormy summer's evening, been split down the middle by lightning.

Kate had once attested to an electrified static that had traveled from the polished wood of the vanity through her arm, making her hair stand on end. Cat listened as the kettle in the kitchen blew, and she made her way down the hall to pour some tea.

On that day of the cleaning out, she remembered cracking the vanity's drawers, exposing scattered bobby pins, loose lipstick tubes, and stacked handkerchiefs stitched with Kate's initials.

She haltingly confided to Sophia and Lily before they had even opened a drawer that she didn't know what she feared more, finding some deep dark secret—an affair, a murder, a wicked fetish (*Now, Cat,* Lily warned, reminding her of Sophia's presence)—or finding out that there really was nothing more interesting other than bobby pins and handkerchiefs.

"You don't want to be discovering some secret of a woman who'll never be able to defend herself," Sophia had said, and folded her arms.

Cat blew across the teacup as she made her way back to her office. She sat down in the swivel chair and remembered the gathered courage that helped her clean out the last vestiges of the old woman's life.

As it turned out, it hadn't been a disappointment either way. She discovered a gold band ringed by etched thistles, one that she'd never seen before; a box of unopened sketching pencils, more surprising to her even than the ring had been; but it was the small silver flask of whiskey that really floored her and made her laugh out loud.

No unsolved mysteries. But some nice revelations. She and Lily had drained the little flask of its liquid under Sophia's disapproving gaze. For Will, she kept her grandfather's pocketknife, and she slid Kate's gold thistle ring onto her pinky.

This room had come to belong to her, she thought. Not all at once, but over the years. A few months after it had been emptied she and Lily had lined its walls with bookcases. There was a poster of Virginia Woolf.

Feathered quills and inkwells had become a collection filling two shelves of her bookcases. In the corner on a wooden stenographer's desk was an old black Olivetti whose keys still sprung and snapped against the roller. Lily had given it to Cat one birthday, saying it'd be simpler for everybody if Cat would just collect glass pigs or shot glasses.

Lately, lots of things would be simpler if she wasn't a writer. The quiet of her life was suddenly loud. Will coming back married; the upcoming book tour; fantasies of traveling; and on and on. Then maybe, there would be a new story, a mystery, an adventure, the love of her life all waiting for her somewhere else.

The face that crept up between her reality and her fantasy

brought with it worry. Lily. What would she do about Lil? What would she tell her? What about the job? What about pool nights? What about the fact that they hadn't been apart for more than a week their entire lives? Lily would be a wreck without her.

Or would she?

That Lily would probably be fine pained Cat some. In the loneliest sense of it. Lily had Hannah and her giant family and Cat suspected Lily wouldn't mind giving up pool night for an extra long dip or two in the hot tub with Hannah. Lily would be just fine.

It was Cat who would be alone: without the girlfriend, without a giant family, without the hot tub. Cat, who'd never been without Lily her whole life. The idea of wandering around in another country looking for a story to write and a woman to love reduced her to feeling pathetic.

Maybe Lily was right, maybe it was just time to settle down here, now, with a nice girl. Especially since the book was done. Now was the time to kick back and enjoy.

This time though, she thought, she'd fall in love carefully, slowly, with somebody smart. No more desperate affairs with crazed chicks or dates with cuckoo clowns. Cat pecked at a key on the Olivetti, it snapped and stuck—*L*. She pried it from the page and settled it neatly back in line. And then on second thought she struck: *ist—List*. As the word appeared, so too, through her mind, did a string of qualifications for the next woman in her life. She'd be very specific. There would be depth and commitment and loyalty. This time, she would be discerning. *Number One—Green eyes,* she typed. The ribbon was still good.

Cat was asleep, her face pressed against the cold steel of the typewriter's keys, when she was shouted awake by Lily.

"Hey! Wake up, for *creep's sake!*"

The no-cursing policy had forced Lily into a diverse, creative vocabulary.

Cat groaned and Lily headed to make coffee.

"You look like some old writer sleepin' off a drunk; like Hemingway or ..." Lily stopped at the door. "Who was it that slept with Humphrey Bogart?"

"Humphrey Bogart?" Cat peeled her face off the keys.

"In the movie—about that falcon?"

She groaned again, trying to sit up. "What are you talking about?"

"Lillian Hellman!" Lily slapped the door in a triumphant high-five.

"Go make coffee, Lil." Cat pushed past her. "I'm getting in the shower."

"Make it quick; I need to go see Daniel for an adjustment."

Daniel was Galways' chiropractor and was known simply as Daniel.

"So, we gotta go before work," Lily said, as she made her way to the kitchen.

When they arrived, it was Daniel himself who greeted the pair, but it was Cat for whom he'd been waiting. Shaking her hand and patting her shoulders, he fawned over her reading performance of the night before.

She had been stopped again at the lumberyard, where she'd assured Dizzy that his gift of daisies were safe in a vase of water on her kitchen table. It wasn't until lunchtime, as they were leaving the Soup Kitchen, a take-out place that they frequented every Friday, that two strange women accosted Cat as she tried to leave and bombarded her with accolades and questions. When she finally got to the van, Lily was halfway through her soup.

"I thought we were going to go sit down by the lake and eat?"

"Yeah, well, you were takin' so long with your *fans.*"

Cat sighed. On their way to work that very morning, Lily had counseled Cat on being a celebrity. She herself, Lily had explained, knew something about fame, having experienced her own brand of it as the only woman carpenter in the whole town.

"Think it's easy keeping your privacy when the press constantly hounds you every time you swing a hammer?" Lily seemed to be only half-joking.

Cat ought to start thinking of herself as a business, Lily had said. Make nice with her public. She'd heard some actress confirm this on the *Rosie O'Donnell Show.* Actresses, Lily cautioned Cat, knew about these things.

But now Lily was just staring ahead of herself, finishing her lunch. She tossed the empty container behind the front seat of the truck and gunned the engine.

"Hey, I can't eat this hot soup while we're moving," Cat protested.

Lily turned off the motor, sighed, and leaned back against her seat.

"Eat your sandwich." Cat handed her the fat bread wrapped in wax paper. *"Eeh, you've got a sore hand,"* she said, mimicking her grandmother.

"What does that mean, anyway?" Lily turned on her. "You say that every time I eat a sandwich and it never has made any sense."

Cat shrugged and bit into her own.

"If you don't know what something means you shouldn't be saying it all the time," Lily said chewing.

Cat turned and looked at her. "What's the matter with you?"

"Nothin'."

"You're being awfully cranky." Cat finished and stuffed her own empty container in the bag.

"Is that what that means—*cranky?* Am not."

Cat closed her eyes. She was not going to participate in this pouting game. She changed the subject.

"Did I tell you that I got a message from Zoe last night?" Cat had almost forgotten about it herself.

Zoe was an old motorcycle pal. A tall dark thin woman with long black hair (Cherokee blood, she claimed), who had bedded half the dykes in town—Cat and Lil excluded. She was also an officer at the nearby women's prison. At one time she had been hot on Cat's trail, or so Cat had thought. Until it came out that what Zoe was really after wasn't Cat at all, but her motorcycle. One night, after a few beers, Zoe begged Cat for a chance to buy the Glide. She'd said no, but hoped they could still be friends. Too drunk to lift her head, Zoe had sighed and said she really didn't need another friend, what she really needed was the Glide.

Lily looked up at the mention of Zoe's name. She'd been fascinated by Zoe's wild lifestyle: of motorcycles, bars, girls, and maybe even of her job at the prison. Zoe liked to say all the girls there—even the straight ones—wanted her.

"What'd she want?" Lily asked.

"She's having a fortieth birthday party for herself down at OzGirlz this weekend."

"Zoe Wright is forty years old?" Lily's eyes brightened. Her grin spread. This was the best news Lily could have. "I mean, it doesn't surprise me that she's that old. She does have all that gray in her hair, you know. And she is a little rode hard." Lily started the truck. "So, Zoe Wright is forty, hah!"

"Want to go with me? You and Hannah?" Cat pulled a

cigarette from her pocket and lit it. Lily snapped her fingers and Cat handed her the smoke and lit another one. She propped her boot up on the dashboard and burned a loose string from the bottom of her jeans.

"You know Hannah can't stand Zoe," Lily said, watching as Cat slapped at the small flame she'd ignited. "You're gonna set yourself on fire." She backed the truck out.

Cat said, "So come alone. Hannah doesn't need to be there."

Lily slowed the van to a stop at a red light. She glanced at Cat, sucked her bottom lip, and shook her head, making Cat feel as if she'd just proposed murder. Lily started her tired bit about how she would never leave Hannah alone on a Friday night. It was not what *couples* did. If Cat would just get herself a permanent relationship, she might understand.

"You can't just forget about the other person."

"Right. Never mind."

"Are you goin'?" The next best thing to being at a Zoe Wright fortieth birthday party would be to have your best friend there, Cat thought.

"Possibly." In fact, Zoe had enticed her with the prospects of meeting some new single dykes in town. And since she was now on her quest for that *permanent* relationship (although she'd never tell Lily about her plans), she thought it would be a good place to start.

"Zoe hired The Girls and Tony to play." Cat mentioned the hot local band that always drew a big dyke crowd. The skinny-ass guitar player had a voice that made you want to weep and the drummer had some wicked-bomb biceps, if Cat recalled.

"Zoe said she wants to introduce me to that drummer."

Lily nearly set them off the road, shocked at this latest news. Her mouth dropped and then she looked hurt.

"I can't believe you'd let Zoe Wright fix you up with some drummer and you won't even let me fix you up with a doctor. A doctor!"

Cat was glad to have gotten the upper hand. So what if she couldn't get her own dates? At least she could give somebody else with a different idea of a match a shot at it.

"Where we going?" Cat asked, tiring of the battle.

"You remember that job we went on with the thirty bug-eyed Chihuahuas? When we got fleas all over us?"

Cat nodded. She remembered how she and Lily had stood in their underwear in the bathroom of an Amoco station, trying to shake the hundreds of tiny black fleas from their overalls and T-shirts.

"What about it?" She sighed, knowing it wouldn't be anything good.

"Well, this new job's got a couple of Chihuahuas on it." Lily told her. "Hope you're prepared."

The van made a left into a subdivision and a quick right up a hedge-lined driveway. As they curved around to the large brick house, Cat saw a couple, a man and a woman, standing in front of the big garage doors. The woman, Britta, was wearing green framed sunglasses and holding a matching pair of Chihuahuas, each cloaked in a red saddle jacket. Beside her was her husband, Bob, who wore a weighted fishing hat. His navy cardigan, with the college insignia, was buttoned wrong.

"The Lemons," Lily said fumbling with her seatbelt. Cat tried to ignore the feeling of impending doom. She climbed out and went around to the back of the van to grab the tool belts, then she joined Lily and the Lemons at the garage.

"Hey, little dogs," Lily said to the shivering Chihuahuas. Before her fingers reached its head, one of the bug-eyed beasts snapped. Lily pulled her hand back and held it behind her back.

"Oh, they don't like strangers," Britta said. She had a slight German accent. "Missy." She rubbed the little dog. "Be nice to the carpenters."

Cat handed Lily her tool belt and strapped the other across her waist. After the pleasantries had been exchanged, Cat left the group to begin unloading the van. She never could stand hanging around listening to homeowners explaining how they'd envisioned them doing the job. Lily called for her and the foursome made their way into the now open garage.

Before either of them knew what was happening, while Britta babbled at Lily, Bob pulled Cat to the side.

"You. Let me *zee* your tape measurer, there." He pointed to her. The hair on the back of her neck raised. He snatched it from her belt. "Let's measure this baby."

Wrestling the flimsy metal off its reel, the jittery man pulled it across the length of the garage and called out meaningless numbers. He seemed to be on a mission to take the measurements before either she or Lily could get to it—as if they couldn't be trusted. Without warning, he then let go of the tape, sending it whizzing back across the room, slicing through Cat's thumb.

"*Fuck!*" she yelled, bringing the bleeding finger to her mouth. Lily ran over to Cat, grabbing her hand.

"Let me see."

It was deeper than a papercut but carried the same sting. The blood was coming fast.

"God damn it."

"No cussin'," Lily said under her breath.

Cat repeated the profanity. In the van she pulled the last bandage from the emergency kit, tearing the sheathing with her teeth. As she was wrapping her thumb, there was a sharp pinch at her ankle. One of the Chihuahuas was struggling with her pant leg and some flesh between its needlelike teeth. She kicked the dog away, sending it yelping and Britta running.

"Ach, my precious, my liebling!"

Cat pulled up her pant leg exposing two small punctures.

"What did you do to her to make her bite you?"

"What did *I* do?" Cat looked to Lily. "I was standing here wrapping up my bleeding *thumb*—" She wiped the blood from her ankle. "That ... that ... little drumstick of a dog attacked me."

Lily bent down.

"Lemme see it."

Cat swatted at her. "Let it be."

Lily turned to the Lemons and suggested they try to keep the little dogs out of the hard-hat area. "Wouldn't want them to get hurt," she said. Before the clients left them, Lily asked directions to the bathroom.

"Uh ... we ... uh ... use the one upstairs ... our niece lives downstairs. She shouldn't be disturbed."

Lily and Cat exchanged glances.

"OK, fine ... so show me where." Lily followed the Lemons through the door to the house.

As Cat was kicking the steel legs of the saw-bench open, snapping them locked, Lily reappeared at her shoulder.

"Don't be needin' to pee." Lily climbed up the bumper and untied the ropes around a stack of wood on the roof.

"Why?"

"It's a dang maze they got you runnin' through. First this door, then another one, then stairs, then seventeen canaries ..." Lily slid the boards from the roof and Cat piled them beside the garage door.

"Canaries?"

"Yeah, She's got a bunch of little yellow canaries in cages up there."

"Canaries and Chihuahuas." Cat shook her head.

With the concrete nail gun, Lily pointed across the garage. "We're going to shoot down those one-by-fours to the slab floor."

Cat's gun slipped on the first shot, sending the nail sailing through the air, knocking out a florescent light bulb, which shattered. They looked at the trashed bulb and then at each other. They both burst into shocked laughter.

Cat was leaning against the wall, trying to compose herself when Bob and Britta appeared at the door.

"There is something funny?" Britta said, looking around suspiciously.

Lily smiled. Cat swallowed.

"We don't like that," Bob said.

"Don't like us laughing?" Cat fumbled with the nail gun, nearly dropping it.

"No, no we don't," Bob said almost thoughtfully now. Britta nodded vigorously, her hand loyally on his shoulder.

"Workers should work," Bob said. His *w*'s had sounded like *v*'s. "Well, that's how we work," Lily said. "We talk, we laugh, we work. We get the job done."

The Lemons were staring silently. Lily didn't flinch and eventually they tucked themselves back inside the doorway.

Lily circled and said, "I'm gettin' pissed off. You?" She nibbled the skin on the side of her thumb, not waiting for an answer. "All we've got to do is lay this floor. Two days—tops—then we're outta here."

"I've got to pee." Cat wiggled.

"So go." Lily looked at her. "Good luck," she said.

But Cat wasn't going in there. She did not want to walk

through a maze, or pass a bunch of canaries, or run into Mr. and Mrs. Whacko. No. She'd wait till she could go in the safety of the Amoco station. She looked at her watch. Her bladder was already anxious.

Lily pointed. "See that electrical wire over there? Take these vice grips and pull the staples out." Lily herself headed out the door toward the van.

As Cat struggled with the first staple, Bob approached from a side door and handed her some rubber gripped cutting pliers.

"Here try these," he offered. He said, *"zeez ..."*

She took them and decided they actually might work better.

Easing the sharp edge under the staple, she pulled gently.

"Here, let me show you." Bob knelt beside her and stuck his hand out.

"No, thanks."

"You're not doing it right." Bob reached for the tool.

"This is a hot wire," she explained. "I don't want to get shocked."

"You're not using enough leverage."

Cat stopped and slowly rose above Bob. He stared up at her from his haunches and watched as she slapped the pliers in her palm.

"Listen you ..." She smacked, again. "I've been a carpenter for ten years; you don't think I know *something* about lever- age?" She moved in on him, her knees nearly touching his nose. Lily had come around the corner. Bob stood and backed away toward the door, muttering about just wanting to help.

"What'd you do to that poor man?" Lily poked her.

"Asshole. He's in my way."

They loaded cartridges and nails into their guns and began shooting the boards to the concrete.

Finishing the last run of sleepers, Cat stood and pressed her hand to her kidney.

"Lil, my teeth are floating."

"Well, go then." Lily threw her ear protectors down.

"I'm working on it." She paced a circle. "In a minute."

Britta came slinking from the rear of the garage, guiding a half-full glass of water in her hands. When she arrived in the center of the room she knelt and placed it on one of the newly laid runners.

"My brother said I could check for level this way."

"Well, that's good for about three inches," Lily said.

Britta was down on all fours squinting across the top of the glass.

"My brother said it would work."

"Yeah. Maybe your brother ought to come over here and lay this floor, then."

Unbuckling her tool belt, Cat dropped it with a clatter to the floor.

"I'm going to the bathroom."

"Oh, dear. Well, go upstairs, remember." Britta wrung her hands.

Cat closed the door behind her, and stood still, waiting for her eyes to adjust to the darkness. *Through a door and up the stairs,* Lily had said.

Except there were four doors, not one. Cat ruled out the door with the sign saying *Big Bob's Den.* The rock music playing behind the second door, she'd decided, probably belonged to the scary niece. The third smaller door looked like a closet. Behind the fourth door, she thought she heard a vacuum cleaner. Bob vacuums? she thought to herself. Whatta guy. *I choose door number four.*

She yanked open the door. This was no Bob and no vacuum cleaner. Bending nearly upside down, was a young woman.

Blonde hair touched the floor as a hair dryer blew against it. She straightened and turned off the blower. Her black belt hung loose around her small waist. She smiled shyly.

"I'm sorry," Cat said, tripping over a puckered floor rug. "Damn ... I mean ... I was looking for the bathroom." So, this was the niece. A baby dyke. No doubt about it. She could tell by the gaydar reflecting in the girl's own eyes. So, Mr. and Mrs. Whacko were trying to keep the big bad dyke carpenters away from their pretty little lipstick lesbian. Well, well, well, this might be an interesting job after all.

"It's OK." The girl thumbed behind her. "You can use mine."

"No ... they said there was one upstairs." She turned.

"Really, I don't mind. I'm almost done anyway, c'mon." She tugged on Cat's arm.

Cat sidled by her, avoiding contact, and closed herself into the cupboard-sized bathroom. After all these hours, she suddenly couldn't pee. The fact that the cutie was standing just inches from her, on the other side of the door, was the cause of her suddenly shy kidney. *Breathe,* she told herself. How was it that all the good-looking women were suddenly showing up in bathrooms? Twisting the water knob at the tub encouraged a slow painful trickle. When she finished, in what seemed like an hour, she opened the door to find the girl blocking her exit.

"I'm Ellen."

"Oh ... I'm Cat."

"I heard you read last night." She continued to hold Cat's hand. "At Mari's?"

Cat hadn't recalled seeing this face. But there were so many *people* there, how could she remember everyone? Ellen's eyes were dark. After a silence, Cat made a move toward the door. Ellen held on. Was she being detained?

Cat gulped and stepped back. With her came Ellen, now pressing her into the sink. Cat turned and pointed. "Mind if I wash my hands?" She twisted the knob and began running her hands under the water as Ellen's hands made their way over her shoulders. Jesus.

Sweat was beading under her hair. In the mirror, Ellen's reflected likeness pressed against Cat's back, mouth to her ear, a stiff nipple moving up and down Cat's arm. Oh, God. She looked into her own eyes. As if snapped from the moment she twisted and grabbed Ellen's shoulders. Up close, Cat could see that she was only about eighteen years old. Her full lips began a slow pout, and just before she could place them, Cat turned her head and moved away.

"Look," she began, swallowing. Her mouth was dry. "I don't even know you." She took a step toward the door.

"That's the beauty of it," Ellen said, leaning back against the sink, legs parting. She pushed her breasts up, revealing nipples at attention. "Don't you think? Spontaneity. Right here, right now."

Cat slammed the door behind her and rushed back into the darkened corridor. *Holy* mother of Sappho, a nymphodyke! No wonder the Lemons were whacked. They must have known. She'd have to tell Lily. Get them both out of this job before it was too late. But she didn't have the chance. When she opened the garage door, loud voices echoed around the cavernous room. Bob's voice was booming and he was flapping around like an agitated penguin. By the time she reached Lily, Bob had planted himself in front of her and was jamming a pointed finger in her face. Tiny spit globs had formed in the corners of his mouth.

"When I hired Girls with Hammers," Bob was saying, "I wasn't expecting *homosexual girls!*"

Cat placed her hand on Lily's back and pulled her back just a bit.

"What's going on here?" Cat looked at Lily.

"He says he ain't gonna pay us 'cause we're dykes."

Cat started toward Bob and it was Lily who'd grabbed her shirt.

"No Cat. C'mon, we're outta here."

She bent down and started gathering up her tools. Cat followed suit. What came next, she almost couldn't believe even though it was happening right before her very eyes. Britta and Bob began running all over the garage. Bob yelled, "You vohn't get avay wiss thiss," and kicked a hammer from Cat's reach. Britta scooped a tape away from Lily. "You haf our down payment! Give it back!" A screwdriver spun out the door, pliers clanked against the washing machine. When Bob made an unsuccessful punt at Lily's nail gun, she grabbed the front of his sweater and jerked him.

"Keep your freakin' hands off my tools, idiot. You ain't paid for nothin' but the materials." She stomped the floor. "And you're standin' on 'em."

Britta screamed and Cat made a dive for Lily, grabbed the back of her belt and pulled her back. Bob rushed to Britta, showing his torn sweater. Britta threatened the police.

"Assault and battery," she accused. "Ve'll tell zem you took our money and destroyed our home vis your sloppy verk."

"You're crazy," Cat said, pushing Lily out the door. Suddenly, Ellen appeared. Everyone stopped and turned as she carefully stepped over tools, making her way toward Cat. She handed her a pink square of paper.

"Give me a call," she said and kissed her full on the lips.

Lily jerked Cat out of the garage.

"Screw this, we're outta here."

They tossed their tools into the back of the van and pulled away.

They were silent until they hit the main road.

"What the fuck was that?" Cat finally asked.

"Scammin'," Lily declared.

Cat looked at her.

"My daddy told me about it," Lily said. "Never experienced it myself, though. Homeowners who get you to do part of a job and then go all crazy so that you'll walk off."

"I don't get it," Cat confessed.

"Well, see, Big Bob there probably thinks he can lay a floor. What he couldn't do was shoot down those runners."

Cat nodded as she began to get the picture. "So once that's done, he goes nuts and we leave, sorry to lose the money but glad to get away, right?"

"Exactly."

"Shit."

They rode in silence, both replaying their own versions of the incident.

"What's up with that chick?" Lily finally asked, lighting a cigarette.

Cat told her about the bathroom episode.

Lily grinned and poked her. "That's pretty hot."

"Yeah, if I'd have been drunk in a bar and looking for raw anonymous sex up against a wall, I'd a had it made."

"No, this is even better, spontaneous anonymous sex in a *bathroom.*"

"For cryin' out loud, Lil. I'm getting too old for this shit."

Lily patted Cat's shoulder. "Maybe you're growin' up."

Cat lit a cigarette and watched the smoke curl loose, swirl, and whisk out the window. That's how things were feeling lately, she thought. Like she was drifting. Crazy people pushing physical space, Lily crowding thinking space, women crashing sexual space, like she was smoke, without weight or integrity—nothing. She rubbed her sore neck. She was getting too old or too tired for this work anymore. It was dirty and dangerous, she thought, reaching down and smoothing her bandaged thumb over her bandaged ankle.

She stubbed out the cigarette in the ashtray and stole a glance at Lily. *What the hell are we doing?* she wanted to shout. *Is this it for the rest of our lives? For the rest of my life—?*

But she said nothing.

The truck lurched over Cat's rutted driveway and came to a stop.

"So, where's this birthday party happening tonight?" Lily asked.

"OzGirlz," Cat said, climbing out. "Sure you don't want to come?"

"I'll just wait for the reviews."

OzGirlz was humming. The parking lot was packed and so Cat pulled the Glide into a skinny place near the side door. The bar was housed in an old brick factory building that hung over the river. It had once been a sawmill. Although long since gutted of its big-toothed saws and razorlike planers, the smell of freshly cut wood permeated. Zoe, dressed in a silver biker's outfit replete with dangling fringe on chaps and sleeves, greeted her guests at the door, pinning pink carnations on all comers. Cat figured it was this part of the gesture that had given Zoe the idea in the first place. She accepted the light brush of fingers and humored Zoe's half-joking guess that the rattle inside the little gift box was, she hoped, the keys to Cat's Glide. In fact, it was a miniature likeness of the bike, in die-cast metal. Cat wandered into the belly of the beast that was humming with the rocking sounds of The Girls and Tony, urging the room to motion. As promised, the guitar player, from what she could see, was cute, and the drummer did have some wicked biceps.

High above, hanging from rough-hewn rafters, were brass and wood ceiling fans pulling the thick fog of cigarette smoke up and out of the crowd. The walls had been left their natural brick and decorated with the works of local artists. Primarily local lesbian artists. Green fronded palmettos and tall ficus trees were placed strategically in corners and along walls. All the woodwork, including tables and chairs, had been painted in the same warm cream color. It was a pretty big bar with an upstairs pool hall and an outside deck overlooking the water. The stage and slick dance floor had been waxed to a sheen.

Cat squeezed between two big women at the bar. The one on her left, she noticed, had a black tattoo snaking out of her shirt collar. The fanged mouth of the cobra, ready to strike, was poised at the woman's own jugular, just below the line of her shaved head. When she turned, Cat winced, catching the matching silver studs piercing her eyebrow, nose, and bottom lip. The woman's call for another beer clicked the stud in her tongue against her front teeth. The hefty girl to her right had green hair.

Ruthie came around the bar for one big hug and then retreated back to her post. She was sweating profusely. Handing Cat a beer over the head of the silver-studded woman, she waved away her money.

"On the house, honey."

Cat turned around to scan the party, smiling at the streamers screaming out Zoe's crossover into middle age. Was forty really *middle age?* Only six more years for the number to claim her own life. She ought to be careful what she said. Now, Zoe was being carried around the dance floor

145

on the shoulders of a big, muscle-bound leatherhead, whom she was whipping with a toy cat-o'-nine-tails. This was going to be a wild one. Cat felt a nudge at her elbow. Little blonde Candace, her agent, was trying to wrestle her way through the crowd at the bar.

"What are you doing here?" Cat yelled above the music. This was no place for a straight girl. Not that it held true for all lesbians, herself included, but there were some dykes who got off on bringing out het-women. It was the same kind of mentality in men who fantasized about bringing a lezzie back to the fold. Candace was fish food in here. Cat guided her across the bar into a corner that had missed occupation.

"I thought I might find you here," Candace said, talking fast.

She was a Yankee. A New York City girl. She'd moved south a year ago after putting her time in at a major publishing house where she weeded the crap from the slush pile. Somehow along the way she'd absorbed the rules of what made something publishable. Though straight, Candace had been singled out to cull through submissions of gay writers. The company wanted to get with the New Enlightenment. They wanted to get the fresh stuff.

"What they didn't get up there in the Big Apple," Candace had said. "is that there's this untapped reservoir of good Southern lesbian writers down here. I'd pick something out and my boss would practically cross her eyes and say are you crazy? That's the damn Bible Belt."

In their first conversation on the phone, during which Candace told her she had read one of Cat's stories in a galley of an anthology, she had imagined a tall dark woman with a neat bun pulled tight. When she'd met Candace for coffee at Mari's the next day, she had been startled to see this little wisp of a woman, fair with blonde hair and gray eyes that stared back. On the table between them, Candace had opened a briefcase and spilled her admissions. She was serious about her business, but Cat would be her first client. She knew what to do. She had contacts in New York. What, she had finally asked, did Cat have to lose? At that moment, with the book nearly completed, Cat hadn't a clue as to how to find a reputable agent. And so she had hired Candace on commission.

As it turned out, Cat had been Candace's first sell.

Now, she put her arm around Candace's shoulder and waved her beer bottle at the crowd of writhing lesbians. There were women dressed in tight leather, circling one another like lions at the Colosseum; there was a cluster of sports dykes, all starched, hair shellacked in place, white button-down shirts and steam-creased Levi's. Floating by were three women dressed in blue flowing gowns, with wreaths of silver stars woven through their hair. On their cheeks, in blue and yellow, were more stars. Each carried a woven basket piled with gold and silver glitter, from which they tossed handfuls into the air as they passed by.

"Are you out of your mind coming down here?" Cat asked. "What, are you looking to be a lesbian entree?"

"Oh, stop. I'm from New York, remember?"

This, Cat had learned, seemed to cover everything for Candace. If she appeared weak or tough, smart or ignorant, serious or funny, all modes of operation were caused or dependent upon Candace's home of origin. New Yorkers thought the world began and ended in Times Square.

"You better get yourself out of here," Cat warned. "I can't be watching over you all night."

"Whose party?"

Cat pointed to Zoe, up on the stage singing a duet of "Me

and Bobby McGee" with the guitar player. "Just turned forty."

"Pretty hot for forty," Candace said and gave her an awkward hug to the waist.

Cat smiled and hugged her back.

"Will they think I'm your—date?" Candace whispered, flirting.

"Probably not. You're not my type."

Candace pulled back, hurt crossed her face.

"Straight." Cat teased. "I don't do straight girls. Anybody in here who knows me, knows that."

"What about that Zoe?" Candace stood on tiptoes to see the stage.

"Oh, you better keep away from Zoe; she loves straight girls."

"Darby would have a fit." Candace looked around the room. Darby was her boyfriend whom she talked about constantly. Cat had thought she could have picked a guy with a more masculine name. But when she'd met Darby, all preconceptions went out the window. He was six-foot four and blew up buildings for a living.

Now Cat wondered if Candace was a little afraid of her own fleeting fantasies about women and that's what was making her nervous. And this was what was so surprising about her presence here tonight.

"So, what do you need that can't wait until tomorrow?" Cat asked.

"OK, I've got three book signings lined up: The Purple Crayon in Winston, Alice's Brownie in Greensboro, and It's a Drag in Raleigh."

Cat's mouth and eyes widened simultaneously. Before she could protest, Candace interrupted.

"Say yes and I'll leave."

Blackmail. She'd have to take time off of work. Just a couple of days here and there. God, that sounded good. Lily would probably be OK with it. And Candace was looking so hopeful. The girl was really working her stuff.

She said yes and escorted Candace to the front door and watched her make her way across the parking lot to her car. Cat turned back into the bar and was swallowed into a passing group of dreadlocked Earth-Girls. The mix of body odor and patchouli choked her. When one of the women tripped and tossed loose a Birkenstock, the entire company, save Cat, bent to search for it. She stood feeling like a sprouted daisy in a kindergarten Easter pageant. She climbed over the backs of two bent Earth-Girls and with the help of an outstretched hand she was pulled free.

The outstretched hand belonged to an old high school friend, Jody Taylor. "*Married* Jody Taylor?" Cat laughed. "Two-kids Jody Taylor?"

"*Was* married, being the operative word. Till I found out the bastard was banging my sister." She'd had it with men. "Divorced—thank God," Jody said. She thought she'd give girls a try. Cat could barely hear her above the din from the stage.

Cat feigned a full bladder and excused herself to the ladies room.

As she battled her way through the crowd (a mosh pit, she decided) Cat spotted a flicker of coppery curl near the dance floor. Her heart sped up. And she changed directions. Moving slower now, she rounded the dancers, keeping the top of the head in sight. Through a break in the crowd she could see the woman's back. Cat moved forward and waited. Finally the face turned. Yes! Cat smiled. It was the woman from Mari's, the one who'd given her the paper towels in the bathroom. She was laughing and talking with someone. Every now and then her eyes would leave her companion's face and scan the room. They were still as green as Cat had remembered.

The band had finished their first set and were going to take a fifteen minute break, according to the skinny little guitar player, who spoke with a Virginia twang into the mike. As the floor cleared, the wave of women making their way to the bar made Cat feel like a salmon in a rush up river. She saw that the green-eyed woman was also riding a current that was pulling her way. As she approached, her companion was swept behind Cat's back and away. The redhead smiled, and leaned close to speak.

"You did very well last night."

Cat nodded her thanks.

"I wanted to have my book signed," she said, louder now. "But I had to go to work."

Cat held an imaginary pen and scribbled her signature in the air. "Some other time," she shouted and offered her hand. "I'm Cat." The woman's hand was smooth and soft in her palm. Her fingers long.

"I know." She touched her collar. "Mel." Before any other words could pass between them, Cat was set on from behind by Zoe, a little tipsy, who pulled her into the still-roiling crowd.

"Come on," Zoe yelled. "I've got that drummer for you to meet."

Cat's protests went unheeded; she twisted to look over her shoulder, but the space she'd only seconds before occupied was filling in with people, blocking her view of the stranger whose name she was pretty sure she'd heard as Mel. By the time Zoe had managed to plow her way through the crowd toward the band, Cat and the drummer had just enough time to shake hands. The break had ended. Cat quickly found her way back to the spot where she'd left the stranger, then circled the bar once more and climbed into the loft of the pool hall. Leaning over the rail, she tried to spot the copper curls from above, but they were nowhere to be found. The woman was gone—again. Cat turned to the stairs, slipping through the crowd, and headed home on the Glide.

Chapter Nine

Lily and Cat were lying in the sun, eating their lunch on the front lawn of the home whose kitchen they were remodeling. The morning had been spent tearing out old cabinets and knocking out plaster walls. It was barely noon and already they were sweaty and dirty and starting to ache.

"You never got her name?" Lily asked when Cat finished telling the story.

"Mel. That's all she said. And then she took off, I guess." Cat shook her head. "Story of my life."

An old battered Oldsmobile pulled up across the street and they both leaned forward as the door opened. The emerging woman wore black tights under a flowered skirt and white running shoes. Snaking down her back was one long braid. Her hair was completely gray. She wrestled two bags from the trunk and then made her way down the steps toward the house; she disappeared inside the front door.

"Premature gray," Lily said. She chewed the last bite of her sandwich. "Her hair's gone gray before its time."

"How do you know that?"

"Too young." Lily sliced an apple and ran the blade of her pocketknife, a three-bladed Uncle Henry, between her teeth.

"Lil, people go gray at forty." Cat pulled strands of her own hair through her fingers, noticing the silver threading through the gold.

"No way, did you see her thighs?" Lily pointed at Cat with her knife.

"Hey now, I've seen some pretty tight over-forty thighs. Look at Tina Turner, for God's sakes."

"She doesn't count; she's a star."

Cat carried their coolers back to the van, thinking about the woman with the copper curls again. Why hadn't she waited? Cat could swear she'd been attracted—maybe had even deliberately gotten herself swept toward Cat in the bar-throng.

Returning to the entrance of the now nearly demolished kitchen, she bent and picked up her tool belt, buckling it across her waist. Behind her, Lily was going on about some movie she had watched the night before.

"I haven't heard a word you've said," Cat said finally, pulling her hammer from its holster. She eyed the remaining wall and punched a hole.

"Lovesick." Lily beat against the plaster, cracking it. "You gotta find that girl."

Cat loosened a big piece of wall at her waist. Lifting it, she threw it to the mounting pile in the corner. Sure, she'd just take out an ad: *Redhead beauty lost at OzGirlz. Please return to Cat Hood. Reward.*

Lily pulled some wall back with a small crowbar. "I hate when you get in these moods."

Cat went on beating the plaster, landing chunks on her foot. Chips and dust flew high into the air. Lily pulled her bandana up around her nose.

"Take it easy."

Chunks of plaster were falling independently, loosening

153

the steel lathe. Neither Cat nor Lily saw the plank of wall begin its peel away from the studwork, its weight yanking and popping the nails that had been holding it in place. Suddenly, the big square freed itself and came crashing down on the top of Cat's hand; caught now between her hammer and the jagged steel, her flesh tore.

"Fuck!"

Lily jumped to wedge her fingers under the heavy sheet and together they heaved the plaster to the side. When Cat pulled her hand away, the flap of ragged skin folded—ripped open at the knuckles.

"Fuck!" she yelled again.

Blood poured from her hand and down the arm that Lily was trying to get her to hold up. Fiery pain seared across Cat's fingers and she imagined cracked and broken bones.

Lily dragged her into the bathroom and sat her down on the seat of the toilet. She yanked a delicate towel off the rod. Its hand-stitched flowered embroidery was worn but still beautifully claimed by tiny initials in the lower right corner.

"Here, press this on it," Lily said. She knelt to rummage through the drawers beneath the sink. Cat pinched the corner of the linen between two barely clean fingers and held it away from the bloody edges of the wound.

"Lil, I can't use this. It's somebody's antique thing." Lily grabbed it back and dropped it to the floor.

"Hold your hand over the sink." She twisted the water on. "You're bleedin' everywhere." Her panic hit a pitch when she glanced into the basin filling with pink water. She intensified her search for a compress. "Sugar, fire, and save matches," she pseudo-swore. Over her shoulder she tossed a toothbrush, curlers, and tampons.

Cat's hand was turning a dark blue and the fire in it was

raging. She couldn't bring herself to look for very long. "Don't we have an emergency kit in the van?" she suggested.

Lily ran.

Cat waited, holding her hand, watching the basin water darkening. "There were no bandages in the kit," Lily huffed, leaned against the jam, defeated. In her right hand was a roll of silver duct tape and in her left was a sanitary napkin. Cat looked from one to the other.

"You are not wrapping my hand in a panty liner."

"It ain't a panty liner. It's a Stayfree Maxi Pad." Lily kneeled down. "It doesn't matter, Cat." She carefully placed the pad on top. "The most important thing is to stop the bleedin', OK?" Her voice had become soft. "This won't be so bad. Shoot, no one will even notice or care."

The emergency room was busy. The throbbing in Cat's hand had increased to a low drone with each pulsed heartbeat. They approached the desk and the admitting nurse asked to see the wound. She turned it over in her chubby fist, trying to peek beneath the silver tape.

"What's this?"

Cat frowned and elbowed Lily.

"Look, we're carpenters," Lily said, clearing her throat. "She got cut."

The nurse lifted an eyebrow.

Lily ducked her head. "It was all I could find."

Without pulling away the tape, she peeked under the pad. "Well, it stopped the bleeding. Leave it on. Y'all are carpenters and you don't carry an emergency kit?" She dismissed them to the waiting room.

Cat sat down next to an old black man in red suspenders and tried to balance her elbow on the armrest between them. He leaned to his right and snapped open a newspaper.

"Want me to get you a pillow or something?" Lily asked. "Magazine?"

"No, thanks." When Cat shifted her arm, her fingers made a grinding noise. She cringed. Something was broken in there. Lily squirmed beside her, flipping through a magazine without looking at the pictures.

"Thirsty?"

Cat could see that this was going to be a long wait. An even longer one if Lily was going to be fidgeting around like a four-year-old. So Cat pretended to be thirsty and Lily bolted from her seat to the drink machines.

Leaning back, Cat closed her eyes, trying to remember the last time she'd been hurt this badly. There had been a careless swing of a slowing circular saw that had carved a two-inch cut into her thigh a couple years ago. It had just missed an artery and had required fifteen stitches. That was probably the last worst one. She squinted at her hand. This was definitely the next worst one.

A little girl had climbed onto the old man's knee and was whispering into his big ear behind a tiny, cupped palm.

"Hush, now, Jolie," he said and pulled her closer. His eyes avoided Cat's and he twisted his back to her.

"But, Grandpa, it *is*." Jolie, whose hair was plaited in tiny rows, tugged on her grandfather's suspender.

Lily came back and handed Cat a Coke. Jolie slid from the old man's lap and leaned against his knee.

"You be still, now." His old gnarled hand rested on his granddaughter's head as he glanced nervously at Cat. "Leave this lady alone."

Instead, Jolie took two steps closer and pointed to Cat's hand.

"My mamma uses that kind, too."

Lily choked.

Cat closed her eyes and sat silently, willing herself not to think about the sanitary napkin swaddling her wound. It was all too Lily-ish—too ridiculous to even be faced. She'd keep her eyes closed until some kind nurse or doctor came to remove the offensive thing.

Instead she opened them, hearing Lily's voice coming from some distance away.

"*This* is where you work?" Lily was saying. "My God, what luck—I've got Cat right here."

She was steering a woman in a white coat Cat's way. It was the familiar coppery hair and matching look of surprise on her face that made the pounding in Cat's hand spread to her head. She felt faint. Next thing, Lily was introducing her to the woman as if they'd never met before.

Or rather, the woman was introducing herself.

"Melissa McHeaney."

"*Doctor* Melissa McHeaney." Lily nudged Cat's ribs.

"Finally," Cat said. "A whole name."

Melissa motioned for them to follow her down a narrow hall.

Lily whispered, "It's the *doctor/artist* me and Hannah been tellin' you about."

The three entered a small cubicle barely big enough for two. Melissa made Cat lie on the crinkly white paper lining the hospital bed and carefully snipped away the duct tape. Even more carefully, she lifted the napkin. The wound burned as the air hit it, but the bleeding had slowed.

"Lucky for you, you're women carpenters," Melissa said and washed around the cut with a warm soapy sponge. "I pack those things when I go hiking. Best thing to use, really." She smiled as she poured the cold liquid antiseptic over the cut, watching Cat's face.

In the light, the woman's green eyes had changed, deepening

to emerald flecked with bits of gold. Cat stared, unable to even blink, wondering if she was suffering from blood loss. She didn't care. A close-up of those eyes was worth this whole painful experience.

"Sometimes you gotta improvise in a situation," Lily was saying. She was glad to have done something right, Cat could tell.

"You were pretty resourceful."

In spite of the doctor's gentle touch, Cat's face screwed up as wild pain coursed through her arm when Melissa attempted to wiggle one of the fingers of the wounded hand.

"I think we might have some broken digits, here," she said to Cat. "We'll need to get X-rays. But I'll have to stitch you up, first.

A nurse came in to give Cat a shot. "This'll make you feel like you got a dead fish hanging from your elbow," she said.

Cat laughed in spite of herself and leaned her head back on the pillow. Her throat was dry and hot.

"How you doing there, Cat?" Melissa asked, looking down at her.

She couldn't answer and so she nodded. Then closing her eyes, she let the soft hands begin to stitch. She dozed. Most of the next few hours were hazy for her. She remembered being wheeled from this cubicle to X-ray where they made her flip her wrist into unnatural positions while they took pictures. There were other stops and other hospital people who asked questions that Lily, not Cat, answered. Cat herself was quietly drifting in the air somewhere between Lily's voice and the darkness behind her own eyes.

"It was the end of my shift," Melissa was saying as Cat squinted awake.

She was resting an arm on the bed where Cat lay. Her doctor's garb had been exchanged for street clothes. The soft green of her sweater tucked beneath her chin reflected in her eyes.

"That was nice," Cat said. "Thank you. Must have been some great drugs."

"I'm sorry that we met this way," Melissa leaned over.

"We weren't getting very far before." Their eyes met and stayed and Cat said, "First, you rescue me in the bathroom. Then, you're torn from my grasp and swept away in a sea of people, just like in a movie."

They both laughed. Cat leaned forward.

"Slow," Melissa said, getting up and wrapping her arm around her patient's shoulders. "Take it easy. You'll get a head-rush."

"I'd love a head-rush right now." She felt Melissa's laugh wrap around her. But a shot of pain fired through to her fingers and she winced. She squeezed her eyes shut against the ache.

"Hey, hey," Melissa ducked around in front of her and held her gently by the shoulders.

Cat opened her eyes as the scorching in her hand began to wane. She blew out slowly and tried to focus but there were twos and threes of everything. She leaned forward into Melissa's shoulder, resting her head.

"Dizzy," she said.

As the fuzz began to wear off, she recognized the scent of Plumaria and felt the warmth beneath her cheek where she rested it against Melissa's shoulder.

"You OK?" Melissa's fingers were in her hair. Breath on her neck.

"Hey, buddyroo," Lily plowed into the area pushing a wheelchair. "Ready to rock and roll?"

"Easy, Lil, I'm a little woozy."

"Oh, sorry. Of course." She looked at Melissa. "Hey, you been here all the time?"

"Yes," Melissa moved to the side but held steady to Cat's elbow as she slid from the bed. "Easy with this hand now," her tone was gentle. "You've got smashed bones, ripped tendons, and torn flesh in there, remember."

Cat stood, tentatively. "Damn, I could have lived all week without hearing all that," she said, cradling her broken hand against her breasts.

"Sorry." Melissa faced her. "I tell the truth, and ..."

"And?"

Melissa frowned, " ... and I don't play games." She pulled a marker from her back pocket and wrote her name and phone number on Cat's cast.

The black letters were thick and bold. Cat looked from her arm to Melissa's face. It was an Irish face; her nose was straight but her chin was curved. A dimple appeared on the left side when she smiled. And her teeth, Cat noticed, were white and even. She had a thing for teeth.

"Do we like each other?" Melissa looked at her. The question surprised Cat and she thought it probably showed on her face. She stuttered.

"Well, yeah ... I mean, I like you. It'd be good if you liked me back."

They were quiet.

Melissa cleared her throat. "I'm not in favor of pretending."

Cat searched the green eyes, now gentle.

"Hey," Lily, smiling, interrupted. "We ready to get outta here? I'm starving." She rolled the chair back and forth in front of Cat. C'mon, hop in. I'll push you home."

Cat looked up at Melissa. "I will call."

Melissa only smiled, nodding. Cat noticed a small wisp of a curl that bobbed just over one eye, independent of the rest of her hair. It made her seem a little less the calm, cool doctor—a little more a woman taken suddenly, pleasantly, off guard.

"So, what do you think?" Lily asked, driving.

Cat didn't answer. Her hand throbbed, but she knew she was smiling.

"Crazy, huh? The woman you've been stalking all this time turns out to be the same woman I've been trying to fix you up with."

"I haven't been stalking her. I've just been noticing her."

"Stalking—noticing, same difference."

"Lily, it is not." Trust Lily to push the magic of the moment.

"So, do you like her?"

Cat lifted her casted hand. "Do you really think I have anything other than *pain* on my mind?"

"Maybe me and Hannah can have you both over for dinner."

Cat leaned her head back against the seat and closed her eyes.

"Let it go, Lil."

"You already admitted that you like her. So have dinner at our house."

Cat said, "Just this once, Lil, maybe I'll do things my way."

She slept till they hit Maskas Creek Road, when Lily awakened her by trying to talk her into staying overnight at her house.

"It makes sense, Cat," she said. "Hannah and I can take care of you." Cat could just picture this: Lily disturbing her every five minutes with some weird new organic soup that was good for broken hands.

"No, take me home. I just want to sleep."

161

"But your hand is smashed to smithereens."

"Lil, quit saying that. Every time you say *smithereens* my hand aches."

"Sorry. Tore up, though ..."

"Lil!"

Cat leaned forward and blew through her teeth. All she wanted was to get home, smoke a joint, and go to bed. Pot would take the edge off the pain. She traced her fingers over the black lettering on her cast. Did she really have to wait till morning?

There were several cars parked at the cabin. Cat limped out of the van and rested against the front bumper, noticing all in a row: Hannah's truck, Delores's mini-van, and Sophia's ancient station wagon. Marce's jeep was up by the barn. Cat looked quizzically at Lily, who was exiting the truck.

"What the hell did you tell them? It looks like a fucking wake."

"They were worried."

The front door opened and Will and Matthew made a grab for her.

"Let go." She shook Will from her. "It's my hand, not my leg."

The house was filled; not only had Marce come with Will, but also Mamma had come with Matthew and Delores; and Sophia, who barely ever left her own home, was there in Cat's kitchen, brewing tea. Cat worried that she hadn't cleaned up the bathroom that morning and imagined the dried toothpaste spit in the sink. She was suddenly a stranger in her own home. Mamma's ribs and chicken were cooking on her stove, filling the house with sumptuous aromas.

The couch had been made into a bed, piled high with pillows and a couple of blankets. Mike had already taken

162

his place at its foot. Marce was kneeling, attending to the fire in the woodstove and Hannah was pouring glasses of wine.

"Give her some room." Will swept a nonexistent crowd from the entrance, nearly tripping them both as he guided her around the couch, helping her sit, like she was some old woman. He unlaced her boots and pulled them from her feet, and Hannah placed a glass of wine in her good hand. Cat looked up to faces lined in a half-moon around her.

"What are y'all doing here?" she asked.

"Now, child," Mamma had begun, "you didn't expect us to just leave you here on your own, did you?"

"It's what's expected," Sophia concurred. "It's what families do."

But she hadn't expected it.

She'd prayed for a quiet moment alone, with a big fat joint pinched between her good fingers and Melissa on her mind. Instead, what she got was a surprise party.

"You need to eat," Mamma told her.

As Cat settled back against the couch, she watched them all busy themselves around her: filling plates and glasses, dragging extra chairs from the kitchen, bumping around the room like tops. Finally, each settled and balanced a heaping plate on his or her knees.

With her own dinner precariously tipping on her lap, Cat, lefthanded but never ambidextrous, tried to butter a piece of cornbread. Lily leaped to her side and took the knife away, quickly smearing the muffin with two swift slaps of butter. Great. They'd be trying to spoon-feed her next. Cat looked at the clock and wished for time to hurry so that they would all leave her alone.

As they cleared their second and third helpings from their plates and raised newly refilled glasses to their lips,

Will stood, calling for their attention, clearing his throat for an announcement, he said. He turned to Cat.

"We're going to build a place next door." He thumbed over his shoulder. "So we can be a family again."

The pounding in her hand and head doubled its pace, pushing, she imagined, her brain up against the inside of her skull. It had never occurred to her that Will would ever come back, let alone move in next door. Or build a next door to move into, even.

"So, we're going to sell Marce's place over in Sellarsville …" Cat heard him saying, looking now everywhere but at her.

It would pay for the new house on his land. *His land,* he said. These words and Will's eyes finally did land on her, as did everyone else's. She knew she should say something— something good. They were waiting. But there had been no time between the collapsing walls of this morning and the proposed raising of these new ones now. She didn't know how she felt about any of it. They waited. Lily was the first to begin her nervous foot tapping. Finally, Cat raised her glass.

"Sköl," she saluted them.

And they all raised glasses wishing the couple well. As they talked of earthmovers and contractors, Cat's mind doubled back to a different place. She didn't want to hear or think about any of this. Certainly she didn't want to talk about it until she'd had time to feel it. Right now, what she was feeling was a sore pulse throughout her whole body, emanating from her hand.

An outburst from Lily swayed everyone from their individual circles back into a group.

"Hey everybody—guess what?" she said loudly. "Cat's in love!"

All the eyes flew back to her. Pink patches burned her cheeks.

"Lil!"

"Who with?" Delores asked.

"Where'd you meet her?" Hannah wanted to know.

"When did this happen?" Will weighed in.

"I am not *in love,*" she said to them.

"It's Melissa." Lily put an arm around Hannah. "She was the doctor at the hospital today. Same person Cat's been stalking this whole time."

"Lily!"

"Same person Hannah and me were trying to fix her up with in the first place."

"Can you shut up!" Cat grimaced, feeling the shot of extra pain launched by her fury.

"All right," Sophia said. "That's enough. Lily *Nelda,* you leave Cat be, now."

Ha, Lily Nelda. Cat felt a childlike rise of malicious revenge upon hearing Sophia's use of the middle name that Lily despised.

Again, Cat accidentally leaned on her sore arm and another shot of pain buzzed her molars. Sophia put her plate down. With one hand around Cat's shoulders, she gently eased her back into the couch pillows. "Now, honey, you need to rest. Don't you let her pick at you."

"Sometimes she can be so stupid," Cat said. Tears welling now. She felt a flood of them coming on. *Oh God, please don't let me lose it. Let them all leave before it comes.*

"Yes, she can." Sophia wiped a runaway tear from Cat's chin. "So, why do you let her get you so mad?"

Lily knelt beside them. "Cat, I'm sorry. I guess I got carried away."

The room had quieted, everybody watching to make sure Cat and Lily made up. After they hugged and kissed and rubbed each other's heads and said things like *"I love you, buddy"* and *"I love you back, you dog,"* the room hummed into motion. Everyone cleared, scraped, scrubbed, rinsed, dried, and put away the entire dinner within ten minutes. In the next five minutes, Mamma and Sophia brewed tea and set up a tray with water, pain pills, the phone, and the remote to the television. Soon the house had emptied of all but Will and Marce, who planned on spending the night.

She was finally able to kick back and smoke her joint.

Marce had gone to bed and Will sat in the lounger across from her. An uncomfortable silence hovered between them.

"Sophia told me she thought you might need a good cry. How come? Hand hurt?"

Cat's throat thickened. She watched her brother. He fidgeted in the chair, like a little boy who had something great on his mind and no words to begin the purge.

"You pissed at me?" he finally asked, not looking at her.

"Will, you just sprung a pretty big deal on me in front of the whole world. How'm I supposed to feel?"

"I thought you'd be happy."

"I thought you hated it here?"

"I did," he said, looking up at her. "There was so much bullshit. I hated everything back then."

"So, what's different? I mean besides Marce?"

He got up and went to the stove, pushing around the dying coals, flaring a flame. He blew it bright and threw in a small log. When he stood, he held the poker limply in his hand and looked at her. There hung that moment of intimacy, the one where self-revelation transcends time and space and things become no longer the same as they were. She waited.

"I'm different, for one thing," he finally acknowledged. "I've been running my whole life. Mostly from myself."

She frowned. She was still mad at him. "This is news?" she said.

Will came near and seated himself beside her. "Did you ever wonder what it is inside that drives you?"

"What do you mean?"

"Like, what makes you write? What makes you act? What makes you cry?"

Now she was really confused. She raked her fingers through the tangled hair on his forehead. "Keep going."

"Cat, for me, I think the drive has been anger. Maybe even rage." He leaned into her.

It was the most honest thing she'd ever heard him say. *Sure,* she wanted to tell him. *Don't you know that's what always separated you from Kate? From life?* But she kept the thought to herself.

She thought he might be crying, his face turned away. How long had it been since Will had been able to cry?

"Aw, Will. C'mon." She wrapped her arms around him. Held him while he wept. His big hand swept at his tears. Then he laughed a little. "There's something else, Cat."

She felt him fill his lungs. His blue eyes were wide, and still glittery from tears. He looked like a man ready to spill a river of news.

"Marce is pregnant. We're going to have a baby."

"What?"

"Yeah," he laughed. "A little Hood. What do you make of that? Me—a dad."

Cat slid around to face him. "Oh my God, Will." She pressed her palm to his cheek. A baby in the family. A baby. Will's baby. Their eyes caught and tears brimmed. "You're going to be a father." The notion, spoken, set them both to laughing.

"Ha! You're going to be an auntie."

"Oh my God. It's a damn miracle! I didn't think either one of us was going to reproduce. I knew I wasn't, and I figured that even if you ever did, you probably wouldn't know about it."

"Hey, now."

Cat wrapped her arms around her brother's neck. "You're going to be a dad. Oh boy, this kid's going to be spoiled to death."

"No way."

"Yeah, this baby's going to get all that good stuff you should've had, Will."

His eyes filled again.

He pulled a Kleenex from the box Sophia had left for Cat and blew hard. She wiped her own eyes, and punched his shoulder. "God help it if it's a girl, though."

"Why?"

"She'll never be allowed to date."

"Not till she's twenty-one and only with an escort—namely me." He turned for the stairs. Before he went up, he looked back at her. "Do you see now why I want to come back?"

She nodded.

"Do you want me here?" He waited. "Can we be a family again?"

She studied him and then looked around the room. There was an odd sudden feeling of detachment inside her, as if she were not connected to any of it. "I want you to be happy," she said, finally. "I've wanted that since you were ten years old. If this is going to make you happy, then I want it."

She stood on the porch for one last smoke. Will's question lingered. Wasn't that what she'd always wanted? To be surrounded by a big family like Lily's? To build a life with someone? Someone who would understand about her writing; about the *kind* of time required—the hours on the porch staring and smoking. Scribbling at coffee shops and the predawn leaps from sleep to write until the sun rose. Her way of being creative? She wanted someone who would want her to do all of these things. Someone who needed that same *kind* of time for her own passion. Was she dreaming up someone who couldn't possibly exist?

She blew smoke toward the inky sky and thought about her other recent imaginings—the ones where she was traveling back to her beginnings—to where Kate began. Scotland. In between Cat's bouts of loneliness and her crazy little crush, she had found her way into a hunger to know more about her grandmother—her story, her family, and the fate that had brought her here. Scotland, Cat imagined, was cold and stony and laced with a kind of mystery. It spoke of heaths and glens and misty highlands; and of a young woman sent away into exile. More—it called to her, at night, in a voice familiar, like home.

Chapter Ten

Her sleep had been wracked with pain that throbbed in her hand and traveled up her arm. At four in the morning she awoke to swallow a pain pill and some water, then decided to go to her office with the intent of working on the story. Her swollen fingers were bluish and cold hovering over the keys. One peck with the left index sent a searing message to her brain. She would not be typing with this hand for a long time to come. She'd have to use the old hunt and peck method with her right, which behaved as if it had been palsied. Oh boy, she thought, there's going to be a lot of time to kill in the next few weeks. Better get a system going here, Ms. Right Hand.

When it became apparent that no words could move beyond the throb, she gave up and grabbed a book from her shelf and went back to the couch to finish her sleep. It had taken only three pages to flip by before the painkiller kicked in and made her drowsy enough to doze. It was the gust of wet air whipping into the house from the back door that had awakened her again some three hours later. Mamma had arrived with breakfast as promised.

"Now, you just lie there, honey," Mamma said before Cat could attempt a rise. She went straight to the kitchen. Soon after the rattling of pots and pans, the smell of coffee and bacon filled the house, rousing Will and Marce from above. As the three ate, Mamma washed up.

"I'll stay here with you today, Cat," Will said between bites of biscuit. "Marce has to go back to work."

Cat shook her head. "No, I want to be by myself. I'm fine." After a debate that brought them each to a childish huff, Cat turned pleading eyes toward Marce.

"Will, leave her be. If she needs anything, she'll call." Marce gathered their dirty plates and took them into the kitchen where she began drying the stacking pile Mamma had washed. "You will call, won't you, Cat?" She asked, peeking around the corner.

"I will. I promise." She smiled at Will. "You know, you could go get me some stuff from the store before you leave." This task and Marce's encouragement seemed to be enough for Will to agree to leave her alone. When Mamma finished, she brought her coffee to the couch and sat down beside Cat.

"We're right next door." Mamma patted her knee. "I'll be bringing over your meals every day." She raised her hand to Cat's protest and continued, ignoring her. Reaching into a canvas bag at her feet, Mamma pulled out a handful of bread bags and a twisted bunch of rubber bands. She handed them to Cat.

"What are these for?" Cat held the bags and shook them.

"You're going to need to wrap that arm up to take a shower."

Cat had been so grateful to have her hand stitched and plastered and finally eased of its fiery intensity that she hadn't considered how inconvenient this whole thing was going to be. She wished she had wrecked her right hand instead. At least then she could have managed better. How was she going to wash her hair? Her mind flashed through the steps of the seemingly mundane task. She could see how dependent the whole procedure was upon her left hand. Shit. She wanted them all to leave. She felt a big damn cry coming on—the one she had managed to stave off.

Before Mamma left, she announced her return at dinner-time. No arguments. And there weren't any. Cat knew better. Will followed Mamma out and went to the grocery store. Marce had poured them each another cup of coffee and seated herself across from Cat. They were quiet. Some of what had hung between herself and Will the night before was now hanging here between the women. Finally Cat grinned.

"So, rumor has it that we are not alone."

Marce smiled and looked over. "Will told you?"

Cat nodded.

"Well?" Marce asked.

"I've got to admit I'm a little stunned."

"Stunned in a good way or in a bad way?"

"I just never thought we'd continue." Cat looked up. "I mean as a family. The Hoods. Don't get me wrong, I'm loving the idea of having a baby in the family, but I can't quite move beyond the fact that I had sort of settled into the idea that this branch of the clan was at its end."

"Kind of morbid thinking."

Cat shrugged. "Look at us, Marce. Me? I'm a dyke. And up until you came along, Will wasn't exactly the family-man kind of guy, if you know what I mean. No offense to your choice in men," Cat grinned, "but I never thought that there was a woman alive who'd put up with his shit."

Marce laughed.

"But seeing him last night, talking about being a dad? He's going to be great at it."

Marce nodded.

"You've brought him back," Cat said. "Back home and back to himself."

Marce seemed to swallow back tears. She smiled.

"And you'll be Auntie Cat, right next door." Marce teased. "Babysitter extraordinaire!"

When Cat didn't laugh and instead looked away, Marce frowned. "I'm sorry. I was kidding about the babysitting part."

Cat raised her hand. "No, it's not that. Of course I'd love to be the eccentric old lezzie aunt next door." She smiled. "But there's something else. Something I've been seriously kicking around but I haven't really told anyone."

"Go on. Remember, I'm the sister-*out*-law. It's my role to gain favor with you."

They laughed.

"I'm thinking I want to go to Scotland. I want to write this story about our grandmother, Kate. I need to find out about her family."

"That's the big secret?"

"I want to go for a year."

"Oh. Now I get it."

"At least a year. Who knows ..."

"So, we're talking a big move. Quitting the job, packing up, leaving here?"

Cat nodded and poured out to Marce all the reasons she thought she was ready, including this new reason, this new baby. This return of the prodigal son to the land. It gave her a chance to leave. This land would not be abandoned. She could close everything up and be at peace knowing Will and his new family would take up the mantle of guardianship. "Somehow all the pieces are fitting."

Will roared into the drive and barged into the house with brown grocery bags in each arm. He had brought a little

173

bunch of yellow flowers, and shyly placed them in a vase, dropping an aspirin in the water. Cat shut her mouth against the remark that almost escaped her. Where had he ever learned about aspirins in vase water, she wondered. Or about being sweet, for that matter.

But it had been Marce, not Will, who'd insisted they stick around for Cat's first shower experience.

"In case you have trouble," Marce assured. "Just for today."

She managed to slide the first Wonder bag over her cast and slipped the rubber band tight around its opening. Twisting water knobs backward with her right hand had been difficult, but squirting shampoo and lathering soap with one clumsy hand had proved most challenging. All the while Marce helped her hold her bagged arm above her head. Will stayed decently behind the bathroom door, making anxious suggestions.

"Get lost," Marce finally ordered. "She's doing fine."

By the time she dried and dressed, she was exhausted. Will and Marce, having seen proof of her competence, finally left her with her damp head wrapped in a towel.

Alone and seated with a cup of tea in front of the television, Cat noticed the smeared ink on her cast. The watery letters of Melissa's name had blended into the runny numbers of her phone. Fuck. How was she going to call her, now? Mike gently nudged her sore hand with his nose. He looked up at her, worried.

"I'm OK, pal," she said. He climbed up beside her and settled into the curve of her side, licking at her hand. Dogs were funny, she thought. Wild animals living in your house. The points of his fangs reminded her of this, and yet, he was an old soul, she believed. Maybe, although she wasn't entirely convinced, they'd known each other in a different life. Wolves together, they'd run in a pack a million years ago, across some frozen tundra. Or better still, they had been Celtic pagans, draped in fur skins, dancing around a bonfire on some craggy outcropping, sacrificing wine to the gods. Celtic, Pict, or Scot. The two of them roaming the Highlands.

Cat drifted.

Rain and wind pelting against the windowpane awakened her from her nap. The painkillers were rendering her helpless, but without them, she ached. Sheets of heavy rain blew sideways across the valley. Puddles had filled the road and drowned the newly planted tobacco in muddy rows across the creek. Wind howled warnings around the house and hail beat a dismal rat-a-tat on the roof. She managed to stuff a log into the stove and stirred the coals to flames. If she thought that she was going to be left alone to recover in peace, she was wrong. Like a storm of its own, the phone began to ring.

"Hey! What happened?" Candace's concern lilted over the wires. "You *will* be able to go to the reading next week, won't you?"

And David Webber's office.

"We heard about your accident." Mona-the-secretary's concern, Cat thought, sounded more sincere than Candace's.

Then Lil.

"You need anything, buddy? Keeping that arm elevated?"

Will called with two excuses.

"Think we should build facing south in that lower field?" and "How's your arm?" Then, "Marce thinks we should face east on account of the creek being there," and "Need anything?"

Lil, again.

"Comin' over. Want me to get you a movie?"

Just as she'd settled into the couch and an old Tracy and Hepburn flick, the phone jangled again. *Damn it, Lily.* She grabbed for the receiver.

"For Christ's sake, Lil, I'm fine. I've swallowed my pills, eaten my lunch, and taken a healthy shit. Don't come!"

There was quiet on the other end and then a slow eruption of laughter. Finally, the voice managed to calm and articulate words.

"Well, you sound fine."

Unfamiliar.

"But about that last part—"

It wasn't Lily.

"Who is this?"

"Melissa."

"Oh God."

"Getting a little *too* much care?"

"You have no idea," Cat said. She sat up on the couch, pushing at her messy hair as if she could be seen through the phone. "I'm glad you called," she said. "I took a shower and your phone number smeared."

"Oh no, then we'd have to go through all that *stalking* business all over again."

"That sounds like something Lily would say—*stalk*—has she gotten at you already?" Cat asked.

"You could say that."

Cat's embarrassment reared. "Need to kill Lily."

Melissa laughed. "She loves you."

"She smothers me."

"But in a good way."

There was quiet again.

Finally, Melissa cleared her throat.

"I was wondering—of course only if you feel up to it—if you'd want to have dinner with me tonight? I'll bring it to you."

Cat felt herself smiling in spite of the rush of blood to her hand and head.

"Oh, you don't have to bring it!" She explained the meals on wheels that would be delivered that afternoon by Mamma. "I guarantee, there's always more than enough food."

As she replaced the phone in its cradle, she looked around the cabin. It wasn't in too bad shape. Lots of clutter, though. She made a sweep of the house, which left her fingers swelled to plump sausages. Oh, that's attractive, she thought, and gently squeezed a fat link. It was only after she'd whipped through a cleaning of her bathroom that she caught a glimpse of herself in the mirror. She was still dressed in the flannels that she'd worn for the last twenty-four hours. Her hair looked like it had been the nesting place of a couple of rats, and so she tied it up in a ponytail.

By the time she'd clumsily changed into clean sweatpants and jersey, the red Jeep, shiny with rain, had pulled in behind the truck.

Melissa entered dripping and cold with a basket of bread and wine and cheese hidden beneath her rain gear. When she loosened her jacket, she brought out her second surprise, a game of Scrabble.

"I might be making a big mistake bringing this here," she said, making herself at home. Cat directed them into the kitchen where Mamma's chicken soup was simmering; they unloaded the bread and cheese neatly onto plates.

Cat excused herself to the bathroom and when she returned she found Melissa standing before an old printer's type case hanging on the wall.

"What are these?" she asked, referring to the small shiny porcelain figures filling the rectangular boxes of the case.

"Wade Whimsies." Cat came over and pulled one out. It was a tumbled *Jack* with a tiny spilled pail of water by his side. "They're made in England. They come in stuff."

Melissa frowned as she turned a small blue whale in her fingers. "Stuff?"

"You know, like for promotions in boxes of Red Rose Tea, like prizes in Cracker Jacks."

Melissa smiled and put a blue whale back in place.

"So, I put them in here. I mean, I don't go out hunting for them. Just if they come to me."

"I see," Melissa said and moved to the far corner of the room where a round table held a scattering of round glass snow globes. She picked one up. Inside, Dorothy, the Tin Man, Scarecrow, and Lion were skipping along the Yellow Brick Road on their way to the Emerald City, diminutive in the background.

"Turn it over," Cat said, encouraging her to turn the key. "Somewhere Over the Rainbow" tinkled from the base and tiny gold glitter floated down onto the smiling foursome trapped inside the globe. One by one, Melissa reached for the other globes, turned them upside down and twisted the keys on their undersides. A chorus of chiming tunes rang through the fall of plastic snow.

"This is quite a collection," Melissa said.

"It's not a collection. I don't collect stuff—it sort of just comes."

Cat led Melissa down the hallway, past a line of old blue Mason jars and glass milk bottles on a shelf above them. Melissa pointed. "Not a collection?"

Cat shook her head. She opened the door to her office and they stepped across the threshold. Melissa moved around the room, cocking her head to read spines of books, leaning over framed photos of family and friends, pausing at the shelf holding the ink wells and quills. Their number suddenly seemed great to Cat. There were at least a dozen. She hadn't counted, just kept sticking them in there. On the shelf above were wooden and cardboard pencil boxes, some a half century old; these were less numerous, harder to come by. This she knew because she had in fact been scouring antique stores and flea markets looking for them.

"So, you're *not* a collector?" Melissa's brow raised in skepticism.

Cat knew that the incriminating evidence surrounding her was going to make a lie out of any denial she'd attempt. She turned them out of the room and back down the hall.

"Not on purpose."

Melissa directed Cat to unfold the board. Seated at the low round table in the living room, the two sipped wine and ate cheese, admiring the fire Cat had built. The Scrabble game began. "If I lose this in a humiliating defeat," Melissa warned, "the next time, I'll be bringing over Trivial Pursuit. I'm a whiz at that."

Cat suffered her own humiliation, especially since she was supposed to be some kind of writer. She'd managed to fill the board with two and three-letter words. But the conversation weakened her focus on the game. As she struggled with four *E's*, a *Q*, and two *R's,* she listened to Melissa tell about being born and raised in Boston, and then about the other places she had lived after leaving home. Cat found a *U* on the board and spelled out *queer.*

"Oh, nice," Melissa said. "Trying to tell me something?"

Cat laughed. *"Queer* as in *odd,* she defended.

Melissa placed her letters on the board. *"Z-Y-M-O-T-I-C— zymotic,"* she said.

Cat frowned suspiciously. "What's that? Some doctor

word? That's why I'm losing; you people have your own language. Plus, I'm having a hard time playing with this busted hand."

Melissa laughed. "It has to do with fermenting wine. I learned it from Trivial Pursuit."

"This is like playing with my brother," Cat recalled. "He'd study the dictionary for an hour and then ask me to play." She sipped her wine. "When I found out, I beat him up."

"I always wanted a brother," Melissa said. "I forgot about the violence part."

She was the middle child of three sisters, she said, and the only one who'd left the home state. Her mother had been a teacher and had died when Melissa was still a teenager. The wound was still fresh nearly twenty years later.

Cat said, "I think it would be harder to lose a mother you knew than a mother you couldn't remember. Why'd you become a doctor?"

"My father was a cop," she said. "He'd come home and tell us all these gruesome stories from his beat." His stories, she described, included discovering loose body parts in ditches, removing victims of stab wounds from crime scenes, and delivering babies in the backs of squad cars. "I thought it was so cool."

Cat tried not to look disgusted.

"My sisters, on the other hand, would wrinkle their noses, like you're doing right now, and beg him to stop." She grinned as Cat smoothed the bridge of her nose with her thumb and index finger. "Once, when he told us about finding a guy with an arrow through his skull, my little sister, Jaynie, threw up right on the table."

Cat laughed outright. There was an easiness between them, she thought.

"For the first time, I finally have the space to do my

painting." Melissa sipped her wine. "Galway has so many galleries. Reminds me of P-town," she said. "Have you ever been there?"

She hadn't been *anywhere,* she admitted.

"We should go there sometime. I have a friend, Arthur; he owns a gallery there. We could stay with him. You'd love Arthur. He's just as queer as he can be."

Uh oh, Cat thought, here they were in only the first conversation and Melissa was already planning a romantic vacation for them. Too quick, too quick. But before her mind had a chance to sabotage the evening, Melissa interrupted her paranoia.

"Every summer," Melissa said, "Arthur invites lesbian artists and writers. It's a great retreat. And it's free. I'll see if I can hook you up."

Now Cat wasn't sure if she was disappointed or relieved to find that this P-town getaway was more a professional jaunt than a romantic suggestion.

Melissa's eyes sparkled as she spoke of her painting, distracting Cat from any further meanderings. As the wine bottle drained, she found herself leaning into Melissa's shoulder, which seemed to happily support her. When Mike tried to insert himself between them, Melissa hugged him around the neck, kissed his nose and then whispered into his ear that she wasn't moving for now, and he could just wait for her departure. He gave a begrudging huff, and settled close to the fire.

"So," Melissa started, "why are you single?"

The question caught Cat off guard. Should she start with junior high school and work her way through every roll with every girlfriend who'd come along? Or should she start with the clown? Should she admit to often—if not always—growing bored? Liking her alone time? Say that

181

casual sex used to be her hobby but she was no longer very interested in it? Or should she start with Jamie?

"I thought I was in love once," Cat fiddled with the four *E*'s she still had, unable to make a word. "She was a piano player. lived here with me. We were all about trying to live a creative life together."

"That sounds good. What happened?"

"Well, I was writing my head off in the beginning. She was all twisted 'cause she felt blocked. Her *block* got all over me. We wound up smoking too much pot and fucking all the time. No words on the page for months. Then one night I came home and found her fucking some bimbo in my bed."

"Ouch."

"Yeah. Big time ouch. You know what?" Cat looked at Melissa. "She didn't even cry. Packed up her shit and left without one word. Later, she sent me a note saying I'd been stifling her creativity. She was glad she could feel free again."

"Bitch," Melissa said.

"Whore, actually."

They laughed.

"Do you think that you were?" Melissa asked. "Stifling her creativity."

Cat shrugged. "I think we were stifling each other. But I picked right up again as soon as she left. The book got underway after that."

"And her?"

"Hooked up with a party crowd, spends a lot of time in bars, drinking, doing coke—not playing her music. I heard she's with some woman who cheats on her ... Guess things come around."

"And you?"

Cat looked up. "I made a list. Of everything that I do and do not want in a relationship and I keep adding to it."

"How many pages?

"Twenty-seven."

"Wow." Melissa ran her fingers along Cat's arm. "Must have it pretty well narrowed down by now."

"Oh, I'm picky as hell."

"How'm I doing matching up to this list?"

"You're here, aren't you?"

Melissa smiled. "Here, and about to kick your ass at Scrabble."

"Yeah, well you do what you need to, but that's number seventeen on my list."

"What? *Must let me win at Scrabble?*"

"Something like that ..."

"Well, don't expect any surrendering ..." Melissa leaned into Cat and breathed against her ear.

"No surrendering at all?" Cat asked. "Not here?" She touched Melissa's arm. "Or here?" Her hand went to Melissa's cheek. "Or here?" She leaned into her neck and kissed.

Melissa eased away and looked at Cat. "Watch it, sister, I won't be seduced into losing to you. Let's just get that straight right now. Your turn,"

After Cat's overwhelming defeat at Scrabble, blaming her sorry loss on the wine and the throbbing in her arm, they settled into the back of the couch where their shoulders pressed together. How, Cat wondered, could the fluttering in her chest be winning over the throb in her arm? Curls, burnished copper in the firelight, spilled over Melissa's shoulders and onto her own. She leaned closer until a soft strand brushed her cheek. Her good hand reached for one of Melissa's and they wound fingers together and smiled.

"What about you?" Cat asked. "Relationship-wise, I mean."

Melissa took a deep breath. "I had one for a long time. Her name was Leah. She was a painter. Beautiful. We met when I was in med school, older than me, by about fifteen years. It was good at first—great in fact. I was mad about her."

"So what happened?"

"It wasn't till we'd been together for awhile—like a year—when I found out she had a nasty habit."

Cat frowned.

"Heroin." Melissa closed her eyes. "But, at that point I was in love with her. Wanted to help her. Wanted to get rid of this one small thing, because the rest was so good. I wasn't going to abandon her. We lived together. Leah painted by day, taught at the community college at night. There were no signs or clues of the addiction, initially. Which is probably a lie," Melissa said more to herself than Cat. "I probably just ignored them. It wasn't till I'd found a syringe behind the bathroom wastebasket that I knew for sure."

"Jesus." Cat let herself shift closer again.

"There's some stuff I'm not proud of in all this." Melissa voice had become soft. "I tried to help. Wean her off. Pretty soon I was the one who was shooting her up with morphine at night. Stuff I was writing prescriptions for ..." she winced. "Stuff I should have known better about."

Cat was silent, her breath shallow. Waiting.

"It might have helped, too, if she hadn't been double dosing the heroin during the day."

Cat shook her head. "So, you finally got out?"

"No, Leah got out." Melissa looked away. Cat could see only shadows on her face now, moving shadows cast by the fire. "I came home one night to find her dead in the bathtub. She had a needle still in her arm."

Cat reached to hold her. "I'm so sorry."

"I don't usually talk about it," Melissa said. "Tried to block it out."

"I'm glad you told me."

She felt Melissa's fingers in her hair. They glanced shyly, then looked away. Embarrassed by their mutual affection.

"I might just be a groupie," Melissa had confided. "I could just be infatuated with the romanticism of writers."

Cat laughed. "Oh yeah, this is romantic all right. Infatuate all you want." She squeezed the hand. "But there's no mystery; it's merely insanity."

"Don't wreck it for me," Melissa whispered, "though I'm not sure you could, actually."

A flood of heat traveled up Cat's body, bypassing her injured hand and arm, but pressing all practical thought out of her mind. She brought Melissa's hand to her lips and kissed. That was all she wanted to do and now she could die happy. But Melissa tucked their joined hands beneath Cat's chin and slowly brought their lips together. The last thing Cat saw, just before her lids closed, was the green of a gulf sea that she willingly let herself be swept into.

It was Lily's bedtime phone check-in that rattled them from the moment. Cat let the machine pick up, but Lily's voice coming from the speaker sounded concerned. A personal visit threatened. Cat picked up.

"You mean *she's* there? What are you doing?"

"Lily, what do you think?" Exasperation chased the pain back down into Cat's hand.

"Like—kissin'?"

"Knock it off." Cat smiled across at Melissa. "I'm hanging up, Lily."

"OK, buddy," Lily conceded. "I can hear that you're in good hands."

But by the time she'd hung up, Melissa had gathered her belongings in the picnic basket and was making ready to head home.

"You could stay ..." Cat said, looking outside at the gray sheets of rain that muted the outline of Melissa's Jeep only a few feet away.

"Early shift at the hospital," Melissa said. "Or I might have taken you up on it," But she didn't leave without inquiring about Cat's schedule for the next few days.

"I have a book signing in Winston-Salem—Thursday. Want to come with me?"

Melissa's eyes grew devilish, and she came close.

"I would love that. I can help carry your pen." Cat swatted at her, and told her she could collect the money from the book sales instead. Then she was in Melissa's arms, pressed warm against her.

"We're kind of like a jigsaw puzzle, no?" Cat imagined as breasts and thighs fit neatly into place.

"Puzzle?"

Cat breathed her in—the Plumaria, the faintly flowery scent of her shampoo.

"You know—the way a jigsaw puzzle fits together—once you find the right pieces. Like when you have one with a certain color ... or something about it that you need. The puzzle becomes whole,"

"Oh," Melissa said. She kissed Cat and held a hand against her cheek. "I like puzzles, too. They can be a challenge or a breeze." She lifted her hood and ran into the rain.

After the headlights disappeared down the cove road, Cat turned and without thinking jumped into the air, landing hard. The sharp pain of her arm and hand buzzed all the way up to her teeth, and her eyes filled with tears. *Fuckfuckfuck.* She danced around the room. Mike watched her from the place by the fire. The sympathy he'd previously mustered was by now replaced with apathetic groans.

"Quit it," she said and tossed a sock at him. He buried his nose.

"She's nice. Don't you think she's nice?" Groaning loudly, he rolled to his back. When she kneeled over him and ran her fingers through the golden fur on his belly, he gave in and licked one forgiving kiss to her nose. "You big jealous baby." Cat rose and made her way upstairs to her bed. The hand hurt, but she was not going to think about that now.

Chapter Eleven

The road, rutted and sloshy from the rain, curved along through the Carolina woodland out of Galway for about ten miles before they hit the smooth highway and traveled toward Winston-Salem. Somehow, something seemingly beyond her control, had infiltrated her plans for the day. She'd allowed herself a romantic fantasy centered around a long intimate drive alone with Melissa, conjuring a candlelit dinner at a little Italian restaurant. Her imaginings had even gone so far as to include bringing the pair back to the cabin for an evening nightcap ... and?

Well, it didn't have a chance to get that far, she thought, as she found herself in the backseat of Candace's car, heading for the city with Melissa by her side and Lily (for God's sakes) in the front seat chattering away about the time Jay Leno's *people* (was the word she'd used) had contacted her and asked her to participate in a hammering contest with the man himself.

"Now how did they come to know about you?" Candace asked, again, not having gotten an answer the first time she asked, a few minutes ago.

"Oh, hazards of fame," Lily said, turning around in her seat, grinning at the pair. "Right, Cat?" She launched into her legendary tale of becoming the first woman to become a master carpenter. She'd had lots of media attention.

Oh, boy, Cat thought.

It was why, Lily confessed, she wanted to take this trip with Cat, so she could keep an eye on Cat's fans. "You gotta be careful nowadays," Lily said. "All kinds of whackos out there."

Melissa smiled and twisted her fingers around Cat's. Between Candace's overzealous attention to her one and only client, and Lily's overprotectiveness of her oldest and dearest best friend, Cat was beginning to feel smothered. In six girlfriend-less years she'd had all the alone time she could bear. Now she found somebody she wanted to be quiet with and she was hauling around an entourage instead. If this was a glimpse of fame, she wanted no part of it.

From the moment they had entered the bookstore, and all the way through the reading and follow-up question and answer session, to the closing of the last signed book, Cat struggled to focus. Lily had taken charge of making sure she had water and a chair and *Did she need to take her next pill so that she would be pain free but not drowsy before the reading?* Candace handled all the schmoozing with the bookstore people. And Melissa cracked jokes in her ear, reminding Cat not to burp through her reading, but to definitely work the word *sex* into her responses.

A small gray-haired woman in the front row asked, in a thick Southern drawl, "I was wondering, is there any thin' *physical* that you do for yourself to get those juices flowing?"

Cat frowned, at first confused by the question. She glanced at Melissa, catching her mouthing the word *sex*. Cat then blushed and looked down. "Um," she fumbled, "what do you mean by *physical?*"

This caused the audience to titter, and she tried again.

"I mean, what gets your juices flowing?"

The little old lady cocked her head at Cat, oblivious of the snickering crowd.

"What do you do to keep the story *comin'?* Exercise? Run? Yoga? Anything?"

Cat pressed her lips together and nodded. "That's exactly right, ma'am," she said, seriously. "I run." She raised an eyebrow at Melissa. "That's it. I run."

The romantic Italian dinner had instead been a Chinese buffet back in Galway. Candace, thankfully, had excused herself, but Lily had joined the pair for dinner.

"Once, we had this job cutting bricks in half with a masonry saw," Lily said sitting across from the couple. "It was hot and we were sweatin', 'member, Cat?"

"We wore these goggles," Cat added, "so our faces were orange except around our eyes. We looked like raccoons or bandits."

"But by the end of the day we were totally covered in red dust. Our hair stuck out like cotton candy."

Cat remembered how they'd been like a couple of coal miners. But neither of them had thought anything about this when, at the end of the day, they'd strolled right into the Winn Dixie for groceries.

"A couple of little Pigpens," Cat agreed. "Totally unaware." They had tracked a rusty trail down the shiny white aisles.

"They asked us to leave!" Lily said between crunches of an egg roll. "Can you believe that? I've seen farmers covered with cow shiii ... poop who never got asked to leave."

Cat thought Lily's determination to quit cussin' was

waning. She felt Melissa's squeeze to her good hand, checking in.

"Cat show you her tattoo, yet?" Lily asked the wildly complete non-sequitur. "We got 'em together." She lifted her shirt sleeve to reveal the small red hammer that was more often than not concealed by her watch band.

"We got drunk at a Harley rally in Virginia when we were eighteen." Lily smiled. "We didn't even know it happened till we got sober two days later."

Cat shook her head.

"Where's yours?" Melissa asked her.

"Show her, Cat," Lily urged.

And so she rolled her right sleeve to reveal the small blue quill pen on the inside of her upper forearm.

Melissa touched it. "How'd I miss that?"

Cat shrugged. "Too dark?"

Melissa's beeper went off. She frowned at the flashing numbers and excused herself to carry her cell phone out the door. When she returned, she immediately gathered her coat and hat.

"Lily, would you mind taking me to the hospital? There's an emergency. They're calling all of us in. I'm sorry, but I have to go." She reached and wrapped a finger around a loose strand of Cat's hair. Both her eyes and her words were filled with regret.

"I'm sorry," she said and kissed the top of her head.

"I'll be back in a minute," Lily said. "Pay the bill; I'll pick you up outside." With that she threw money on the table and the pair disappeared out the door.

Somehow, Cat thought that the universe was deciding the pace of this new relationship. It was going slow. Maybe that's what made it hopeful; it was different in almost every way from any other she'd ever had before.

⌘⌘

Melissa's call came to say she'd have to be working fairly solidly for the next few days. The conversation dallied for a half hour, then Cat laid the receiver down on its hook, feeling frustrated that she couldn't just drive over and snatch Melissa away from her job.

Lily was visiting, keeping her company and commiserating with Cat about her no writing/no loving state. They'd been rocking on the porch, listening as the world bustled home: cars humming and tractors rambling along the creek road, turkey buzzards swooping for one last dive at dinner. Lily, still dusty from her day, passed the joint over. Haltingly, she began.

"Listen, I found somebody to fill in for you ... while you're laid up." She kicked at the top of a nail head that was popping up from a floorboard. She didn't look at Cat.

This was news. This was somehow unexpected, but of course Lily would need help. Cat looked at her fingers whose purplish bruise was browning along the edges. This wasn't a stubbed toe, but a *wreckage*. It was going to take a lot more than a few days to fuse itself back together.

"Who is it?" She braced herself against the answer, kind of like waiting for a car repair bill.

"Her name is Dolly and you'll love her, Cat."

"Dolly? What kind of name is Dolly? Why should I love her?"

"Whatdya mean what kind of name is it? It's a normal name."

"It's a stupid name for a carpenter." Cat toked and toked again.

"Ain't any stupider than *Cat*." Lily sat back and scowled, watching the fast burn of the joint in Cat's fingers. "Hit it and pass it."

Cat handed it back. "Well, does she know anything about carpentry?"

Lily's mouth tugged a grin. "That's the beauty of it. Her daddy was a carpenter just like mine and she was *site mite*, just like me! Can you believe it?"

What was there not to believe? Unless this Dolly was a liar. Cat lit a cigarette and drew hard.

"How old is she?"

"She's only twenty-two and let me tell you what," Lily leaned back easily. "She's strong and fast and flexible. Didn't realize how much age matters till I saw her moving on that first day. *Speedy Gonzalez.* Not like you and me, gettin' a little sluggish and rickety."

Cat stood and walked to the rail where she propped her elbows, her back to Lil. *Sluggish and rickety?* Jesus—what the fuck did that mean?

"And she's smart," Lily said. "She can figure out anything. You know how we're always getting things backward?"

Cat turned, *"We* do not always get things backward. *You* are the one who gets things backward."

"Yeah, but Dolly, well she just looks at something and knows it ain't right. She saved my ass twice in the last couple days."

Cat leaned back against the rail.

Lily went on to explain how Dolly was not only an experienced carpenter, but was also a fiddle player. "Has her own Celtic band. Even went to Ireland to learn music from famous Irish people."

"What do you mean famous Irish people?"

"You know, like famous Irish musicians. I can't remember who they are, but I'd heard of them on WNW. You know, Fiona Finch for the *Pipes and Fiddle Show?*"

"So what's she doing working carpentry if she's got all that?"

Lily got up and draped her arm across Cat's shoulders.

"She's like you, working carpentry so she can do her art. 'Cept you're a lot closer to getting famous. Dolly doesn't have a CD out or anything."

Cat threw her cigarette over the rail. "Does she understand that this is just a temporary job? I mean, she knows she's just filling in for me for the time being, right?"

Lily nodded and headed for the door. "Oh, yeah. For sure."

But Cat didn't think she sounded sure. She thought she sounded like the idea hadn't even crossed her mind.

Lily paused, "How long did Melissa say you'd be laid up?"

"About six weeks." Cat frowned suspiciously. "Why?"

"I'll let Dolly know tonight when she comes over for dinner."

"For dinner? During the week?"

"Both Dolly and her boyfriend Padraig are coming." Lily grinned. "They both meditate. Just like me and Hannah. Can you believe that?"

Cat believed it.

"So, don't you worry about work. Enjoy your time off, Cat. You deserve it." And then Lily disappeared.

Enjoy, Cat thought. She wished she could. She wished that all the time she'd had on her hands could be spent writing, but the broken fingers would only allow spurts of this before they'd pound in angry protests against the task. Instead, with Mamma's home-cooked meals in her belly and the remote control in her good hand, she was getting fatter by the day.

It was during the third week of her confinement that she'd been scheduled to appear on the David Webber radio show. Candace would be there, handling the details, she'd assured. Before Cat left the house she'd thrown on an old pair of Levis and a raggedy sweatshirt. She didn't think it mattered since she was going to be on the radio and no one but that old geezer was going to see her, anyway.

As soon as she walked into the lobby and Candace saw the holey sweatshirt with the frayed cuffs, she'd yanked Cat into the ladies room, demanding that they trade shirts.

"There is no way in hell, Candace." Cat raised her arms and moved away from the little woman as she began unbuttoning her black silk blouse with the gold embroidery.

Candace's fingers paused in their uncoupling descent and raised eyes to Cat.

"Turn around," she said. "No watching me do this."

"What!" Cat said. "I don't even *want* your damned shirt!" But she turned.

Candace said, "Look, I haven't worked my ass off for the last year trying to sell both you and your book to sit back and let you sabotage it just because you don't have any respect for yourself. Take off your shirt."

"What's that supposed to mean?" Cat stepped sideways and crossed her arms over her chest. She was still carefully not watching Candace taking off her shirt. "I do so have respect for myself." But unease coursed through her.

There was a deep sigh that came hard from Candace. It forced Cat's eyes down and her arms to untwine. She scraped one thumbnail with the other without looking up.

"I've seen it before," Candace started quietly. "In other women." She laughed. "Hell, even in myself."

Cat waited, her back to Candace.

"You don't believe you're good enough."

"For what?"

"For this," Candace reached around her and pointed to the world outside the bathroom door. "You feel like you're this huge fraud and that somebody will find you out. And

195

so you sabotage." She pinched the back of Cat's sleeve in evidence.

Cat shifted her weight from left to right. Was this true? She looked down the length of her own body; in addition to the near-shredded shirt, she saw the smears of orange-colored paint across her left thigh, and on her feet were her work boots, still caked with the red clay from the last job site. Well, she had to admit this was extreme even for her. She knew better. But had it been sabotage? Why would she want to wreck something that was good?

"Why the hell would I do that?"

"Because that way, no one, including yourself, will ever expect anything more out of you." Cat heard Candace walk to the sink and begin washing her hands.

"Sounds like you know something about it?" Cat said to the reflection in the mirror. Candace was standing there in her little black lace bra, clearly having forgotten her exposure.

"Why do you think I left New York?"

"You wrecked something?"

Candace dried her hands and faced Cat. She closed her arms across her chest, modest again. "Yes and no. Yes, I felt like a fraud; yes I did little things to try to ensure my failure. Give me your damn shirt." She hunched her shoulders. "But no, in that I'm not a fraud. I'm good at what I do. I know books, I know writers, I know publishers, and I know how to get everybody together and make them all happy."

Cat stared at her. Then pulled her sweatshirt off, handed it over, and slipped on the blouse, surprised that it fit.

"Now I had to leave New York and come here and work with you to know all that." Candace was smiling shyly. "You did write a book. You are who you are." In one swift move, she pulled Cat's tattered sweatshirt on and stood looking ragged but determined. "So, don't wreck this for either of us," she said.

Then she marched Cat from the rest room as if she had just singlehandedly captured a battalion.

They waited together on a loveseat, Candace going over notes and Cat fidgeting through an old *Time* magazine, when finally a tall woman with a tight brown bun nodded at them. They reached the door leading into the "pulse of the station," as Candace called it, and The Bun turned on them, nailing Candace with a haughty look.

"Mr. Webber will be seeing Ms. Hood alone," she said.

Cat would later swear she saw Candace somehow raise inches above her diminutive height and lean forward as if she were going to spit. The woman's bun pulled tighter, tugging her eyes to slants. The air between them (Cat would swear again) fairly sizzled. Before Candace could be the one to sabotage everything, Cat tapped her shoulder and whispered into her ear.

"I'll be fine."

Then she stepped across the threshold, and Candace ordered, "Make nice. This is important."

David Webber was seated behind a big faux Louis XVI desk with gaudy gilt swirling around its edges. His great white mane was combed neatly back and was (Cat could smell) lacquered stiffly in place. He was tidy, his mustache and eyebrows trimmed in neat arches. Instead of taking Cat's extended hand, he pulled her to him in an awkward embrace and Cat *thought* she felt his hand brush her ass.

"Catherine," he began, leaving his arm around her, guiding her to the couch. "I was hoping for us to get to know each other a little better before we go on the air." He spoke like an Alabama boy trying to get into Oxford.

When it became apparent that he intended to seat himself beside her, Cat broke from his hold and sat in the chair across from him instead. Nonplussed, he pulled out a notebook.

"So, you were born and raised in Galway, right?"

"No, up north in Little Galway."

"Brothers? Sisters?" he asked.

Boring, she thought. "One brother, Will, " she said.

"Single?" He kept his eyes on his clipboard.

Single? She frowned. *Will? Or does he mean me? And what does that have to do with anything?*

Her stomach had that creepy feeling she got whenever she found herself alone with Richie down at the lumberyard.

Webber raised his brow, "Well, are you single? Alone? Without mate?"

"Oh, me, you mean. Who needs to know that?"

He put his pad down.

"I do." Then he winked.

It made her want to kick David Webber in the crotch.

To groped women everywhere, she thought with righteous indignation as she imagined the slamming of boot into balls.

The Bun entered. Both Webber and Cat turned to see her thin lips draw closed, as if pulled by strings, into a tight purse.

"David, it's time for you and Ms. Hood to go on the air."

The two filed into the recording booth, where each was directed to opposing chairs at a small round table. After Cat had seated herself, Webber leaned over her shoulder and whispered, "Drinks and *more* after the show."

And then his fingertips brushed her left breast. This time she was sure of it. Her fists tightened. Before she had a chance to follow through with a clip to his chin, a soundman was behind her, miking her for broadcast.

She could barely think, anger crowding out all thoughts of book, characters, next project ... all the questions for which she'd so carefully prepared. What a waste of time, she thought, sure her disgust was obvious.

"So." Webber's smile slid slyly to one side as he started the interview. Clearly nothing of what she was thinking had registered on his ego-blown radar. "Has this injury impeded your creative or *otherwise* activities?" He winked.

You asshole, she thought.

She answered carefully, "Only that I'm a little slower on the computer."

He chuckled. "Well, I hear that some of those cyberers like it that way."

"Then one of us is listening." She couldn't stop herself from saying it. She hoped Candace wasn't listening too hard.

Cat watched as he laughed again, only thinner—tinny.

He covered himself. "Uh, yes. Well, you can't be in this business and *not* know. Ha ha." He actually said, *ha ha,* just like that. "Of course, we have been getting personal off the air today. Isn't that so, Cat?"

It startled her. It was like Lumberyard Richie copping two hands worth of a feel before she even knew he was nearby. Only Richie was a poor dumb-ass who didn't know any better. Compared to this pig, with his big hair, fake accent, and dinky mustache, Richie was a prince.

Before she could respond, David interrupted and, in a more serious voice, spoke into the mike. "We'll be back in a few minutes for more conversation with Cat Hood, our own local hometown writer."

As soon as it was clear that they were off the air, Cat rose—shutting her mind down to what she was about to do—and quickly walked around to David Webber's side of the table. Shielding his body from view with her own, she reached down between his legs and grabbed his balls.

"Listen, you little prick." She squeezed hard, before he had a chance to grab her wrist. "You wanna do this interview with your mouth full of your own 'nads?"

He shook his head, wide-eyed and pale. She tightened her grip. "Make nice."

He gulped and exhaled and she stepped back away from him. The rest of the interview went smoothly. She'd be damned, she thought, sitting here in Candace's black and gold silk blouse, that she was going to let anything or anyone get in the way of all the hard work she'd done. Candace was right. She needed to own what she'd created. Even if it meant making nice with this dumb sonofabitch pig. When it was over, she threw down her headphones and headed for the door without a word or look at the radio host.

The Bun was waiting at the end of the hallway for her.

Cat stopped. "You work for that little motherfucker?"

"I'm *married* to that little motherfucker," The Bun said.

"I'm sorry." Cat moved past her.

"Me, too," The Bun called after her.

They were finally about to be alone for the first time since the accident, or so it seemed. Cat followed the directions to Melissa's condo. If she could just get there, for crying out loud. She smacked the steering wheel, as she once again rounded the same bend. There was no sign on the left announcing the condominium's existence. *The Place* did not exist as far as Cat could tell. Finally, she pulled into a gas station, got out, and dropped thirty-five cents into a pay phone.

"I'm lost," she said after Melissa's hello.

"What do you mean, lost?"

"I mean, there is no sign on the left saying *The Place*."

"Where are you right now?" Melissa asked.

Cat looked around. "I'm at a Citgo, next door to a restaurant called ..." Cat angled her body to read the sign above her.

"Docker's Row," Melissa said for her.

"Yeah, exactly."

"OK. Now, are you paying close attention?" Her voice hummed against Cat's ear. "Look right across the road and tell me what you see."

Turning toward the two-lane on her right, Cat saw before her a twenty-foot sign with green lettering reading *THE PLACE*. There was silence.

"See you in a minute," Melissa said.

The heavy oak door opened before Cat even knocked. She hardly had a chance to admire the wrought iron strap hinges, with their hammered nail heads, before Melissa whisked her inside. Here there was even more to admire. The wood floors were polished to a glossy warm gold. Brick walls reached high above them; Cat estimated sixteen— maybe twenty—feet. Four large windows opened up on the wall, reaching to the second floor, where a smaller set of mullioned windows ran along the clerestory. From the room's center, a staircase of wrought iron and oak spiraled up into a loft.

"Whoa," Cat said softly.

"Used to be an old bakery and warehouse," Melissa said, showing Cat through the cavernous room.

Heavy beams separated the upper and lower levels. Cat could see the same black iron and oak of the staircase snaking a railing along the second story's edges. There were no perimeters of walls separating the living room from the kitchen and dining areas. A soft brown leather sofa squared the space with a matching chair and ottoman.

Drawing attention to a fireplace, so huge it could have swallowed them both, Melissa pointed out, "The original baking oven."

Its massive stonework was split by a thick-beamed mantle. "With some modifications, of course." She demonstrated how the flue had been reworked, cast iron doors and shelving removed, and venting added to blow the warm air into the room.

"This is awesome," Cat murmured, trailing into the kitchen where a white porcelain sink shone against a red-tiled backsplash. The stove stood as part of a center island whose wood-block top served as a counter with swiveled stools on two sides. Fascinated, Cat stooped to touch the frosted glass doors of Melissa's refrigerator.

"It's like some movie star's refrigerator," she said, opening and closing the doors, one at a time.

"You know movie stars?" Melissa laughed, hugging her around the middle.

"No." Cat made a face. "But, hey, I read those magazines, you know."

Melissa kissed the back of her neck.

"You're giving me goose bumps." Cat shivered.

"Good," Melissa said. "Come here and let me give you some more." She took Cat's good hand and led her up the curving staircase. The massive bed sat in the center of the loft. White sheets rumpled, the half-dozen pillows scattered about seemed like a pretty promising sign for later, but it was the sight across the loft that really turned her on.

It was Melissa's studio. An easel stood on one side.

Large canvasses leaned against the perimeter and an old barn door laid out on steel sawhorses was weighted with paints and brushes, pallets, jars, and more. Cat made it past the bed, and slowly made a pass around the room, sometimes lingering in front of paintings, once turning her head sideways. When she looked up she saw Melissa, stretched across the length of the bed, her upper body propped against two pillows.

"Get over here," she said.

Cat shook her head. "No fair. I want to look at your stuff." Melissa sighed and rolled onto her back, her knees falling open; she beckoned Cat closer with the crook of her finger. "Just one kiss and I'll let you roam."

"You are a vixen," Cat laughed, "luring me to your lair, seducing me with that body, those eyes ..."

"These lips," Melissa suggested. "If you'd just get close enough."

"Oh ..." Cat turned back to the brightly colored people in scenes of restaurants, back porches, and coffee shops—each just a little off, a little askew, a little quirky, but she was thinking about Melissa on the bed behind her.

"I can't choose. You or your paintings? I'm totally charged by both."

Melissa reached her arms into the air above her. "See these hands?"

A tremor passed through her.

Melissa began unbuckling her belt, the sound of leather sliding and silver snapping urging Cat forward, away from the paintings and toward the bed, where she moved over Melissa, straddling her, stilling her hands mid-task.

"Isn't that my job?" Cat asked.

"Oh, I thought I might have to do it all by myself," Melissa said.

Cat tried to pull the belt the rest of the way through its loops, but it stuck. Single-handed maneuvering was proving awkward.

Melissa, laughing, said, "Looks like you do need some help," and pulled the belt loose.

Cat leaned forward, covering Melissa's mouth with her own. When she felt fingers reaching up under her shirt, grazing nipples, her pulse raced harder. It seared her swollen fingers so the hot pain caused Cat to rock back.

"Jesus!" she yelled.

Melissa sat up. "What? Are you OK? Did I hurt you?" Worry deepened in the crease of her brow.

Cat held her arm up and blew cool air across her fingertips. Beads of sweat sprung on her upper lip. That thing about seeing stars, she thought, actually happens. Inside her brain, tiny explosions of yellow light lit up her frontal lobe. When she was finally able to focus, she found the familiar green eyes now filled with doctorly concern.

"Did I hurt you?" Melissa asked again.

"Not exactly," Cat smiled, a little sheepishly, she imagined. "I mean sort a, *geezus.*"

"Sort of?"

They both leaned back, side by side, heads cozied on one big pillow. Cat held her hand above them. She sighed and then sighed again, not quite able to find the words. She rolled over and pressed her mouth against Melissa's ear. Whispering and not looking were the only ways she could admit to what had happened.

"You know that surge you get? The one that usually shoots to that place?"

"Which place?"

Why, Cat thought, was she making this more difficult than it already was? "You know, *that* place," and she spider-walked her fingers down Melissa's rib cage and belly, landing on the spot.

"Oh, *that* one," Melissa sighed. "Yeah, what about it?"

"Well, that whole thing landed in my hand."

Sliding sideways, facing her, Melissa turned and traced one finger along Cat's shoulder and arm. She was smiling, but gently, as if her heart had been touched. She wrapped her arms tightly around Cat.

"Well, then we'll be holding off on that surge-making for awhile." She kissed the top of Cat's head.

"It better not be too long. I'll go mad."

The phone ringing nearly two hours later woke the pair. Curled around each other in the center of the big bed, Melissa's hair webbed across the pillow, tickling Cat's cheek. The two started, like a couple of drunks, up from the bed. Cat relaxed back into her doze; it wasn't at home and it wasn't her phone. Except Melissa tugging at her shoulder awakened her.

"It's for you," she said and handed Cat the receiver.

The fog was still thick as she heard Candace on the other end.

"How'd you find me?" Cat asked, now annoyed. With a light finger Melissa was drawing circles across Cat's back and all she wanted to do was focus on that. She held the receiver away from her ear as Candace's voice came loud in staccato bursts. Cat rolled her eyes and Melissa laughed. She brought the phone back to her ear.

"I don't know," Cat said. "New York's a haul."

Candace burst out with an un-Candace-like curse.

"OK, OK. Don't go getting your panties in a knot. And don't call me here, Candace. Call me at home. Tomorrow."

She hung up without good-bye.

"That woman," Cat sighed. "She's got an interview set up with some New York City lesbian writer who heard me on that stupid David Webber program."

"All the way up in New York?" Melissa's fingers worked into the muscles leading from Cat's shoulders through to her neck.

"I guess. Anyway, she wants me to come talk at a writer's conference up there."

The hands paused mid-massage. "You're going, aren't you?"

"Have to, if I want Candace to leave me alone. God, she's like a dang bloodhound, sniffing me out of every corner."

"She's got plans for you, Cat."

"No kidding."

The massage resumed. "Is that a bad thing?" Melissa asked. "Isn't that what agents do? I mean it is her job, right?"

"I know. I just wasn't expecting all this, you know?" Cat settled into the pillow. "I wanted my book published, for sure. And who wouldn't want to make some money on it? But all this traveling and radio shows and now this conference thing. You know, if my hand wasn't busted, I'd be missing work."

Melissa listened as Cat worried aloud. "I mean, Lily needs me."

"I thought she had someone helping out?"

"Temporarily. But once this hand ..." Cat stretched out her arm, "... once I can work, that stupid Dolly will be on her way."

Melissa sat up. "*Stupid* Dolly? Why is she stupid?"

Cat shrugged. "Just stuff. She acts like she's the best little carpenter since Jesus."

"Sounds like you're kind of jealous."

"About what? Some fiddle player with a dumb name? I just don't like the idea of her getting too cozy in my job."

"I see."

"Anyway, I'm going broke. I gotta get back to work." Cat sat up and looked around the room. There were fine things in this place. Things that cost some *jack,* as Lily would say. Things that came from upscale stores like Pottery Barn and probably Neiman Marcus. She noticed a blue glass vase of white orchids on the bedside table. What was a rich doctor doing with a poor carpenter who only happened to write a book? Cat wriggled from the back rub and stood up from the bed.

"Hey, where you going?" Melissa reached for her hand.

"Gotta go," Cat said, pulling on her jeans. As she moved away, Melissa slid from the bed, crossing the room toward her. Cat headed down the spiral and Melissa followed quickly behind. She grabbed Cat's shoulder as they reached the landing.

"Hey!" She turned Cat around. "What just happened? Did I say something? I'm sorry, about the jealous comment ... I was just ..."

Cat shook her head.

"What then? You can tell me." Melissa's eyes were dark green now, worried.

Cat wondered what was she supposed to say. The truth? *I'm sorry, Melissa, I just figured out that you're too good for me, so I'm leaving.*

Melissa compressed her lips as if she were biting something back.

"It must be scary to have all this coming at you at once: broken hand, interviews, now love affairs." She brought Cat's hurt fingers to her lips. "Feels like it should be exhilarating, but it's overwhelming instead?"

The fear pushing Cat toward the door eased somewhat and she took a deep breath. They found the couch and sat together in silence until Cat's stomach growled and they both laughed. Melissa brought them wine and cheese and bread.

She decided not to mention the whole rich/doctor—poor/carpenter thing. Maybe she would think that one through, first. For now—she still wanted to tell Melissa so many things.

She sipped her second glass of wine, and found herself beginning to talk about Kate. About the ocean crossing made by a frightened young girl, pregnant with Cat's own father.

"I think I want to write her story," she said as she had said to Marce. Melissa was kind, like Marce, she had decided. Smart and understanding.

"I mean, I think I want to go to Scotland." She looked at Melissa for a reaction, but there was only continuing interest. "To see if there's still family there. To see the way it is."

"Makes a lot of sense. Maybe this whole broken hand thing happened for a reason," Melissa offered.

Cat frowned.

"Maybe it's giving you a chance to think about doing other things ... I mean things other than carpentry."

This didn't, as might have occurred in the past, cause Cat to rise in defense of carpentry or to feel guilty about leaving Lily. Instead she nodded, knowing that Melissa was merely voicing something she herself had been thinking about: that maybe it was time to trust the writing to support the life. Especially with Candace mad-dogging her career.

She said, "Now that Will's back and about to have a baby and build a house, well, it all kind of makes sense."

They sat in silence then. She knew that Melissa understood that Cat's going would separate them. But it wasn't time to talk about that, yet.

Chapter Twelve

These thoughts and others had been on Cat's mind as she was on her knees cleaning out the closet in her office. It was the last place to receive her attentions since she'd been cooped up. As she leaned into the darkened cubby her knee tilted a loose floorboard that swung up and banged her forehead. She sat back and rubbed the quickly rising egg. *Please, no more injuries,* she thought. *Damn.*

It was from this vantage point that she noticed something protruding from the gap left by the loosened board. She scooted closer and reached inside. Her hand touched a folder of paper wedged tightly between the joists. Its dusty binding pulled through a lace of cobwebs. Wiping her sleeve across the cover, she discovered the bottom corner was blackened, as if it had barely escaped a fire. *Kate's Diary* was written in the now fading inked curls of her grandmother's hand. Against the tall dresser, Cat propped her back and unfolded her legs in front of her. Carefully penned across the first page was the date—*May 2nd, 1938.* Her heart sped and she ran a shaky finger under the beginning entry.

Dear Diary, I believe I might be pregnant ...

The words on the pages were shaky. Then seemed to grow more firm.

I haven't told anyone ... especially not Angus. I won't burden him. He has dreams that I won't spoil.

And then, *Dad learnt that Angus and I were alone on the crag. Someone, probably Nelly S, spied and told. Dad slammed his fist on the kitchen table. He said he wouldn't have a slut for a daughter. He came at me and would have struck me in the face had Thomas not grabbed him. What will he do if he finds me with child?*

She had planned her escape. *I will vanish to Arran into the hills and raise the babe on my own. I have saved nearly two pounds. I haven't seen Angus in a fortnight. I sent the message through Mary that Dad forbade me to see him anymore. It's for the best.*

But there came a twist. *I finally broke down and told Mary the truth. I have been so afraid. Behind my back she went to Angus. As I was walking home from market, I heard a whistle from above and in the tree I saw him dangling from a branch. He said, 'We are to have a babe'—and that was that. The only other thing he said was that we are to meet—to make plans—he said. Saturday behind the church. I told Mary, first to scold her and then to thank her. She believes that Angus will marry me. I don't know.*

But it was to be this very diary that betrayed Kate before she had even met Angus on that day.

Dad found the diary hidden under my bed after Mam asked his help in turning the mattress. He stormed the kitchen with the book in one hand and his belt in the other. I fell to the floor after the strap crossed my shoulders the first time. Mam curled around me trembling like a leaf, taking the next whipping upon her own backside.

Cat read on. *It was Mary and Thomas who pulled Dad off of me and Mam. He threw the diary into the fire and then slammed the door on his way out. Thomas ran for Angus and Mary and*

Mam helped me pack. Jacko, who'd hidden in the corner, rescued the diary. Everyone gave over every last shilling they had hid. We had to hurry. Mam thought Dad would have gone for a whiskey, but we didn't know and we all knew it would be best for me to leave right away.

Pages later the journal revealed more of the lovers' dramatic departure.

Angus came with his face bloodied. His pack was only half filled. When his Da caught him filling his sack he beat him; first with his fists, then with an axe handle. He said no son of his would leave the farm for some whore who claims to be carrying who-knows-whose babe. Angus left his father face down in a pig trough—where he belonged, Angus said—and then he would say no more to me. We haven't spoken much since then at all. But we have seen the ship. We've booked steerage. I am afraid. Mornings I am sick. How will I do at sea?

There were pages missing, but there was an entry on a torn page. A letter, Cat thought, never finished, never sent:

Dear Mary,

America is a big place. We have come to her wilds and they remind me of the hills of home ...

And that was it. Cat folded the book and leaned her head back against the dresser. She brought the diary up and breathed the charred pages. Cat laid the journal down next to her and stared for a long time as if it were a door she was almost fearful of passing through. But now that she had found it, she knew there was nothing left to do but to go through it.

Her injury-related confinement had helped her achieve some things. She had cleaned out the entire cabin, painted her bathroom, and finally begged Mamma to quit bringing over food, so she could rid the fridge of its molding leftovers.

Her nights were spent on the porch swing, sometimes with her harmonica, occasionally with Delores, and more often than not with Melissa, come to fall asleep with her after a long shift at the hospital.

Today, this would all be coming to an end. Her cast was scheduled for removal that morning. She called to tell Lily she'd be back to work tomorrow.

"Are you sure, buddy?" Lily asked. "Dolly's gotcha covered if you need a couple more days."

Cat hung up feeling annoyed at the good-willed Dolly, who she was sure was trying to take her job away. If Lily's tone was any indication, she'd be perfectly happy with the exchange. Fuck that. She would be back in her old tool belt before the two of them knew what happened. She knocked against her encased arm. Today she would be freed. They had all volunteered to go with her to have the cast removed, but she wanted her minutes alone with Melissa who had volunteered to take it off.

The tiny saw zipped through the plaster and the two halves broke apart in Melissa's hand, kind of like an eggshell. It released a noxious odor and Cat wrinkled her nose.

"Yuk, is that me?"

Melissa looked up, surprised. She laughed and gently took Cat's flaky hand in hers.

"That's you and all your decomposing skin."

Her arm seemed to have shrunk. Its gray pallor and dull weight reminded her of the dead fish that the first nurse had warned her about. Melissa scrubbed away loose papery skin and specks of dried blood that had caked under the cast. Although the job had been neatly done, the dissolved stitches had left an angry jagged scar that was still red and swollen. Its craggy line ran from below Cat's pinky, across four knuckles, and ended just above the flesh of her thumb.

"Man, that's ugly." Cat flexed her fingers. "Guess I'll have to give up my hand-modeling job."

Melissa didn't smile when she looked up from her examination. "I'm afraid it's not going to get much better than this, Cat. It was a bad tear." She kissed the bruised scarring. "I could wish for a neater line, but there was hardly enough unshredded skin to sew together."

"All right, that's enough." Cat squeezed her eyes. "I don't want to hear anymore about it. It works, and that's the main thing, right?" She wiggled the stiff hand.

Melissa kissed the tips of Cat's fingers. "That has yet to be proved." Her eyes slanted upward at Cat and twinkled.

They had avoided the *big surge,* as they had come to call it. Neither had wanted to bring on that pain again, and so they kissed and kissed. Cat controlled her responses but didn't think she'd be able to hold out much longer. Now she sat on top of the hospital bed and watched Melissa move about the sink and mark her chart, waiting. When she moved close enough, Cat grabbed her around the waist with her legs and pulled her closer, capturing her. They giggled as their breaths met, lips nearly touching.

"You're going to get me in trouble here," Melissa warned her.

"I hope so." Cat kissed and let her go. "What time are you coming over? I've got a great dinner planned."

Melissa pulled free and examined Cat's hand more critically. She frowned, worried. Cat forced herself to look at the scarring. It was definitely not a pretty sight. Oh, God. Maybe it was grossing Melissa out.

"I'm sorry," she said.

Sorry? Cat's heart speeded up. Was this going badly?

"I don't want you going back to carpentry until next week."

"Babe, I gotta work. It's a money thing," Cat said, but inside she was touched by this concern.

Melissa pressed Cat's wiggling fingers with a cupped palm. "You have to understand this was bad. You can't just go back to normal. You're going to need physical therapy."

Cat grinned, "OK, let's start tonight."

"That's all you care about, isn't it? You just want to get me in bed."

"Who said anything about bed?" She feigned indignant shock. "I said *dinner*. Which, in my land means food—a meal." She watched Melissa tap a pen against a front tooth. A habit, Cat noticed, that she had while doctoring.

"Now," Cat said, wrapping her closer. "If *dinner* means something different in your world, maybe you should let me know."

Melissa pushed Cat aside. "Yeah, well, dinner in my world usually includes dessert." She glanced sideways. "And it's this that I'm afraid might harm you."

"Oh, please let me be harmed," Cat begged.

Melissa walked her to the checkout desk. "OK. But I'll bring pizza. No cooking for you—you'll probably burn yourself this time."

"And dessert?"

Her query was met with the back of Melissa's shaking head as she turned to go back to work.

"Is that a yes?" She watched as Melissa's hand raised in a wave. "I think that is a yes," Cat called out. Melissa went through the doors.

She swung into the Winn Dixie to collect the ingredients for the monster sub she was planning to make for work tomorrow.

It was while she was standing at the deli counter that she heard Lily's familiar laugh behind her. When she turned,

214

there she was with another woman approaching Cat. They were dressed exactly alike: overalls, boots, and tank tops, and both were covered in the same dirty sawdust. They were giggling like crazy, Lily smacking the other woman's shoulder, saying, "Good one, Dolly. Good one." Lily spotted Cat and grabbed the arm of her companion, rushing over.

Dolly and Cat eyed each other.

Black Irish, Cat thought. That's what Kate would have called the girl with the light eyes and dark hair and smattering of freckles across the bridge of her nose. Her teeth were straight and white and her arms were hard and muscular.

She accepted Lily's big bear hug and then held up her castless arm, wiggling the bandages aside so Lily could see the wound.

"Cool scar," Lily said. She turned to Dolly. "I saved her from bleeding to death with a Stayfree Maxi Pad." They laughed together as Cat nodded, reluctantly. That day suddenly seemed years ago.

"Hey," Lily said. "I'm glad y'all got to meet, since Cat's gonna be working with us tomorrow," Lily said to Dolly.

Cat's gonna be working with us?! She said nothing and kept grinning, feeling like an idiot rag doll.

To Cat, Lily said, "We're still tearing out the innards of that old carriage house." She turned toward Dolly. "A three-man job, right?"

Dolly nodded.

Then Lily playfully smacked Cat's shoulder. "Pick you up, say seven-ish?"

"Why so early?"

"I gotta pick up Dolly in town."

"Fine."

After a few awkward minutes, Lily and her minion went to get groceries, leaving Cat standing alone in front of the

215

deli counter. Suddenly not caring what she might make for lunch in the morning, she left her empty basket and walked toward the door. Before she made her exit, she caught a glimpse of the two standing in front of the frozen foods, considering a pizza box. Cat watched Dolly say something to Lily, whose mouth opened wide as she released that loud laugh that began in her belly. Cat walked through the doors. Halfway down the creek road she realized the knuckles of her right hand, as she gripped the wheel, were white and tight. She relaxed them; then thought of this Dolly-person making Lily laugh that way, and had to relax them again.

It took only a long bath and thoughts of Melissa to help her get past it. She lay in the water and felt the hurt soak away— replaced by a growing desire. She got out of the tub, dried her-self, and put on a cool black tank-top and a pair of tight blue jeans. It was Mike who alerted her to Melissa's arrival. He sat straight up, tail wamping, right in front of the door. His muffled barks were excited as he waited for Melissa to arrive.

"You're a fool," Cat said, shaking her head as he eyed her over his shoulder. "I think you've got an even bigger crush on her than I do."

He whined and then tried a crackling bark, like a lovelorn adolescent.

"Pathetic. You won't catch me begging for attention. No way." She dropped to the couch and flipped open a magazine. "See how cool I am?"

The shepherd was no longer listening as footfalls landed on the porch and the door swung open. Melissa entered without knocking, put down her load, and immediately knelt in front of the shepherd. She hugged him around his neck and kissed his nose. He whimpered and rolled to his back for a belly rub, exposing himself, tongue lagging.

Cat put the magazine down and looked over. "You are ruining my dog."

"Ooh, you're a big scary animal," Melissa said, rubbing his tummy. "Too big and ferocious for me."

Cat came off the couch. "Look at him; he's supposed to be a guard dog. Disgusting. He might as well be a poodle."

Mike gazed up into Melissa's eyes as she scratched under his chin. "You big dope," Cat said to the dog. "You should be ashamed of yourself."

"Don't you listen to that jealous old woman," Melissa whispered into Mike's flopped ear.

"Hey, now," Cat put her arms around Melissa, who was pulling a treat from her pocket. Mike took it to his bed in the corner.

"Something for me?" Cat teased.

Melissa said, "Pizza. Just what the doctor ordered."

Cat poured wine and they sat on the porch, pressed close on the swing, watching the sun sink. It was leaving a pink and amber sky in its wake.

"How's the hand?"

"A little sore, I admit."

"That's why you need another week before you go back to work."

Cat was silent.

"You are going to wait to go back, aren't you?"

Squirm.

"Come on, Cat. *Be responsible.*"

"Aw, now." Cat nuzzled Melissa's neck. "You're not going to get mad at me before our *dessert,* are you?"

Without warning Melissa sprang up and went straight for the phone.

"What's Lily's number? Never mind—I remember."

Cat stood lamely by while Melissa lectured Lily on ripping stitches, tearing tendons, and infection. She even used the word *gangrene,* to Cat's horror.

Cat reached for the phone. Melissa warded her off as the voice on the other end chattered back. Finally, she passed the receiver.

"Are you outta your tree?" Lily demanded.

"Fine. I'll be careful," Cat promised, and hung up.

After dinner, Cat brought their coffee to the porch and once again settled on the swing. It was late and all the peepers and crickets had quieted to sleep. Soon though, there was a rising racket of birdsongs coming from the woods across the road. It sounded like dozens of birds gathering for a late night concert. They each listened, bewildered, until Cat finally laughed.

"What is it?" Melissa turned to her.

"Mockingbird," Cat said. "Odd to hear him out so late."

"Pretty, though."

Cat pointed out the beats between each song and then identified its kind as best she could.

"Mockingbirds are so cool," she said. "They can do it all. That's why other birds hate them. They're jealous."

And this made her think about Dolly and her own rising jealousy. Was Dolly, like a mockingbird, able to do it all? Hadn't Cat reserved that position for herself: writer, carpenter, hot sex machine, if she'd only get the chance?

"Let's go inside," Melissa whispered now into Cat's ear, joining the thoughts. They entered the kitchen and Melissa put their coffee cups on the counter. She brought Cat close, one arm around her waist, running her fingers gently along the ridge of Cat's spine, finding that tender place at its base, sending a shiver through Cat's whole body.

Cat said, "Learn that in medical school?"

"Sort of. From a massage therapist studying the erogenous zone. I was a willing candidate for her research."

Belt buckles click. Curled copper and fine golden strands weave slowly together; fingers lace, unlace, braid, unbraid; palms smooth and cup curves; lips and eyes open, close, search, discover. The joined pair move and sway as one. Slow dancing without music from the light of the kitchen to the dark of the living room. Together, knees bending, lowering. Unfurling skin and bones, layering over and under. Buttons work open, belts loosen; shoes toed free and tossed to corners. Denim and flannel and cotton peel, revealing soft skin on soft skin, matching molds merging. Arms and legs tangle and untangle. Tongues slide, circle, taste. Breaths quicken. Slowing motion, tightropes of muscle grip, wrap, and hold. Bellies heave surges. Each pour and spill over and over again, until there comes a slow receding, a calming to ripples. Their bodies knot as one—wash ashore. They breathe and relax together, falling back, easing grips from the other's rescuing limbs.

Cat's hand, pressing her lover's shoulder, first felt the tremor. Lifting her head, she frowned. Through the dim glow of the firelight, Melissa's hand raised to her mouth. Crying? Cat leaned over. The shaking came in spasms now. What had she done? Jesus. She reached for the hand and Melissa rolled over and into her cross-legged lap.

"What?" Cat asked, hovering above the shaking body. Encircling her with her arms, pulling her close, burying her face in the softness of Melissa's hair, breathing in the mingled scent of their sex. "Please," she whispered. "What's going on?"

Laughter, not crying, had caused Melissa's quaking. Lifting her head, she put a finger against Cat's worried lips.

"You're laughing?"

Melissa tried to compose herself. Cat sat, dejected, trying to make sense of this. She'd never had anyone actually *laugh* at the height of lovemaking. Once, a woman had cried, but she'd understood that. It was emotional. And, once, she remembered she had almost wanted to laugh but she'd suppressed it, stuffed it away, and buried it before it could take hold of her and wreck the whole moment. But here was Melissa just yucking it up all over the place. Cat stared at her, waiting. After a time, Melissa leaned her forehead against Cat's shoulder.

"Oh ... my ... God," she said, catching a breath between each word. "That ... was ... unbelievable."

A laugher. That's what Melissa was. She'd heard about them. Cat found herself grinning, and then giggling, and then laughing outright as Melissa started all over again. Composure lost, each time they looked at each other. Finally, they leaned together in an aching exhaustion. The sweat that had glistened on their bodies was drying cold against their skin.

Cat snatched the quilt from the back of her reading chair and snuggled it around them. She found Melissa's hand beneath the cover and clasped it in her own. They were quiet for a long moment. Watching the fire.

"You're a laugher?" she said, grinning at Melissa, who smiled back.

"Never before you," Melissa told her, raising her hand like a Girl Scout taking her oath.

Cat shook her head. "Damn," she said, reaching out a hand to push curling strands away from the fire-lit green eyes. "I wish I knew what was so damn funny."

Chapter Thirteen

Melissa stayed the night and in the morning, Cat found her talking to Lily in the kitchen. They were talking about her, she was sure. While she'd been in the shower, the remnants of last night's dinner had been cleared, and Melissa was washing up the last plate. On the counter was her thermos and cooler packed with a lunch. Melissa handed Cat a cup of cream-colored coffee, just the way she liked it.

"I found some tuna fish in your cupboard." Melissa's hand brushed her shoulder and inspired a tingling to creep through her. I made you a sandwich and chicken noodle soup, à la Campbell's."

Lily stood grinning.

"Thanks." Cat grabbed her jacket. "What are you all smiling about?" She looked at Lily, who quickly moved around the corner while Cat said her good-byes.

"You are great," Cat said to Melissa.

"No, *you* are great."

"No, *you* are." Cat pecked at her cheek.

Lily's head poked around. "Enough already. You're both great, really. Let's go. We got work to do." She headed for the door.

Cat and Melissa laughed.

"Had fun last night," Cat said, not moving her arms from around her lover.

"Had fun this morning." Melissa's lips found hers.

"You make me weak."

"That, too."

"When will I see you again?" Cat asked.

"You mean, when will we share this precious moment?" Melissa's eyebrows raised in innocence. "Are we in love or just friends?"

Cat frowned.

"Or is that just some cheesy song running through my head?"

Laughing, Cat lifted Melissa from her feet. She was light—lighter even than she looked. "I like you. I mean—" Cat set her down. "I mean, I *like* you."

"You better get out of here before your boss fires you." Melissa snapped a dishrag at her.

Cat turned. "You used to be a jock. Didn't you?"

Melissa headed back to the sink, waving her off.

"What was it? Field hockey?" Cat made an elaborate show of wiping her mouth. "Yuk, I kissed an athlete." And she disappeared through the door.

"I was just telling Dolly, yesterday," Lily said as she turned onto an unfamiliar city street, "how me and Hannah had picked out Melissa for you a long time ago."

Cat stared out the window. If she had heard this once in the last two months, she'd heard it a million times.

"So, are you two thinking of moving in together?" Lily asked this the same way she might have asked, *So are you two thinking of going to the movies together?*

"Lil, we've only been dating for two months."

"Two months and two days," Lily corrected her. "What

222

are you waiting for? She's the best thing to walk into your life. You gotta admit it."

"I do admit it." Cat pulled a cigarette out of the pack. "I just don't think everybody has to live together right away."

"Why not? Me and Hannah been doing it for nearly ten years ..."

"Fifteen," Cat said.

"Yeah, see ... went by so quick I can hardly remember. The point is—living together is a good thing."

Cat lit the cigarette and cracked the window.

"No smoking in the van," Lily said.

"What?"

"Dolly's allergic to smoke. Makes her sneeze. So no smoking in the van."

Cat propped her foot on the dashboard, rolled her window down and dragged slowly on the cigarette.

"I'll blow it out the window."

"Can't you wait till we get there?"

"Look, I'm not quitting smoking in the van—something I've been doing every morning on my way to work for the last ten years—just because of some temporary worker's allergies. How long's she gonna be on the job anyway?"

Lily finally turned the van onto a skinny one way side street. "Well, this job we got is a three-man job, for sure."

"Three-man job? When have we ever needed another person?"

"And with your arm being weak and all, I'm gonna keep Dolly on through the summer."

"The whole summer?!"

"Look, it'll make it easier on all of us, Cat. We're getting older; we deserve to take it easy. And I've figured it out. I can make more money keeping Dolly on."

They pulled up in front of an old brick apartment building.

Lily shifted into park and jumped out. She leaped up the steps and pushed a button beside the big glass doors. Turning, she waved to Cat just as the dark-haired fiddle player emerged from the building. The pair made their way to her side of the van. Lily opened the door.

"Reach behind you there, Cat, and grab that pillow."

She pulled out the soft blue pillow, the one that usually leaned in the corner of her big leather chair up at Lily and Hannah's house. Her pillow. She handed it to Lily.

"Why don't you climb out and let Dolly in there, Cat?"

She did as she was instructed and as she returned to her seat, her eyes met Dolly's. Each tried a smile and a nod. Lily leaned in and placed the pillow on the tool-bench between the cab seats.

"There, Dolly. That ought to cushion your ride."

Dolly climbed over Cat's lunch box, lifted it, and threw it in the back. When the three were settled, shoulder to shoulder, Lily backed out and they drove off in an awkward silence. Finally, Lily cleared her throat.

"You should hear Dolly play her fiddle, Cat. She's really great. Got a band, don'tcha Dolly?"

Dolly nodded. She looked uncomfortable. For an instant Cat felt her pain. Literally stuck in between two friends, whose shoulders had, for over ten years, been the only ones rubbing together in this van. Lily went on about the Celtic music that Dolly's band, Mulligan Stew, played all over town.

"There's even a fella in the group," Lily continued, "who plays a drum with a bone. What kind of bone is that again, Dolly?"

"Deer." Dolly nodded. "It's a deer bone."

"That's right. How 'bout that, Cat?" Lily peered across Dolly at Cat. "A *deer* bone." The van swerved almost onto the shoulder.

"Stay in your lane," Cat muttered.

"I already told Dolly all about you and your book and how you're gettin' famous."

Rather than rallying conversation, this statement halted all real discussion completely. They rode to the job site listening to Lily point out fluffy white clouds in the shapes of power tools. She called to the cows chewing cuds behind barbed fencing, and once slowed to allow a squirrel to cross her path.

"Git along little dogie," she said out her window.

When they finally pulled into the driveway of the carriage house, Cat threw open the door and tumbled out. A burst of uneasy air followed her. As was her routine, she walked to the back of the truck and unlatched its doors, flinging them wide. What she saw shocked her.

Tools that normally would be scattered along the floor of the van were clamped and hung along the sides. A newly installed pegboard held packets of drill bits and Allen wrenches, screws and nails, nuts and bolts. A magnetic strip had been glued along the edge and held an assortment of reciprocating and jigsaw blades. Crowbars clamped; wood, metal, and Sheetrock saws hung in an orderly fashion; mallets and hammers had been strapped under a bungee cord. Along the left side, three rows of shelving were stacked floor to ceiling. These held the boxed tools: nail guns, circular saws, wrenches, and screwdrivers. Along the floor to one side, in a neat row, was the biggest equipment: ladder, miter saw, benches, and the heaviest of all, the table saw.

"Surprise!" Lily slapped her shoulder. "Look what Dolly did!"

Cat turned and glowered at the woman who would not meet her eyes.

"All this." Lily's arm swept across the organized workshop. "It's what we've been meaning to do for years, remember?"

Cat forced a nod.

"Only one mention of it to Dolly, and bingo, it's done!"

Seizing her tool belt that now hung from a special blue hook of its own, Cat wrapped it around her waist. Its buckled ends refused to meet. She pulled again, this time tighter, there was still a good two inches to go. Jesus, had she really gained that much weight since she'd been laid off? No. She looked down at her jeans, admittedly a slightly bit more snug, but not uncomfortable. Not two inches uncomfortable. What the hell? She looked down and noticed that her tools were not in their usual spots. Instead of their seemingly (to some) haphazard placement, each was now lodged in a matching sheath or pouch. Her pencils, (sharpened she noticed), were snug in the sleeve that had been made to hold them. A flat-tipped screwdriver hung in its long loop. Her measuring tape had been clipped to its clasp. When she reached in the pouch for her speed square, she was not as usual, poked by loose screw points. Both Lily and Dolly were watching her scrutiny.

Lily started, "Dolly was using it while you were gone." She reached to a red hook and pulled down a spanking clean belt, its pouches filled with gleaming new tools. On its side, in big red letters, Lily had written, *Dolly.* "Now, you got your own." She grinned.

As Dolly strapped it on, Cat struggled to cinch her own. She hooked her belt and made a reach for a crowbar.

"Nope." Lily grabbed the iron from her. "Melissa says all you can do is watch."

"Oh, for Christ's sakes, Lil."

"Nope. And, no cussin' on the job, either. Remember?"

Cat stormed around to the side door of the truck and grabbed her smokes. She lit one and sucked hard, bringing the tip almost to a flame. Lily came around the side.

"Look, I promised Melissa you wouldn't be worrying that hand. I've got to keep to my promises." She patted her shoulder.

"What am I s'posed to do then? Sit around and pick my ass?"

"Cat."

"Lil, you let me decide what I can and can't do. Believe me, my arm'll let me know when it's too much."

Lily looked at her. "All right then. Long as you promise not to overdo. Lily nudged her ribs. "Don't want to put a crimp in your sex life again, now do ya?"

With the exception of unloading and loading, fetching and retrieving, holding and balancing, Cat was allowed to do nothing. At first it was just Lily who grabbed tools from her hand. But soon Dolly was set to the task. It was Dolly's offer to carry the end of a two-by-four Cat was balancing on her shoulder that sent her to nearly clipping the girl standing behind her.

"I'm fine," she barked. Dolly backed off.

After lunch Lily benched Cat for the day, saying that she could tell she was tired by how grouchy she was getting.

"I brought along some magazines for you to read," Lily said, handing her the slick pile. "Go over there and sit in the sun." She grabbed a neatly folded paint tarp and handed it to Cat, who believed the rags took up less space stuffed under the front seats, the way they used to be.

She flipped the tarp open, finding a sunny spot on the lawn. She hated this. This was worse than not working at all. She hated having somebody else on the job. Anybody. And this woman was driving her crazy. She'd never seen anybody try so hard to be so perfect. And Lily had turned into a fucking cheerleader: *Good thinking, Dolly! Way to swing a hammer! Never saw anybody who could measure so perfect.* On and on, ratcheting up Cat's headache every time she opened her mouth. She pulled the tarp across the grass and into the shade of a big maple tree.

Dolly was fast, she'd give her that. And she maneuvered fine around Lily's clownsiness. She'd learned, during lunch, that Dolly, like Lily, had worked a steel high-rise once.

"She ain't afraid of heights." Lily turned to Dolly. "Cat's afraid of heights. Ever since I let go of that ladder."

Cat glared.

Lily ignored her. "But she'll still get up there. Won'tcha, Cat?"

Cat chewed her tuna sandwich, not answering.

"Like my granddaddy used to say," Lily breezed on without her. "A brave man is the one who admits his fear and goes up anyway. The coward, well that's the one that don't admit *or* don't go up." She slapped her own knee, grinning. Cat wanted to tell her she was acting like a fool.

She was relieved to lie down on the tarp. Get away from Lily's jabbering. She read one page of a magazine and fell asleep.

Lily's boot, tapping her own, awakened her.

"We're done. Ready to go?"

Cat shaded her brow and squinted in the spotty light.

All the tools and debris had been cleared from the site, she noticed. "C'mon, Dolly's waiting in the van."

This was totally humiliating.

Lily slung her arm across Cat's shoulder and walked her

to the back of the van. Together they folded the tarp like a bed sheet.

"Listen, Dolly says she's got to go on a fiddle tour for a couple of weeks. Think you and me can handle this by ourselves starting tomorrow?"

Cat nodded, relieved.

After dropping off Dolly, Cat and Lily rode in an uncommon and uncomfortable silence. Cat smoked and stared out the window while Lily drove too slowly in the fast lane, as she always did.

"Why don't you like Dolly?" Lily finally asked.

Cat looked up, surprised. "I don't *not* like Dolly." She was, of course, lying. "What makes you say that?"

"You were awfully quiet today."

"Yeah, well." Cat examined her cigarette. "So was Dolly. You were the one yammerin' away. Who could get a word in?"

"Well, somebody had to talk. You were being so grumpy."

Cat was suddenly exhausted. "Sorry, I think my arm's just bugging me."

"Maybe if you just spend some time with Dolly. You should hear this Celtic music. Amazing."

"Maybe so," Cat said, and went back to staring out the window.

When Lily dropped her at the back door she promised to be ready for their pool night by six thirty. It had been almost two months since they'd had their Tuesday night game down at The Pocket.

On the answering machine there was a blinking message from Marce telling Cat, "Call me right away. It's not an emergency—it's just something good."

She managed to catch Marce between classes. "Her name is

Isobel Richards and she runs the Literature Department for this girls' school just outside of Glasgow," Marce said. "I met her last week while she was here with her husband for a conference. He's an anthropology professor over there. I had lunch with them and wound up mentioning you and your book. Anyway, she just emailed me and asked if I thought you might be interested in teaching American literature at her school."

"Me?" Cat was dumbfounded. "Why would anyone think I can teach?"

"Cat—you'd be great. Will said you'd read every book in the Little Galway library by the time you were ten."

"Will exaggerates." But he hadn't. From the time she was eight, she'd bugged librarians for every book from *Tom Sawyer* to *Pentimento*. Once, when she was fourteen, she'd demanded the library stock *The Story of O*, and for this she'd been banned from their premises for a year.

"And you are qualified, Cat," Marce said. "You've got your MFA. You've written a book, for God's sake."

"But—"

"Think about it. I'll forward her email to you; just talk to her."

"I don't know, Marce." But she felt something like excitement fluttering inside.

"I gotta run. My students, I'm sure, are waiting on pins and needles for my next fascinating lecture."

Cat laughed and then said, "Thanks, Marce."

"You mean you'll give it a shot?"

"I'll … give it some thought. Honest. You're a sweetheart to think of me."

"Yes," Marce said, with a smile in her voice. "I am."

⌘⌘

The idea of teaching American literature to a bunch of teenaged Scottish girls terrified her. She wasn't a teacher. Then she heard Lily's voice, *be the water* ... something Lily'd picked up in a meditation book and said whenever there was a glitch on the job. This certainly did feel like a hand of fate, as Lily would surely call it. A sign, in fact, bright neon, if she were to take it that way.

Cat looked down at her feet and watched the suds swirl and swish around her toes sliding easily down toward the drain. No obstacles there—paths of least resistance and all that, she thought. She dried off, making her way to her office where she clicked on her email and brought up Marce's forwarded message.

It was a year-long appointment—she read the details. Travel and housing would be provided and a small stipend; Isobel admitted, apologetically, to its meagerness. No, it wasn't a great deal, Cat thought, but it was the perfect deal for her. She wrote back her interest and pressed the *send* button. She thought of the message zipping across the Atlantic on invisible wires ... zooming her words toward her possible fate. After she turned off her computer she called Melissa, but there was no answer. Maybe, Cat thought, she'd stop to see her after pool night, and tell her the good news.

Dave the bartender was glad to see them. He admired Cat's unbandaged purple scar as he set down two Newcastles in front of them. They tapped glasses and sipped through the foamy beer.

"So, this thing with Melissa's going pretty good, huh?" Lily said, chalking the cue stick that she'd pulled from the wall.

"Yeah, I really like her." Cat racked the balls and then stuffed quarters into the side of the table. "She's funny, smart, reads a lot. All those good things. I like her art. It makes me see differently. Think differently." She broke the triangle of balls apart, sending a stripe into a corner pocket. Her healing arm balked at leaning too hard into the shot. "I'm not calling them tonight."

"Not with that arm," Lily concurred. "Are you two thinking about living together?"

Cat sunk the ball, straightened and looked at her, "Will ya cut that out? We are *not* thinking of living together."

Lily came around the table, and broke open a pack of cigarettes. "That's just stupid, Cat." She started in on her. "You've met the perfect woman, an artist *and* a doctor for goodness sakes. You've got the perfect job, the perfect house, perfect friends, hell, even Will's turning out to be the perfect family. You've got it all, just like me and Hannah. What more could you want?"

Cat bent and squinted across the table, hoping for a better set up than what was there. The question made her uneasy— as if she'd done something wrong. Lily thought everybody in the world would be happy if they just lived like her and Hannah. But things were different now; for Cat, this time, there were factors that Lily didn't even know about.

"I've got other things going on right now ..." Cat said, missing her shot.

"What things?" Lily leaned and smacked two solids against each other without even looking. They spun in place, then one teetered and sank into a side pocket.

"Well, I've got this book to sell, for one ..."

"It's selling. The book is selling." Lily waved her stick in the air.

"And, I've got another one to write ..."

"So write it!" Lily shook her head. "You are just making up a bunch of excuses, like you always do. You know what? You are a *saboteur!*"

232

If she hadn't been so serious, Cat would have burst out laughing. "Which means," Lily went on, ignoring her, "that for the first time in your sorry little life you've met the woman of your dreams and you could have everything, but you're too scared and so you wreck everything rather than making it right!"

Cat set the stick down on the corner of the pool table. "You don't know anything about it. You don't even make any sense."

"So tell me!"

"Well, I was going to tell you. But you just go off like a damn firecracker. And I can swear now, because I'm on my own time."

"Yeah? Well, I'm not fire-cracking now, am I? So ... tell me."

Cat swallowed and then looked across the table. "Listen, Lil. There's a chance I might go to Scotland."

Lily stared. "Scotland? For what?"

"I told you I want to write a story about my grand-mother."

"You have to go to Scotland to write about *Kate*?"

Cat felt exasperation itching beneath her skin. Of all the people in the world, you'd think your best friend would be the one who would understand, instead of everyone else around.

"For how long?" Lily gnawed the side of her thumb.

"A year."

Lily stared at her for a moment. "What the hell will you do for work?" she asked, leaning into the table.

"You're swearing. There's a teaching job at a girls' school—American lit."

"Teach? You ain't any kind of teacher." Lily punctuated the air with her stick. "What about carpentry? What about

233

Melissa? What about that new little baby coming into your world?"

"Lily, you don't understand ..."

"No? The hell I don't. And I can swear on my own time, too. You're just like you always are, too selfish to commit to anybody or anything except for your stupid stories ..." The sudden change in Lily's face revealed that even she knew she'd crossed a big line.

Cat threw her hands up in frustration, knocking a beer glass from the table onto the floor.

"Now look what you've done!" Lily yelped, shoving her aside to get to the spill.

"Hey, now." Cat pushed back. "You can be such a jerk, Cameron."

"Me?" Lily body-blocked her. "You, Cat Hood, are an idiot."

Cat grabbed hold of Lily's shirt and yanked her forward. Hustling, Dave jumped the bar and jerked the two apart. He dangled them by their collars like a couple of rag dolls.

"I'm going to have to ask you girls to take this outside," he said, half laughing. Then he gave them each a good shake before shoving them through the door. "Pool is off limits for two weeks!"

Kicked out of a bar. It hadn't happened to them since they were nineteen. They slunk into the truck cab and slouched into the seats. Kicked out of their favorite bar. Banned for two weeks.

"Well, now you went and did it." Lily lit a cigarette.

"*I* did it? You started the fucking fight!"

Cat threw the truck into reverse and screeched out of the parking lot. If Lily said one more word, she'd dump her sorry ass right out.

As the truck wound into the hills, darkness swallowed the glow of headlights. Neither spoke the remainder of the ride. Lily hunched herself against the door, smoking a pack of cigarettes, one after the other. When they pulled in, Hannah was standing in the driveway with her fists planted on her hips. She motioned for Cat to roll down her window.

"What's the matter with you two?"

They sank into their seats, suddenly allied in their misbehavior. Cat looked to her lap where her hands had landed. She slid her finger along the ridged scar. They'd been tattled on. Dave the bartender had called Hannah, worried that the two might try to kill each other before they got home.

"Did you have to embarrass yourselves in front of everyone? Not to mention embarrassing *me*."

Cat pictured Hannah grabbing hold of Lily's ear and dragging her inside for a good thrashing, which she deserved.

"What came over you? Two grown women. Best friends, supposedly." Hannah motioned Lily out of the truck and pushed her toward the house.

"You go home, Cat." Hannah walked away from the cab. "Good luck explaining this to Melissa."

As she drove off, Cat recalled the very first tussle she'd ever had with Lily. They'd been ten years old.

Together they had entered and won a contest on the back of a cereal box. The prize had been a two-headed troll doll with green and blue hair. Thinking back now, it was a truly hideous thing. One body, two heads, four eyes, two mouths and noses.

The problem? How to share the winnings. After much shouting and yelling, pushing and shoving, the two had wrestled across the floor of Cat's bedroom, the troll yanking between them.

Suddenly, out of nowhere, Kate had swooped in, kicked

235

the two apart and grabbed the troll from their hands. As she made her way down the stairs, the two little girls hung onto her apron, pulling and begging her to stop.

"Keep away," were her only words of warning as she threw the doll onto the cutting board and raised the cleaver above it.

"*No!* Don't do it." Lily screeched. "Give it to Cat. She can have it. I'd rather her have it."

Kate had paused, cleaver suspended.

"I'm no King Solomon," was what Kate said as she brought down the knife like a hurling guillotine, halving the doll neatly in two; leaving each piece with one head, one arm, and one leg. She handed Cat and Lily each half a troll.

"There now, ya both deserve your prize."

Cat laughed in spite of herself now, remembering the scene. *Yeah, well, you were a great surgeon, Kate,* she wished she could tell her grandmother now. *Dividing that doll brought us back together, Gran.* She wondered now what act could unite the pair this time?

Instead of heading home, she made her way toward town, landing at the French Bakery Shop whose service was attended by beautiful European-looking women behind the counter. Cat and Lily had named them according to their regions. Tonight it was Switzerland. There was one free table near the window and Cat grabbed a rumpled newspaper and settled with her coffee. As she skimmed through the editorials, she was interrupted by someone leaning over her paper. Marce.

"Hey, fancy meeting you here," Cat said. When they hugged, a little shyly maybe, Cat could feel a rising mound of baby beneath Marce's coat. Without thinking, she opened the jacket to admire.

"Whoa, mamma!" She grinned.

"Getting big, aren't I?"

"I'll say. How much longer, two months?"

"We're into the weeks—six weeks," Marce said, as Cat first helped her take off her jacket and then pulled out a chair for her. "Not long, considering. "

"How's my brother handling all this?" she asked, handing Marce the sugar and unwrapping utensils from a napkin, which she carefully spread out on Marce's nearly imperceptible lap. She then seated herself, looking up expectantly.

"Exactly like you," Marce said, shaking her head.

"Ouch." Cat squirmed. "Kind of annoying, all that special attention, huh?"

"Oh, you'd think I had some crippling disease. Sometimes he acts like I'm dying."

"You've wrecked my brother, turned him to mush." Cat smiled.

"He's cute to see like this, don't you think?" Marce stirred her coffee.

"Makes me think he's going to be a great dad."

"Me, too. Have you talked to him today?"

"No. Why?" Cat asked.

Marce shifted in her discomfort.

"You can tell me. We're supposed to be family, right?"

"Well, the house in Sellarsville has a bid—looks promising."

"That's good news, right?"

"Yes and no. Yes, we've got the money now. No, because we haven't even broken ground to build the new place. I want to rent a place near school till it's done. Will wants to hook a trailer up to your cabin while we build."

It was Cat who now shifted in her discomfort. "Well, now, I uh ..."

"Cat," Marce said, touching her shoulder. "I live with him, remember? Look at me."

Cat looked.

"I want you to tell him no." Marce nodded. "He refuses to listen to me. You stand up to him. Don't let him bully you into this. I'll be right behind you."

"Tell him to come around and see me," Cat said, not wanting Marce to worry about any of this. She had enough to worry about with the baby coming along. "We'll talk things out."

They were quiet for a moment and then Cat laughed. "I kind of like having a teammate."

"Teammate?"

"You, I mean."

Marce smiled and put her hands over her belly. "Can I tell you something ?"

Cat waited.

"It's a giant secret." Her sister-in-law raised two fingers and pointed to her middle.

Cat frowned. "There's two in there?"

"I just found out." Marce dug into her briefcase and pulled out a very fuzzy copy of what she said was a picture of two babies in a womb. She pointed to a few circled knobs, explaining there were the second pair of feet and hands, and then showed why the doctor thought one was a boy and one was a girl. Cat couldn't see any of it, but she didn't say.

"Twins."

"The doctor said she's been hiding behind her brother for the last few months." Marce ran a finger across the picture.

"Will doesn't know?" Cat asked.

"No. You're the first."

"Oh, boy."

"I know."

"How do you feel about it?" Cat asked.

"You know, when the doctor first said it I thought, *Oh my*

God, I'm thirty-eight years old. As if that were a bad thing. But then I thought, *Oh my God, I'm thirty-eight years old. I get a whole family in one shot!*"

Cat laughed.

"Could be our one and only chance at this parenthood thing."

"Well, there's little to do about it, except be in awe."

"Nice, Cat." Marce sipped from her teacup and then looked over. "Did you decide about Scotland?"

"I emailed Isobel. No word yet."

"Will you go?"

Cat shrugged. "I'm not sure, but I'm leaning toward it."

"How do you think Melissa and Lily will take it?" Marce asked.

"Melissa will be the easiest, I think. I gotta admit, though, I hate the idea of leaving her. Of leaving *us* right now. I think I might be falling in love with her, Marce. But this book is real and this job might be real. I can't just ignore it all."

Marce sipped her coffee. "You can control just about everything in a relationship, except timing. But if Melissa is all that she seems to be, she'll want you to go."

"That's what I'm thinking. Lily says I'm sabotaging the relationship."

"Are you?"

"No. I really do want this to work out."

"And it can, Cat. People have all kinds of relationships: long distance, live-in, live-out. It's up to you both to decide how you'll do it. What's right for Lily and Hannah is not necessarily right for you."

"Well, don't tell Lil that. She can't believe that someone wouldn't want to live the exact same fucking life that she's got ... Especially not me."

"Ouch," Marce's eyebrows raised in question.

Cat dismissed the ferocity of her tone with a wave of her hand. Sorry," she said. "Lily and I just had a fight. I told her about Scotland and she went ballistic. We got kicked out of The Pocket, for *brawling*," She tried a smile. "Can you believe it?"

"Sounds like she's afraid to lose you."

Cat said, "I think Lily's mostly afraid of change. She's happy as long everything remains static in her life. For a long time, I think I even believed that. You know?"

Marce nodded. "Have you ever wanted anything different from her before now? Have you ever told her that you do?"

"No, I guess I haven't." Cat's eyes searched Marce's, "I can't not write this book, Marce. I can't not go to Scotland. I want them both."

"Then you already know what you'll be doing."

"I guess so. You probably think I'm stubborn."

"You are a remarkable woman, Cat. Much, I imagine, like your grandmother was. Determined."

"You mean headstrong, don't you?" Cat smiled.

"Like Kate. You and Will are both like her, in your own ways."

Cat sat back and stared at Switzerland wiping down the counter. "Kate took off into the world because she was forced to," she said after a minute. "I don't really have to go. No one's making me."

Marce picked up her coffee. "Kate is making you," she murmured. "I think you know that. And I think you know she's right."

Chapter Fourteen

It was nice, Cat had to admit, having a girlfriend who really liked you. It was nice to hear the voice on the other end of the phone be glad that you called. And it was nice when that voice admitted to wanting to see you, too.

But a relationship like this brought responsibilities she'd not known before. Rounding the last curve before Melissa's house, she wondered how it would be possible to follow her dream without sacrificing the two of them. Marce had been right, she needed to tell Melissa about Scotland and to make this all manageable, because it was and it could be if they really wanted it.

Melissa must have heard her coming. The door opened and she was there, smiling and whisking her inside, clearly happy for the surprise visit. She immediately pulled Cat up the stairs to the studio above. She was covered in paint, her white Oxford shirt with the turned up collar and cuffs and long tail speckled in rainbow colors. A streak of blue crossed the bridge of her nose. Beneath the shirt she wore a pair of green silk boxers, also splattered with paint.

"I admit it," Melissa said, lifting a glass of wine to her lips. "I've been drinking and painting all night and I'm a little drunk by both right now."

Cat smiled. She'd never seen Melissa so loose. But she didn't mind being pushed back onto the pillows that Melissa piled on the tarp on the floor. She really didn't mind when a giggling Melissa slid the boots from her feet and unzipped her jeans, and then quickly lifted her shirt over her head. She was somewhat (pleasantly) startled when her pants were tugged from her legs. Lying there, watching Melissa pull off her own clothes then trip across the room to fetch the bottle of wine, her sweet ass bouncing slightly as she went, excited Cat and filled her with tenderness. Melissa slid a glass of red wine into Cat's hand and told her to lie still; she felt herself go weak in the rising desire.

Melissa kissed her neck and throat. "Close your eyes," she whispered. "Are you ready?"

She was ready for anything. At least she thought so until a chilly wetness tickled her nipple. Her eyes flew open to catch a quick glimpse of the slick paintbrush touching her skin. Bright orange swirls circled her breast. Her nipples stiffened even more—a reaction unexpected and a little embarrassing, Cat thought.

"I'm going to paint you." Melissa knelt above her. "In the nude."

"You are not," Cat said, covering her exposure.

"But you promised I could. Just the other night." She pouted.

"No, I didn't."

"Yes. You said I could paint you in the nude someday. Remember? We were on your porch."

Cat started to get up. "I thought you meant paint a picture of me—naked. Not paint my actual naked skin. Are you nuts?"

Melissa pulled her back down across her lap, cradling her. She whispered, "Just relax." With small strokes, she dabbed designs of orange around Cat's other breast.

Cat drained her wineglass and closed her eyes. She tried to slow her breathing but mostly everything was on fire. Moist, fingerlike tips ran across and over her skin. Yellows, greens, and blues, Cat imagined, conjured lines of some ancient sacred geometry around her own sacred geometry. She held up her wineglass to be refilled. Melissa slid her gently from the triangle of her thighs back onto the pillowed floor. She held the glass steady in her hand, but before she had a chance to sip, Melissa had tilted back her head and pressed her mouth down. Lips coaxed open by a quick tongue, she felt the hot wine dribbling from Melissa's mouth into her own. The burgundy missed some of its mark and ran over her chin onto her chest. The feathery brush was now dusting down her spine.

"What color?" she whispered.

"Dark red. Like the wine." Melissa's voice seemed far away behind her.

Cat shivered.

"Lie back. Stay still." Melissa gently ordered, spreading her arms and legs wide, as if making her ready to fan a snow angel.

"Oh God," Cat moaned.

Melissa then engaged three or four or a million—there was no counting—different brushes, producing a sensation like the sweep of a thousand individual strands of hair over her body. The finest brush tickled her lips, a fat brush grazing between her legs, in fast whisking strokes each insistently closer to her deepest places. Cat thought she might go mad.

With every smooth caress, she imagined another color—and her body responded with another quiver. Sparks exploded behind her closed eyes. The more strokes she felt flicking her skin, the more strokes she wanted. She imagined she must look something like a tattooed lady, head to toe covered in colors and this drove her even more insane. She reached for Melissa, but each time her fingers only slid through paint and warm sweat.

She could take the torture no more. Grabbing Melissa's wrists, she pulled. Together they slid naked and slick with paint into each other's arms.

Mouths searched as they gently wrestled positions. Cat stretched, spreading the length of matching limbs. Swimming together, their colors lathered, blending into one—a grayish blue. Melissa's face was streaked in yellow and green, her curls slicked with orange and peach.

It was Melissa who'd straddled and leaned back; Cat curled into her, first pressing cheek to belly, pulling thighs close, gently stroking with tongue and fingertips, hands grabbed hair, pushing mouth and tongue deeper. They held onto the wild bucking moment. Bursts of breath and sweat and sex erupted simultaneously. A single sneaking finger pressing up inside, igniting more explosions and the two rocked, holding on as they came together. Side by side, each on her back, catching breaths in long gasps.

"Jesus," Cat finally said.

At length, they managed to become upright. Melissa was looking at her, a slow smile spreading her mouth wide. She took Cat's hand and led her to the bathroom, where they stood looking at themselves in the long mirror. They were both blue. Smeared from toes to tits to tongues— slate blue. Cat thought of her ancient Pict ancestors, described as *berserkers* by her grandmother who loved the great tales of the fur-clad, blue-faced warriors.

"No wonder Hadrian built that wall," Cat said.

Melissa laughed. "We do look ferocious. That's for sure."

She leaned over and turned the knobs, filling the

oversized bathtub with warm sudsy water, and then she floated small lighted wax candles. One behind the other dipped into the Jacuzzi, balancing small glasses of Grand Marnier. She and Cat sat across from each other in the water, the candles rocking a little when Melissa started up the low jet, but then finding a steady rolling rhythm.

"Look up," Melissa said, pointing to the ceiling.

Above them was a huge square skylight, revealing a star-filled sky. It wasn't the first time Cat had been in this Jacuzzi—but it was the first time that the stars were out.

"It's not the same as your porch ..." Melissa said.

"Hey, it's great. Stars over the bathtub."

They gently washed the paint and sex from each other's skin and spooned around each other sipping Grand Marnier and resting.

Finally, after some quiet moments, Cat said softly, "I have something to tell you." She could feel the soft curve of Melissa's back against her chest. Water sounds, drips and plunks and trickles echoed. Steamy air swirled around the soft flickering lights of candles and stars. Cat imagined, for a moment, that they were tucked away in some mystical, tropical rain forest, where they never would be found. The water around them shimmered blue and gray, and she watched, silver at times.

Did she really want to give this up for a whole year? She caressed Melissa's shoulders and reached around to stroke her breasts and thighs. Did she even want to disrupt this one small fantastic moment in the interest of bringing up a colder reality?

Melissa was quiet, waiting, pressing Cat's hands closer as they journeyed over her body.

"I might have a chance to go to Scotland—for a year."

⌘⌘

It went as Marce had predicted it would go, maybe because Marce had seen something in Melissa that she, Cat, had not quite believed until that moment.

I'm in love with you, the beautiful doctor said. *This will merely rearrange time for us.*

The bath scene, its swirling blue water, and Melissa in her arms were still on Cat's mind as she rolled the truck into her driveway the next morning, almost hitting the back of the work van. Lily was strutting around the yard, looking at her watch.

"Where the hell have you been?" she demanded. "I've been waiting for fifteen minutes."

Cat got out slowly and looked at her own watch, "Yeah, well that's your problem. You're still five minutes early." She left Lily standing in the driveway. She had to change, and feed Mike. Thank God, she had washed the last of the paint from her hair at Melissa's.

As they rode in silence to the job site, the fight of the previous evening simmered to an angry huffiness. Tested only occasionally by a monosyllabic exchange between them, each smoked and watched the road.

The sun was barely up by the time they reached the job site. Already beads of sweat were rolling from Cat's hairline down her skin. It was going to be a true scorcher today—temps in the nineties. She looked across the lawn to the house where they'd be working. Although palatial in size, both grounds and structure seemed just a little worn. The yard, barren of trees, was beginning to shimmer in the heat, like one of those weird sci-fi movies where any minute a silver spacecraft is going to land. At the center of a wrought iron table, an umbrella was stuck at half-mast, useless against an already brutal sun.

"Dang, it's hot," Lily said as she surveyed a thick concrete wall jutting from the house. "I can't remember the last time it was this hot, this early."

The wall stood at about shoulder height, six feet long and two feet thick, a combination of granite rock, cement, and steel rods. Cat suspected it had been slapped together years ago, probably by some enthusiastic homeowner after he'd read a how-to book on stonework. Girls with Hammers had been hired to knock it down and replace it with a screened-in porch. But the porch would come later.

"Gimme your hammer." Lily snapped at Cat.

"How about *please?*" she said, handing it over.

With the claw, Lily loosened a staple pinning a fat wire to the house. She grabbed at it and pulled. "We gotta move this."

"Must be connected to that meter." Cat pointed over Lily's shoulder to the glass-globed clockworks protruding from the side of house.

Lily got a foothold on the wall and hitched herself up. Grabbing a jutting rock, she caught her toe in a grout gully. Cat watched her scramble to the top of the wall and straddle it, resting before she stood up and walked its length to the corner of the house. She reached above and peeled back a shingle to peek under it. Yanking it like a loose tooth, she tossed it down over her shoulder, just missing Cat's head.

"Hey, watch it." She danced clear.

"I can't see a thing." Lily dislodged and flung another one.

"Quit throwing that shit at me." Cat kicked at the shingle by her foot.

"No cussin'."

"I'm cussin'; get over it."

"Well, get outta the way, then." Lily ducked for a different view. "I can't see a friggin' thing." She jumped down. "We're gonna have to go into the attic."

The pitch of the roof rose high above them; black shingles steamed as the sun's rays vaporized the morning dew. Outside, it was ninety-five degrees at least; inside, up there in that attic—Cat visualized no windows and itchy insulation under their feet and who knew what nesting above their heads—it would be a hundred and ten.

"Now?"

"Yes, now ... what do you think ... we're gonna wait till Christmas?"

They headed for the back door, halting just short of the threshold.

"Holy shit." Cat said. They both stopped in their tracks. The rotting smell, coming from inside the kitchen, was gagging. They wrapped their arms across their noses. Along the counters were stacks of unscraped dinner plates and forks and knives caked with old food strewn along the Formica. The sink, void of water, was full of cold coffee mugs floating chunks of soured cream.

"Are they home?" Cat whispered as she caught sight of a wooden bowl on a small table across the kitchen. It was piled high with blackened bananas.

"Holy Fred Sanford," Lily choked.

There were damp heaps of soured clothing squished between ragged piles of newspaper on the floor. A garbage bag leaked coffee grounds and eggshells. Above it, hovering in a black cloud, were millions of tiny fruit flies.

"Maybe they're dead," she said.

"For God's sakes, quit that." Lily's foot hit a kitty litter box, bumping to life an acrid acidic fume that stung inside their nostrils. They flew outside, each close to vomiting, and stood looking back at the house like it had personally assaulted them—which, Cat thought, it *had.*

"Freaks. How'd you snag this beauty, Lil?"

"I didn't know. I don't ask about the housekeeping situation when I quote, Cat."

"How could you not know? Didn't you come do the estimate?"

"I never went inside. I looked at the outside and just winged the rest." Lily sat down on the overgrown lawn.

"Perfect." Cat got a water bottle from the van. "What are we going to do?"

"What do you mean, *what are we gonna do?*" Lily turned on her. "We're going to work. What else?" She surveyed the stone wall. "I'm making some serious jack on this job."

"You're kidding, right?"

"You know, you're nothing but a princess carpenter." Lily grabbed a flashlight. "Dolly wouldn't be acting like such a baby."

Cat ground her molars. Lily, headed to the van, was continuing her lecture, which had now veered to the American work ethic.

"People gotta live up to their commitments. Especially about jobs. You think I can just walk away 'cause the house is a little messy?"

Cat managed to keep her mouth shut. They went back into the pig-house, holding their breath, and down a hallway. It took some searching to find the cut-out leading up into the attic. It was located in the ceiling of a stuffy little closet crammed with winter coats, an ironing board, and several overstuffed shoe boxes spewing Christmas tree ornaments.

"Where the hell is anybody?" Cat wondered, clearing a spot to put a ladder.

"Here," Lily handed her the flashlight. "You finish clearing this out. I'll be right back." And she left.

⌘⌘

Sweat had soaked through to Cat's underwear, and her socks were soggy by the time she'd finished pushing junk out of the closet.

"Lil?" she called down the hall. When it was clear that Lily was nowhere in the house, she made her way outside. It was the sound of the van's rumbling engine that caught her attention. She found Lily inside sipping a bottle of cool water and talking on the cell phone. Arctic wind, Cat imagined, from the AC was blowing her hair from her face. Cat knocked on the window, startling Lily from her conversation.

"I'll be right there." She yelled from inside the van. She thumbed over her shoulder. "Get the ladder from the back."

Cat felt fury rising.

They struggled the ladder up into the hole and Lily ascended with her flashlight. "I'm gonna need the battery drill," she yelled as her head disappeared into the attic.

I'll give you the battery drill, Cat thought, *right up your ass.* She walked back to the van. *Screw you, Lily,* she said, but only to herself.

She climbed back up into the attic with the drill tucked under her arm. Her eyes took a moment to adjust to the dark. The air hung heavy—pressing her breath back down into her lungs.

"Christ ... Lil," she choked. "It's a fucking steam bath in here."

"What was that?"

Cat didn't repeat it.

Her feet were feeling along the tops of joists hidden beneath pounds of prickly pink fiberglass.

"Easy going there. Stay on the beams. There's nothing but a half-inch piece of Sheetrock between you and the kitchen floor. I don't want to have to be patching up any big holes."

"God forbid you might have to do that." Cat worked her way closer. Sweat was stinging her eyes. Suddenly, there was movement under the pink batting.

"What was that?" Cat grabbed at the rafter above to steady herself.

Lily shone the light down between her boots, "Probably just a little mouse. You ain't afraid of a little mouse are you?"

Cat stilled and watched the insulation.

"C'mon, don't be such a baby." Lily turned back to her work. "Shine your light over here so I can see what we're dealing ..." A quicker louder shuffling came again from beneath the fiberglass. Cat swung the flashlight and caught the head of a black snake as it slid up on top of the pink batting.

"Holy shit." She backed up.

The snake wound its long body out of the crack and slithered toward Lily, who managed to jump the length of its elongated body, miraculously landing both feet on two joists.

"Move ... move ..." She yelled, pushing Cat in front of her. As they descended, Cat swung the lantern one last time; she saw two more snakeheads popping out of the insulation.

"Fuck me, man ..." Lily said as she ducked down the steps.

So much for quittin' cussin', Cat thought.

"Well?" Cat asked as Lily climbed out of the truck, having gotten off the phone with the homeowner.

"I told him I wasn't going back up there until he got rid of the snakes." Lily leaned against the van. "But he still wants us to bust out that fuckin' wall."

Cat looked at the great gray monstrosity standing like a solid chunk of molten lava cooled up against the side of the house.

"Anything else?"

Lily walked away from her. "Yeah, quit gripin' and get the sledgehammers—the big ones."

Grunting as she heaved the sledge over her shoulder, Lily, with one great shift, brought it down against the wall. It barely made a dent.

"Jesus, this is a mother. Come on. You think you can handle this?"

Cat scowled and hefted the heavy steel over her shoulder. Following its weight down with the force of her own, slamming the concrete, the vibration traveled up her bad arm and buzzed in her teeth. She ignored it. The two began a rhythm of pounding and smacking sledges widening the crack. Pieces of wall began flying.

"Put that at the curb," Lily ordered. Another blow crashed against the loosening mortar. Cat clenched her teeth together, absorbing the hits to the concrete. Sweat poured stinging salt into her eyes. Her arms, especially her healing one, were beginning to feel like rubber. She rested the hammer between her feet.

"Can't handle it?" Lily looked at her.

Remaining silent, Cat lifted the sledge back to her shoulder. They took turns crashing blows to the wall as they inched toward the house. Lily managed to smack the bigger chunks away, moving fast, leaving Cat behind clearing through the rubble.

"Would you slow down?"

"Can't handle it, huh?" Lily taunted.

"Fuck you." Cat threw down her hammer. "I quit."

"Yeah ... and good riddance, I say."

Before Cat could stop her, Lily leaned back and swung the sledge up behind her. Its steel head smashing the glass-globed housing of the electric meter. The shattering sent splintered crystals into the sky, suspended for a moment and twinkling in the sun. Almost pretty—like snow, Cat thought, numbly watching. But then the tiny shards of razor-sharp confetti rained down onto Lily's head and shoulders and into her overalls. Cat she ran toward her.

"Shit. Stand still here."

A sprinkle of glass dust sparkled in Lily's hair. She had shut her eyes tight and staggered.

"Hold still," Cat warned again, brushing at a rivulet of sweat on Lily's shoulder. Five tiny pinpricks appeared there, oozing blood.

"*Ouch!*"

"Sorry, sorry. Damn, Lil ... you are covered in glass. I can't tell it from your sweat."

"Is there a hose somewhere?" Lily put her hand to her face, preparing to wipe away the sweat and glass.

"Don't, Lil." Cat grabbed her wrist. "You'll rub the glass." She searched the grounds and the garage for a hose. *How could they not own a hose?* Cat wondered. She squinted into the well-manicured lawns of the houses surrounding them, each set far back from the road, fenced in, but without so much as a sprinkler anywhere to be seen.

"There's only one thing you can do," Cat said as she made her way back to Lily, empty-handed, "You're going to have to get in their shower."

"No way," was all Lily could manage but she allowed Cat to guide her through the garbage minefield of the kitchen till they came to the bathroom. Cautiously, Cat pushed Lily into the small room and undid her bib buckles. The shower was black, but she spared Lily the details. Mold had crept up the walls and curtain. There were slivers of slimy soap clogging the drain. Wet tangles of loosened hair had been flung and stuck to the tub's edges.

"Fuckin' A." Lily tilted her still-closed eyes toward Cat. "It stinks in here."

"Yeah, well, just be glad you can't see."

Lily hung her head. For one moment, as Cat turned on the cold shower, she almost felt sorry for her. While Lily washed the glass from her skin, Cat searched for a towel. After encountering a third sour-smelling clothes basket, she gave up and ran for some clean paint rags from the truck. She thrust them through the door.

"Is that all you could find? This place is disgusting."

"Just dry off."

"I can't put my shirt back on. It's full of glass."

Cat headed back through the house and went into the master bedroom, surprisingly tidy compared to the rest of the house. She found a white T-shirt folded in an open drawer. They had, long ago, pledged a carpenter's oath to never snoop through drawers or closets, and certainly never to steal; this time would have to be an exception.

Lily emerged from the stinky bathroom and stood with the paint rag around her top. Cat threw her the T-shirt.

"It's clean. I checked." She brushed past Lil and headed for the door.

"Hey," Lily tripped after her. "Where you going?"

Outside Cat turned and surveyed her. Lily's hair was hanging in wet tangles and tiny trickles of blood were still apparent on her neck. Each waited for the other to speak, but the chasm between them seemed thicker now than even the rock wall they'd just busted through. Cat turned and headed for the road.

"Hey, aren't you gonna help me pack up?"

"Do it yourself." She turned. "I told you, I quit."

When Cat reached the main road she stuck out her thumb.

She supposed that it was her disheveled sweaty self that caused drivers to turn and swerve their way around her.

Lily did not go by, so she figured she'd stayed to continue the job or took another route altogether.

It wasn't for another two hours, at the head of the valley road leading home, that a dark blue minivan slowed and stopped. It was Delores. Cat hopped up into the seat, and then, after straining not to, burst into tears. Through sobs, she told the whole long story as they drove home.

They pulled into the driveway behind the cabin and Delores cut the engine and turned to face her.

"I think it's just your world changing, Cat," she said. Her tone was gentle. "And because of that, Lily's has to change, too. Neither one of you is willing to let it move easily to its next phase. The two of you have been joined at the hip for almost thirty years." She looked to the skies. "The Universe is saying that it's time for you to separate."

Cat pushed at the tears on her cheeks. "I didn't ask for all this," she said. "I mean, I wanted the book to sell, but I didn't want to lose my best friend."

Delores said, "Sweetie, you two just need to figure out how you'll be different in each other's lives now. You're not losing anybody." She touched Cat's arm. "Just give Lily some time. She's earned it, Cat. She loves you."

Cat leaned over for a hug. "Ah, you're right, Delores. And anyway, maybe it's getting to the move-on time." She got out of the minivan, managing a smile now.

"I'm right next door if you need to talk." Delores waved, and then backed out of the drive.

Cat grabbed a beer from the fridge and made her way to her office where she flipped on the computer. Pressing the cold bottle to her forehead she waited for her email to connect.

How did she want to be in this? Well, she didn't want to be angry. She didn't want to lose her job, her girl, or her best friend. She sure didn't want her whole life turned upside down for her writing. To become famous ... as Lily would say.

True? The nag in her persisted.

She thought, people who say they write only for themselves are full of shit. She'd decided this a long time ago in grad school, when she'd admitted to a fellow writer, "I want my books crammed on the shelves of conglomerate bookstores—nationwide. Call me a whore—you'd be right," she had said, bravely.

Big talk for a little writer, she thought to herself, now. You had wanted all this back then, didn't you? Cat stood staring out the window over her desk, seeing the fields in the back baking slowly in the afternoon sun. You had envisioned it. Dreamed about it. Worked it. Planned it. Hired Candace to make it all happen, for God's sakes—just fucking admit it—you asked for all of this, Cat Hood. The voice inside would not leave her alone.

The *shift*, the one she'd created, had already happened, she now knew. So, now what?

Be the water ... Lily's words floated into her mind. *Go the easy way ...*

Fuck the water, her own brain answered. *It's not always that simple.*

Be the glacier ... she let herself hear Kate's voice, so real that she turned, expecting to see her grandmother. *Forge your way ...* Oh, that was Kate's way, all right. Steady and implacable.

Fuck that—too exhausting.

There was a momentary quiet inside her head. As far back as she could remember, familiar voices came out of air, like phantoms.

Be your heart, then ... Melissa would say something like that.

But what the luck does that mean? She wondered silently.

Cat pressed her palms into her eyes. God, she was making herself crazy.

The ever-familiar, "You've got mail," sounded on her computer and she leaned in to read her messages, immediately clicking open Isobel's from Scotland. Reading, her heart pounded.

They wanted to hire her, Isobel said. The powers-that-be were impressed by her publications. They were delighted that she was a carpenter. Isobel wrote that it had been decided that Cat would be a good role model for their girls. Attached, the message informed her, was a file containing literature about the school and her contract. Finally, Isobel said she would phone to discuss the details.

A contract.

Cat sat back, staring at the screen. Reading and rereading the words. She sighed maybe a dozen times, she wasn't sure why. Then she read the whole email over again.

Be yourself. Another voice. It startled her, because it was one that she didn't recognize, couldn't remember ever contriving to hear. Cat waited, staring again out at the woods, the fields. It was as if she were waiting for someone walking from far away to come closer—and closer still. She closed her eyes. *Mother?*

Be yourself Cat. Be true. Everything will come.

Chapter Fifteen

It seemed that everyone was worrying about them, Cat and Lil. She replaced the phone in its cradle. She wished they wouldn't. She wished she could have told Delores, just then, that things would be OK between herself and Lily, but she hadn't. Or earlier, she had wanted to reassure Hannah that it would just take time, but she couldn't. Talking about it made her one of two things—pissed off or even more pissed off. There was only the night with Melissa that she'd let true feelings surface. In the end it was grief, not anger, that had taken over.

"I think this is for the best," Cat had said through tears. "Lily's all happy with her new best friend, anyway."

"Now, Cat." Melissa had kissed her forehead.

"No, I mean it. She'll only be happy with me if I live the way she wants me to—that's the way it's always been. I always did what she wanted."

Melissa frowned. "Hey, it doesn't look that way from here. I mean, you went to college, you wrote a book, you live on your own. You sure *look* like an independent woman."

Cat had smiled to herself, glad Melissa saw her that way.

"Lily has been there for you through all of that, Cat. I'm

sure she's going to hate having you gone. But she'll adjust."
Curling tightly into Melissa's arms, she then let go.

Cat tapped her fingers against the phone and closed her eyes. There were too many layers to peel away before she could leave. She imagined hands unclasping, eyes turning, voices evaporating, skin beyond touch, and suddenly an aching so great, so filled with loss and sorrow, that she opened her eyes and blinked it from her mind.

To counter her sorrow, she forced herself to think about the pig-house incident, as she had come to think of it. Lily needed to apologize. She wasn't going to give in this time. And if Lily wouldn't, then Cat would just take off for her new gig in the big world without saying another word.

She sat in front of a pile of bills at her desk. Being out of work this way was starting to catch up with her, she had to admit. Subtracting the outgoing from the incoming was beginning to require some creative mathematics. And when it came to math, she was anything but creative. The numbers were still sketchy, even after the deal she'd worked out with Will and Marce for renting the cabin.

"It'll be the best thing for everyone," she had insisted over a game of Monopoly with them. "When those babies get here they'll need space." She rolled the dice. "I won't have to close up the cabin or worry about Mike." She passed *Go,* and collected her two hundred dollars. "Works out for everyone."

Marce had agreed. "But we pay rent," she insisted.

"I'll take it," Cat said, admitting her straits. "I am so broke."

Will offered a loan, but she had declined.

259

⌘⌘

She knew how she'd work it out.

The idea kept creeping into her thoughts. It had become clearer in the last couple of days and she knew it would solve this money problem. She picked up a handful of billing statements and fanned them out. Getting rid of these would make the rest much simpler. What she needed was a big chunk of change and she knew exactly how to get it. There was no other choice; she picked up the phone and dialed Zoe Wright's number.

"She's in mint condition ... Cash. Twenty-five grand—no less."

Cat barely took a breath, explaining, "By the end of next week—no later."

Zoe attempted a negotiation.

"I can get twenty-seven, somewhere else, tomorrow," Cat countered.

"On it," was all Zoe said and hung up the phone.

Cat stood in front of the shelves in her office choosing books to take or store. There was something comforting in the act. Things were starting to come together, she thought.

Once Zoe paid her for the Glide she'd be debt-free, cash and ticket in hand. And if she were lucky (she thought she might be) she might even get to see the new babies before she left. All was good in Cat Hood's world, she thought. Well almost. She missed Lil.

Ever since the fight—in her head—she had spent time with Lily, almost as if she were a character in a story. They would talk, working out all the anger, guilt, and fear. Sometimes Cat would almost forget what they were mad about in the first place, as if the internal dialogue she'd orchestrated had actually cleared the air between them. Twice now she had picked up the phone to call, only to replace it on its cradle when memory finally served. She also tended to forget that she wasn't working anymore. The first time, she'd gone all the way through to the making lunch part before she remembered. This morning, for the first time in over a decade (she was pretty sure), she had slept late. Mike, especially, seemed concerned about that, she thought, remembering how he'd wet-nosed her awake.

It was the sweetest he'd been to her since he found out she was leaving. He'd somehow known as soon as she'd answered Isobel's email. Dogs were like that, she thought; they could sense things. At first, he had been like a puppy, nosing around in that worried way. He'd come curl under her desk while she was writing. A tight space, she thought, looking down. Twice he tried to crawl into her lap, which at first tickled her and so she helped him up, but when his full, awkwardly distributed weight pressed painfully into her, she'd heaved him off. As she had begun to clean and pack, he'd begun to sulk. This entailed avoiding her eyes, exhaling great sighs whenever she passed, and picking at his food. During this phase, Cat once crawled on her hands and knees into his bed, spooning around him, coaxing him out of his funk.

"It's just a year," she had whispered. "Will and Marce and the babies will be here." Then she thought he might not enjoy the idea of "babies," because after that he just got plain grumpy. He ignored her, or would disappear entirely, coming back home smelling all musky.

"You dirty stay-out," she said that very morning, holding open the door, as the *dawg* swayed past her.

"You stink like the dump."

He had eyed her over his shoulder, clunked to his bed, and began licking himself.

She looked over to the corner for him, but he was no longer there.

"Mike?" She waited, listening for the familiar tinkling of his brass nametag against his collar.

She whistled and when he didn't come she climbed the stairs and peeked to his spot up there. It, too, was empty. After a quick but thorough search of the cabin, Cat made her way to the barn.

She yelled, "Mike!" through cupped hands, like a megaphone. "Come on out, you big goof." The shepherd remained elusive. "I know you're pissed at me," she called into the air, "but is this how you want to part? Angry?"

Lily's face surfaced in her mind, and she winced. *Is this how you want to part? Angry?*

Sliding back the big barn door, she scared up a flock of swallows from the roof and they scattered into the sky. It was cool and dusty and mostly empty. He wasn't here, though. She'd known it before she'd even entered.

"Where are you, you old mutt?" She whispered mostly to herself. Across the landscape, there was a low humming stillness. Shading her eyes with her palm, she scanned the vista of woods and fields shimmering in the sun. Nothing dared move in this heat. It would take too much effort. He was probably down at the creek, lying in a cool, shady pool and watching her search from afar. Feeling great satisfaction, no doubt. She turned back for the cabin.

Before she took the steps, she heard a muffled squeaky sound, like a kitten mewing. It came from a gap in the rock foundation below the porch. When the whimper came again she dropped to her knees and stuck her head through the opening. Blinded by the dark, with only bars of dusty sun squeezing through, she saw Mike—and then saw he had a bloody tear in his side. He lifted his head, looked at her, and lay back down.

"Jesus ... Mike."

His back leg was bent at an unnatural angle and she could distinguish a puddle of blood around his head. He'd been hit by a car, she thought.

"Aw, Mike ..." she cooed, wiggling her body in beside him. "Guy, what were you doing in the road?" He licked her hand. On her knees, she gently tried to move him.

"Come on, big guy, it'll be OK." But she knew it wouldn't. With each tug, he cried out. He was too heavy and the space too small for her to do this alone.

Tears washed her neck. "How come you crawled in here, fella?"

She held him, his big head in her lap. She tried to think. She was not going to get him out by herself, not without doing more damage. Cat leaned into him and whispered.

"Hang tight. I'll be right back. I gotta get some help, OK?"

She left the shepherd and went to the phone.

"Pick up, Lil. Pick up," she whispered into the receiver.

And she did.

" ... broken bones and blood everywhere."

"I'll be right there," Lily said.

Cat crawled back under the porch and waited with Mike. The shepherd's breathing was coming sporadically now. He tried to give a thump with his tail when he felt her hand on his head, but it was all he could do to breathe. Cat buried her face in his sticky fur. "It's OK, buddy. I'll take you to Doc." His eyes rolled. "You remember Doc Oldham. Big guy. Looks a little like a bulldog; got hair growing out of his ears?" Mike's breathing wheezed.

263

Lily's MG pulled up before Cat had much more time to think. She met her at the gate.

"It's bad, Lil. Really bad."

In order to get Mike through the opening, they had to roll him first onto an old blanket and then slide him carefully. Together they pulled him into the yard. The damage was far worse than Cat had seen in the dim light under the porch. He'd been rolled and scraped in more places than she had been able to distinguish. Blood and dirt layered the dog's once shiny fur.

"Mother of God," Lily said, looking at him.

He was limp and his breathing was now even more shallow. Cat looked up at Lily.

"We'll need the truck," but her voice sounded hoarse and frightened even to herself. Lily ran. Mike's tongue hung uncontrolled from the side of his mouth, and his eyes were half-closed. Cat pushed her face into the fur around his neck.

"Good boy," she choked. "You've always been such a good boy." Stroking his head just above his eye. "What'd you do, chase some truck?" She saw his eyes flicker and knew he knew she was there. "Remember when you got hit by Witcomb's van?" She smoothed away the mess on his fur. "You got better. Just like now. It'll be OK." But she knew it wouldn't. "I'm sorry I'm going away."

Gathering him in closer she laid her cheek upon his and rocked gently. As his breathing slowed, Cat held him tighter and fingered the brass heart at his throat.

"Hey, hey." She hugged him to her. "Don't you be leaving me, now. No fair. Everything else is changing. I need something to stay the same."

The wheeze coming from the dog was painful to hear.

"You owe me." She held on even tighter. " I could have dumped you right out of that saddlebag."

This was the biggest lie. That night, when his little black head poked out, she was a goner. When his breathing ceased altogether he went limp and sagged against her.

"Ah, Mike, what am I going do without you?" Closing his eyes gently with her fingers, she sang, like she sometimes sang, on their way to sleep,

Come over the hills,
My bonnie Irish lass,
Come over the hills, to your darlin' ...

Lily backed up the truck, and jumped out, running over. Dropping to her knees beside Cat, she reached to slide her two arms under the dog's body.

"No, Lil." Cat looked up. "He died. He just died."

Lily sat down and wrapped her arms around her friend. After some time, she managed to get Cat to move from Mike's side, ushering her into the bathroom where she leaned weeping against the sink as Lily washed blood from her face and arms and hands.

"You OK?" Lily made her sit on the couch, then stood back, her own face streaked by tears. She picked up the phone and made a call to Matthew, who would be the closest person around.

"He's coming to help," she said to Cat, hanging up.

Cat had insisted on washing Mike's body while Matthew and Lily went up the knoll to the little family plot to dig his grave. She whispered words between tears; rubbing his stomach the way he liked; holding the cowl of his fur in her hands; pressing her forehead to his. She begged his forgiveness for every unkind word, for the diet she'd put him on, and for thinking she could leave him for a whole year. Before she let him go, she unclasped the brass heart from his collar.

265

They carried him to the cemetery in the blanket. Matthew wished him a gentle journey and they covered him in loamy earth. He would keep company beside Kate and Angus and Cat's mother and father.

When Matthew left, Cat and Lily sat on the swing on the porch, each quiet in her own thoughts. The sun had dropped in the sky, blackening the mountains to silhouettes. Lily's lips trembled and tears rolled over her lashes. Cat reached a hand across.

"I'm sorry," she said, and squeezed Lil's fingers. Meaning sorry about everything. "I don't want to lose you, Lil."

"I don't want to lose you, either," Lily said, dabbing her eyes with her sleeve.

Cat relaxed against her. "Everything's changed." Her own tears began again. "Mike was the last piece of my world."

They held each other. "Your old world, Cat. You got a new world opening. You gotta go for it. Fate. Remember?"

She held onto Lily even tighter. "I should have paid more attention to him," she mourned.

"He had a good life with you. This was an accident. It had nothing to do with the rest of it."

Lily took her hand and held it. "Listen, you've created a big life for yourself. You've got to follow through."

Cat tried a laugh. "Shit. Did I ever." She shook her head. "How the fuck am I going to teach American literature to a bunch of little Scottish girls?"

Lily grinned at her. "Well, the first thing you gotta do is quit cussing. You can't be going over there saying *shit* and *fuck*. They'll throw you right out of the country."

That night they drove over to Lily's parent's house and climbed up into the old tree castle they'd built those many years ago. It was still sturdy enough to carry them. They lay on their backs and passed a bottle of Jack and a joint back and forth as they looked through the cracks in the roof boards, beyond the tree branches, to the stars. It was Lily who spoke first.

"We'll always be under the same sky, won't we?"

"Seeing the same stars, and moon, and sun."

"Not so far away, after all, is it?"

Chapter Sixteen

Next morning, after she'd climbed down from the tree house and driven home, stiff-jointed and somewhat hung over, she discovered that an absent dog was a lot harder to ignore than a present dog. By accident, she kicked at Mike's furry toy. Guilt struck as the toy hit the wall. She hurried to retrieve it, scooping it to her chest, and then she had to sit down. From across the room she had noticed that someone, maybe Lily or Matthew, had removed Mike's food dishes. She stared at the emptiness.

Before she had left the tree house that morning, Lily had said, "If you feel any sadder, you call me, OK?"

"Could it get any sadder?" She had wondered, then.

It could—and all morning it did.

Pulling her knees to her chin, sitting on the floor of the cabin, Cat held tight and rocked. Every space around her seemed hollow, as if Mike had somehow filled them all. She sat with the toy clenched in her fist.

In her reverie, she didn't hear the tires coming up the drive or Melissa's quiet entry. With gentle prying hands, Melissa released Cat's hold around herself. She folded in her arms. Together they rocked, Melissa stroking a slow rhythm on her back. At some point they'd made their way upstairs, but Cat had no sense of the time.

She stood, limp while Melissa gently removed her clothes and made her lay down. And then she removed her own. Naked between the cool sheets, they blended, weaving legs and arms. Rivulets of tears crossed Melissa's breast as she stroked Cat. Their breathing began a slow matching and together they fell asleep.

When Cat woke, the sun was high. Melissa was sitting on her bedside, like a good doc, with a steaming cup of coffee. Leaning back against her pillow and rubbing her eyes, Cat searched around her head for a point of reference. What day was it? Her eyes landed on the empty plaid blanket in the corner, reminding her, springing new tears. Melissa handed her the cup.

"Hey," she stopped a rolling drop with the tip of her finger. "You OK?"

Cat wiped her face with the heel of her palm, took a deep breath and exhaled the ache against its will. She tried to smile, but instead sipped her coffee. From the small window behind Melissa a soft yellow light haloed the mass of wild curls. She looked like an angel, Cat thought. "You are beautiful," she said.

Melissa smiled and cupped her cheek with a warm palm.

"I'm a mess, huh?" Cat sniffed.

"Not unreasonably so. It's a big deal. He was your baby for a long time."

"The bad thing is that I don't even remember feeling this sad after Kate died."

"You're trying to equate apples and oranges. You've been conditioned to believe that a human life is more valuable than an animal's." She slid into the bed beside Cat. "You can't measure love for your grandmother against love for Mike. You only have to be in your feelings. You don't have to rationalize them." Melissa reached into the pocket of her robe and from a piece of rawhide she dangled the brass heart that said *Mike*. "I found it on the floor." She reached over and tied the leather around Cat's neck.

As tears resumed and her throat swelled, she wondered if she would ever stop crying.

"Let's go hiking," Cat said, surprising even herself. "I need to get *the stink blown off me*, as my granny would say."

"You sure?"

"Let's take the Glide." *One more ride*, she was thinking to herself, *with my girl*.

Unlike many of her previous girlfriends who'd clung to her in terror as she wound the Harley into the hills, Melissa sat back, holding Cat's waist and occasionally leaning forward to squeeze a little love. The sun was hot but the air whipping by cooled their skin. The heat of the summer had begun to threaten and there were few other vehicles on the parkway.

The familiar rumble of the Glide's engine beneath her made Cat feel powerful. Operating eight hundred pounds of rolling metal was no job for a weeney. She'd learned a lot of lessons riding this bike; meeting her own fears was one of them. But she no longer needed the Glide to feel that powerful anymore.

She revved the motor, pushing the bike harder, up into the hills. The confidence she'd once only felt in the saddle of this bike she now felt in other ways. She had it in her writing, and while standing reading her work aloud. It had driven her decision to go to Scotland, and it guided her relationship with Melissa. Cat reached down and pressed the arm around her middle. No, she thought, she no longer needed the Glide to feel this kind of power.

⌘⌘

They had filled the saddlebags with a picnic lunch and now climbed into the hills of the Pickens Forest. Cat pulled the bike into the nearly empty parking area at the trailhead to Cemetery Ridge. The slow, winding creek trickled its way through a flat valley littered with jutting fieldstones. At places, the stream was skinny enough to step over without getting a heel wet. At others, footbridges had been built and flat rocks planted, requiring an occasional hop and splash.

They spread out their blanket in a shady spot beside the lazy water. Melissa tore apart the round loaf of bread and cut thick chunks from a block of white cheddar while Cat uncorked the wine. They settled back against the tree and ate grapes from the cool cluster Melissa had thought to pack.

The mountains rose from the plateau where they rested. Above them, two hawks circled. Cat squinted and watched them float and soar and bounce from windy gust to windy gust.

"I hope they don't think we're dead," she said as they swooped closer.

"Nah—they like little live things." Melissa stuffed the grape skeleton back into the bag.

Beyond them, a field of sweet grass bowed in the breeze.

Cat sighed as she let her gaze rest on the landscape.

"What's going on in that head of yours?" Melissa asked, leaning over, kissing her shoulder.

"These mountains used to go all the way to Scotland. Did you know that? Before the glaciers."

Melissa rested her cheek against Cat's silken back. "I believe everything you tell me," she murmured.

"My grandparents," Cat twirled a river-smooth stick between her fingers, "and a lot of other Scots came here because it reminded them of home."

"That makes sense," Melissa said, "from what I've seen in pictures."

"But it was never home for Kate." Cat turned. "She hardly ever talked about it. Scotland, her family. Sometimes I'd catch her, when she thought no one was around, staring off into the hills. I think it made her *more* homesick, not less."

Circling a gentle finger, Melissa said, "She couldn't go back, either. Even if she'd had the means. There was no home or family to welcome her. But now you'll go."

Cat turned, surprised that Melissa had somehow made this connection that she herself was just barely coming to understand.

"This going back ..." she paused. "For me ..." Words eluded her. "I mean ..." she stumbled. "It feels *old* in me ..."

Melissa waited.

"Like *I'm* going home. Like I've always had this home-sickness for a place I've never even been before." Cat looked up. "Could that be possible?"

"Maybe." Melissa kissed the top of her head. "Maybe Kate's ache was so deep that it permeated your whole childhood. Maybe that sorrow in her was something you unconsciously understood."

Cat thought of the shadows in her grandmother's eyes. How she had tried, sometimes, to see beyond them, into Kate.

"Maybe it's about coming full circle," Melissa said, brushing crumbs from her front. "You'll get to tell the rest of the story of Kate's life. Those two little grandbabies need to know where they come from. Who better to write that than you?"

"Could be the sole purpose of my existence, no?" Cat laughed.

Melissa pulled her down and kissed her. "No."

"No?"

"You are part of my world now," she said. "Another purpose for your existence."

"To be your love slave?" Cat rolled her over.

"Exactly."

They had dozed in the shade beneath the smoochin' tree, as Cat had dubbed it after a long sweet session of just and only kissing.

Melissa had packed their remains into the pouch and had it slung across her shoulders as she stood above Cat, gently kicking at her boot. "You ready there, lazy?"

"Carry me." Cat lifted her arms.

Melissa leaned over and pulled her up. When she was standing, she threw her arms over Melissa's shoulders and rested her chin and lazy weight against her.

"C'mon, carry me back to the Glide."

Melissa held her under the arms, as if drunk. "Cut it out, you baby."

But this only made Cat lean heavier. Melissa wobbled. Their giggling weakened them both and they finally crashed to the ground, the pack softening their fall. Cat hovered above, pinning Melissa's arms back behind her head and then she worked up a spit drip. Melissa struggled and kicked as the ooze threatened its dangling plop.

"You can always tell the dykes who grew up with brothers." Melissa twisted her face. "What's up with you people? Is this how you all tortured each other?"

The drip hovered closer.

"Don't you know how many germs are in spit?" Melissa pinched her mouth closed to prevent the saliva from entering.

Quickly, Cat sucked it back up and laughed, releasing the wrists.

"That," Melissa said, brushing herself as she got to her knees. "Is gross. You wouldn't catch sisters doing that."

"No, sisters just scratch the shit out of each other. I've seen the scars. I'd take spitting over scratching any day."

Cat leaned over, pressing their mouths together, pushing her tongue between easily parting lips, sliding along sharp teeth. She pulled away slowly and Melissa swayed.

"Now, aren't there just as many germs in that as in a spit drip?" Cat asked.

"Yeah, there are germs," Melissa said. "But I'd way rather catch them that way than the other." They stood and together closed the folds of blanket.

"No more spitwads," Cat promised.

The packing that took all week to finish had also taken her mind off Mike. Less and less she found herself weeping. Her focus was on the *nexts*. There was little time now to think about all the *befores*. Today would put an end to the last leftover one.

Not only had she put the dread on today, she'd put the dread on the dreading itself. She carried another box out to the truck, slowing to admire the Glide, all waxed and shiny, waiting for its new owner. Cat supposed that if there were anyone who'd love it like she did, it would have to be Zoe Wright. It was an incomparably beautiful bike. Even the chrome sparkled.

She shoved the last duct-taped box onto the truck. Everything would be shipped tomorrow and arrive just before she did, next week. *Next week?* The time had slithered up on her. Around this time next week, she pictured, she'd be on a plane to Scotland. Her thoughts zoned out the sound of a motor as a car zipped up behind the truck, startling her. Behind the wheel was Candace, she saw, and climbing out of the passenger side door, was ... Zoe Wright? What were these two doing together? Cat wondered suspiciously.

"Well," Zoe said slowly, extending a hand, which Cat shook. "I can only imagine that this is a sad day for you." Actual tears welled in Zoe's eyes as if it was hurting her to see Cat have to part with the Glide. She said she understood the magnitude of a loss such as this one.

Cat appreciated the sympathy. "Zoe Wright, there's no one I'd rather turn my beauty over to than you," she said, amazed at her own magnanimity. She clapped Zoe's shoulder. "Of course it saddens me. But I think our time has come, mine and the Glide's, to end our love affair. Man—uh, woman and machine must move on."

Zoe pulled a cashier's check out of her wallet and handed it to Cat.

She held it up, read it over, and then kissed it. Waving it, she said, "I must admit, this alleviates my sorrows to a great extent."

"Cat," Zoe said, "You are such a writer. You got great words."

Just then, Candace, holding her cell phone, ran at Cat and threw her arms around her. She patted Candace's head until the little woman let go.

"What was that for?"

Candace sniffled and wiped away a tear. "For everything. For being a great writer. For having faith in me. And most important," Candace sidled over beside Zoe and slipped her arm around the tall woman's waist. "For helping me find the love of my life." Candace stood on tiptoes and kissed Zoe's chin.

What? Cat looked from tall, dark, skinny Zoe to the tiny little blonde and back again, trying to make the picture *not* weird in her mind, but it was. She didn't know what to say. "Uh—" she started. She shut her mouth and held her breath but the laugh wouldn't stop. She couldn't picture the two—and

Candace, the little homophobe, looking so smitten—it was too much. She laughed out loud—then composed herself. Then she picked Candace up and spun her around.

"You little lipstick lesbian, you!"

She put her down.

"Well, I don't know what to say. I hope you kids are happy." She herded the inseparable pair toward the bike, then she stopped and turned to Candace.

"What happened to Darby? The building buster?"

"Gone. I heard he joined a support group for men dumped for a woman." Candace smiled.

Before she drove off in the Miata, she kissed both Zoe and Cat on the lips, saying how *liberating* it was to kiss women.

After showing Zoe all the bells and whistles on the Glide, she mumbled, *"Whatever you do, don't wreck it."* And handed over the keys.

The Glide and its new owner headed down the drive and out the creek road. Cat saw Will's truck heading in. *Uh, oh,* she thought. She hadn't seen him for awhile. His new job flying for the Forestry Department took him all over the mountain region for days at a time. There hadn't been a chance to tell him about selling the bike.

She met him as he pulled in and immediately headed for the truck bed.

"What's all this? Baby stuff?" Cat noticed the box with the crib picture and a bunch of pink and blue stuff.

"Yeah, I thought you could help me put these cribs together," Will said distractedly. He thumbed over his shoulder. "I could've sworn I saw a woman driving the Glide outta here."

Cat dug around the bed and yanked out a box. She turned

and made for the house. "C'mon, let's unload this stuff. I still have to get to the post office."

"Cat?" Will stopped her. *"Was* that the Glide I passed?"

She looked to the ground and he looked down the road and then back to her. His brow inched up with understanding.

"You sold her?" It came out as almost a whisper. Cat looked up and nodded.

She thought he was going to cry, but instead he started pacing. Then his beard started twitching; arms began swinging, nostrils flared; all the cliched classic symptoms of a temper-tantrum about to blow.

"Unfuckingbelievable!!" he yelled. "Are you fucking telling me that you fucking sold the Glide without a fucking word to me?"

She stood back. She'd expected this. *Sometimes it's better to beg forgiveness, later, than ask permission, first,* Will's own words came to her.

"Why?" he finally asked.

She showed him the check.

"Twenty-five thousand dollars? Cat, for Christ's sakes, I offered you a loan."

"I didn't want another loan."

"Then why not sell me my fucking bike back?"

"'Cause you don't need another bike."

"It was mine," he barked. "I pushed it from the dump. I fixed it."

"We pushed it. Don't forget." Now she was getting mad. *"We* fixed."

"I gave you that fucking bike. You had no right."

Suddenly the cell phone on his hip rang.

"You got a *cell phone?"* she asked disdainfully.

"Yeah. I got a pregnant wife, remember?" He flipped it

open, mumbled into the receiver and started shaking. Cat took the phone out of his hand and asked all the right questions.

"C'mon," she said, shoving him toward her truck. "You got babies coming."

As they pulled out of the driveway, she turned to him. "Here come, not one but two reasons why you don't need another motorcycle. You don't even need the one you've got anymore. Will, you're about to be a daddy."

They raced off to the hospital.

They were going to perform a C-section, the nurse told Will and Cat as they each slipped into green scrubs and sterile masks.

"Nothing to worry about," the nurse continued even though neither was really listening. "Her water broke early. Happens sometimes with twins."

Paper wraps covered their hands and feet.

"Those babies are just ready to be born," she finished, as she hurried them to the birthing room where Marce was already prepped and propped.

Will ran to her and grabbed her hand—kissing her through his mask.

She smiled, her face glistening. "Wasn't sure you'd make it."

"Are you kidding me?" he asked. "Why is she awake? What's going on?"

"She gets to participate, Dad. Don't worry—she can't feel it."

Cat watched as the babies were lifted, one by one, from Marce's womb. Tiny slick bodies wriggled, reminding her of kittens squirming to life. The boy came first, tufts of red hair sprouting from his head as he was patted down. He howled as the warm cloth washed his birth from his skin. His sister came next, more quietly, her small head, round and covered in yellow fuzz. After they were clean and wrapped, the nurse handed one each to Will and Cat. Brother and sister carried brother and sister to their mamma.

When they had all settled and brought their eyes up from the miracles laying against Marce's breast, they laughed, seeing each other's tears.

"What'll you call them?" Cat asked, finally.

"You tell her," Marce said to Will. Her eyes glistened, resting on her two babies with their small knit caps.

Cat waited.

"We're going to name this one Stryker McGhee," he said and grinned. "Heck of a name, huh?"

"After my father," Marce explained. "I'm the last of a dying breed of McGhees. No male heirs."

"How do you like that, Stryker?" Will cooed to the baby. "Such a tough name for such a little guy." The tiny mouth opened and let out a wail.

The look on Will's face was pure *goof.*

"Looks like Kate got her wish," Cat said. "I *hope you have one just like yourself, William.*" She tried imitating her grandmother's sternest voice.

They both laughed.

"And what about this little itty bitty one?" Cat let the tiny fingers grab around her pinky.

"We've decided on Mary Katherine," Will said, softly.

Cat looked from Will to Marce.

"Katherine with a *K* for Kate," he clarified. "We'll call her Mary Kate." He picked up the pink baby and handed her to Cat.

"Nice, Will," she said and sat in a nearby chair with the drowsy little girl baby in arms. Suddenly, Cat was engulfed by the smell of her grandmother's lilac talc. She looked down at the baby whose eyes had opened and caught her own.

"Hey, y'all," she asked. "Do you smell that?"

Will sniffed. "What's the matter, did she poop already?"

"No." Cat breathed in the sweet scent. "Don't you smell it? Lilac?"

Both Will and Marce shook their heads and turned their attentions back to the blue bundle on Marce's lap.

Cat looked back down at the baby. She sighed. "But you smell it, don't you, Mary Kate?"

Tiny dark eyes held her own.

"That's your great-gran," she whispered to the babe. "Come to get a peek at you."

Later that night, she would tell Lily, "Right then, she winked at me."

"Babies don't wink, Cat."

"I swear to God, Lil, this one did."

Cat left the new little family after Melissa had come to admire the babies. She would be on nightshift—keeping her eye on them all.

It was after dark by the time Cat arrived home. Before picking up the phone to announce the arrival of the twins, she made a pot of coffee. By the time it had finished its brew, she'd finished her duties. Carefully balancing the coffee laced with Bailey's Irish Creme, Cat carried it our to the porch and eased herself into a rocker.

The figure ascending the porch steps startled her and she jumped, splashing hot liquid onto her bare thigh.

"Damn, Delores, you scared the shit outta me." Cat hopped around while Delores went inside for a cup of coffee and a dishrag. After they'd cleaned up, they sat together on the swing.

"Well," Delores said, "I guess the babies are here and you are on your way."

Cat nodded. "Seems like that."

"Hmm, hmm," Delores murmured.

"What?" Cat glanced over at her.

"Nothing." Delores lit a long white cigarette. "Just, I told you so."

"Told me so about what?"

"Sat right here, not even a year ago, and told you your life was about to change." Delores smiled. "I was right, wasn't I?"

"I suppose you were."

"Never doubt the word of a black woman."

"Gimme a break."

Delores laughed. "Well, that's what Mamma always says."

"And who's going to doubt Mamma, huh?"

"Not me."

"Me, either," Cat said.

The two smoked and rocked, both lost in their own thoughts as crickets and tree frogs slowed to a soft hum. It was a time to share quiet, not words. They both somehow knew this, soaking up each other's presence, till the next time. Before Delores left, they wrapped their arms around each other and held on for a long time.

"We wouldn't be here if it weren't for you, Cat," Delores finally said, wiping a tear as she let go.

"And we wouldn't be here if it weren't for you and yours, Delores."

"Well ... no time at all, Cat Hood, and you'll be back."

Cat swallowed hard as she watched her friend make her

way through the starlit night, back down the long creek road toward home.

Three days later the babies arrived at the cabin. And not just the babies, Cat noticed, but their stuff. Tons of stuff. She couldn't believe how much paraphernalia one little baby could have, never mind two.

Bottles and rattles and *nummers,* as Will called the pacifiers, lined the kitchen counter. A breast pump centered the coffee table. A sight that renewed Cat's appreciation for being a lesbian who would never have children. Soft stuffed animals and bright musical toys scattered the house, still in their boxes. Books, whose bindings wouldn't crack for years, were stacked along a bookcase in what used to be Cat's office, but was now the nursery. Everything was doubled: cribs, strollers, crank swings, diaper bags, blankets, sleepers, and pairs of booties and hats. Two of everything including the hungry babies who had no qualms about squalling in stereo in the middle of the night.

Baby admirers also poured in: Marce's folks had flown in from Florida, a sister arrived from some northern state, four women professors, colleagues from the university, visited together. Lily and Hannah checked in periodically, and Lily's parents came. Delores and her entire family could not stay away. It was getting extreme, Cat thought claustrophobically.

A million pictures were snapped. She found herself either smiling or ducking every time she heard a click. Pictures of a sleeping Will with sleeping babies on his big chest; pictures of naked babies, crying babies, yawning babies; photos of mamma nursing babies, babies throwing up on auntie Cat, were captured at every turn. The wee ones were placed in spots under shade trees, in rockers, propped on pillows.

One night, with his son and daughter cradled in his big

arms, Will wondered if the babies had ever been put down since they were born.

"That can't be good for them, can it?" he asked without giving up either one to their cribs.

"What, are you kidding me?" Cat laughed. "Babies love this stuff."

But the onslaught tapered off. Soon after it had, Cat found herself standing on the porch with Will. The babies and their mamma were all cozy and sleeping inside. Cat leaned on the porch rail, looking out at the stars. Upstairs in her room, she had bags packed and waiting by the door. This was the last glimpse of her night sky for awhile.

She lit a joint. "Last one," she said.

Will raised an eyebrow.

"I'm supposed to be a role model soon." She grinned.

"You and me both," Will said, and thumbed over his shoulder.

She nodded. They leaned against each other. Quiet.

"I gotta head on out of here Will," she said. She had not known, before, how she would begin this conversation; but now here it was, coming out of her almost easily, the inevitable truth.

Will said, "You don't have to leave yet, Cat."

"Yeah, I do." She turned to him. "You all need to get this family thing cranking." She held up her hand to his argument. "And I need some sleep. Anyway, I'm all packed."

She smiled and he nodded his head.

"Going to Melissa's?" he finally asked.

"Yeah. I mean, take-off time's in a few days, anyway."

"You excited?"

"Yeah. I guess." She smiled. "Those are some great babies you got in there, Will."

He nodded.

"And a terrific wife. It's a family, again," she said. "You're a good dad."

"You think?"

"Kate would be proud, Will. Those babies and that woman in there are really lucky to have you. So am I."

He wrapped his arms around her. "I hate that you're leaving," he said. Pressing her cheek against his chest she listened to his beating heart.

"That's why I can leave," she whispered. "'Cause you're here. You can take care of the place. You had your turn to see the world, Will. This is mine."

Cat felt him nod, but he said nothing. She held onto his big frame for a long time, breathing in his baby-powder smell, no longer his alone. It lingered throughout the cabin, on the babies, on Marce, even on Cat herself.

She pushed herself back from him as the headlights of Melissa's Jeep flashed across the bridge.

"There's my ride," she said and went inside to get her stuff.

As they rode up the lane, Cat turned back for one last look over her shoulder. Soft lights burned in the cabin window, framing Will and Marce, hands raised in a wave. There was an all new thing happening in that old cabin, she thought; and she turned back, slipping her hand into Melissa's.

"You OK?" the lady doctor asked.

Cat nodded.

She could not have fantasized about three more blissful days. Melissa had taken time off from the hospital. They ordered Chinese takeout and pizza and giant sub sandwiches; they rented movies, took walks, made love, read to each other, painted each other, and lazed together in the dwindling hours.

On the morning of her departure, Cat woke weeping from a dream. She clung to Melissa. "I dreamed I had to leave you," she said, still half asleep.

"Baby, you do," Melissa said softly.

Cat shook herself awake.

"But I'll see you in two months," Melissa said, kissing her forehead. "In Scotland. We'll hike the moors."

"We'll freeze our asses off," Cat said darkly.

"Just think, by the time I get over there, you'll be all settled. I'll have my very own personal tour guide."

"What if I have an accent?"

Melissa laughed and rolled Cat onto her back, kissing her hands and shoulders and neck and chin, working her way to her mouth.

"Then you'll have to speak slooowly," she whispered, running her tongue along Cat's jaw line.

"All righty, me lassie," Cat tried out. "How sloooww does a Scotswoman gooo?"

"Well, unfortunately," Melissa said, poking Cat's chest, "today, my Scotswoman is going to have to make it quick. She's got a plane to catch."

"You won't forget me?" Cat asked, her fingers tangling in Melissa's curls, her breath catching on her own words.

Melissa kissed her throaty answer. "How could I ever forget those eyes? It would be like forgetting to breathe— physically impossible."

They made love like it was the first time.

Cat checked her bag for her passport, traveler's checks, and airplane tickets six times before they even made it out the door. She ran back for her Yankees cap, and stuffed it into her jeans pocket. Finally, Melissa got her into the Jeep and buckled her to the seat. They drove to Hannah and Lily's in quiet. Cat watched out the window. It was foggy—a mist roping the roadways and lying on the trees like gauze. Trying to memorize it all, she wondered if she would get homesick so far away. But it was only a year. You didn't forget what was inside you in only a year.

When they arrived, Melissa joined Hannah while Cat and Lily walked down to the footbridge over the creek and sat, dangling their legs above the water. Cat watched as little fish swam around the shallow still pools between the rocks, safe from the rushing water.

Lily had carried a brown paper bag with her. Now, she tapped Cat on the knee.

"So, this is it?"

Cat handed her a lighted cigarette and then lit her own. "Looks that way."

They smoked.

How funny, she thought. This moment—two people who had shared everything all their whole lives, and now neither could find the words to say good-bye. They swung their legs in sync—in silence. Finally, Lily cleared her throat and leaned her head onto Cat's shoulder.

"What am I gonna do without you?" Cat put an arm around Lily.

"You know I'll always love you best."

Lily smiled and wiped her cheek. "How could you not?" She sniffed. "I saved you from Stanley Schmidt, remember?"

Cat nodded and they laughed through tears.

Without a word, Lily reached into the bag and handed Cat her old tool belt. The hammer was still slung in its holster. Lily gently laid it across her lap. "It won't fit anybody else," she said.

Kate's voice in Cat's head said, *When one door closes, another opens. Just don't let a drunk in.* Cat never could figure out what that last bit meant, but somehow it seemed appropriate now.

Lifting the tool belt to her nose, she breathed in the familiar smell of leather and steel and sawdust. The smell of carpentry and her life with Lil.

"Wonder what Scotland smells like?" Lily said.

"Uh ... like heather? Whoever Heather is."

Each laughed softly.

"Thanks, Lil. I got something for you, too."

From her back pocket, Cat pulled out the Yankees cap and handed it over.

"It was my dad's," Cat said.

Lily looked surprised. "You sure you want me to have this?" she asked.

"You love that hat," Cat said.

"I do. Always hated having to hide it every time you came by."

They leaned into each other.

Melissa called out from the house, letting Cat know it was time to go. Hannah hugged her four times, and continued to wave and blow kisses from the porch. "I'll miss you, McCat," she called after her. Lily had her arms folded, the cap on her head shielding her eyes.

"I'll miss you, back, Hannah Burns." Cat turned back again. "Take good care of my buddy."

Melissa was waiting. Cat reached for the passenger side door, but before she could open it, Lily raced down the steps to stop her.

She spit into her palm and held it out.

"You do it," Lily demanded.

Like it meant something.

Cat spit.

Cynn Chadwick

Born and raised in New Jersey, Cynn
Chadwick has lived in the South for over
twenty years. When she was (much) younger
she worked for one of the first women in the
United States to become a master carpenter.
Her experience working in the trades has
served to inspire many of her stories. While
the stories are fiction, Cynn does, on occasion,
play the harmonica, drinks single-malt scotch,
and wishes there were a bar—somewhere,
anywhere—called Ozgirlz. She has never
owned, but continues to fantasize about
Harley Davidsons.

Chadwick received her master's degree in
Southern Literature and a master of fine arts
degree from Goddard College in Vermont.
Her work has appeared in anthologies
including *Words of Wisdom*, *The Writer's
Gazette*, and *The Harrington Lesbian
Fiction Quarterly*. She teaches writing at the
University of North Carolina at Asheville.

She makes her home in a spoon-shaped
valley in the Blue Ridge Mountains with her
partner, Elenna, and a German shepherd
named Arlo.

www.cynnchadwick.wordpress.com